* * *

*Curiosity flashed from Dane's blues,
accompanied by a satisfied smile. For a
few seconds he held that Cheshire face,
which managed to make Becca wonder.*

"What are you looking at?" she asked.

Tilting his head, he surveyed her from her
Ferragamo heels to her perfect bob. "You."

She wiggled her finger towards him in an
admonishing gesture. "If you're keeping
anything from me—evidence, intel,
information, anything—I promise you will
regret it."

"I love a woman who can make a threat with
a smile."

"I won't be smiling if I discover you're holding
out on me."

"Me, keep secrets from you? You're too
gorgeous to want to upset, love. Just stay one
step behind me, and try to keep up."

"I never stand a step behind any man."

Available in September 2006
from Silhouette Sensation

Flawless
MICHELE HAUF

SILHOUETTE®
Sensation™

Silhouette, Silhouette Sensation and Colophon are registered
trademarks of Harlequin Books S.A., used under licence.

First published in Great Britain 2006
Silhouette Books, Eton House, 18-24 Paradise Road,
Richmond, Surrey TW9 1SR

© Harlequin Books S.A. 2005

Special thanks and acknowledgement are given to
Michele Hauf for her contribution to
THE IT GIRLS series.

ISBN-13: 978 0 373 51376 5
ISBN-10: 0 373 51376 3

18-0906

Printed and bound in Spain
by Litografia Rosés S.A., Barcelona

MICHELE HAUF

has been writing for more than a decade and has
published historical, fantasy and paranormal
romance. A good strong heroine, action and
adventure and a touch of romance make for her
favourite kind of story. And if it's set in France, all
the better! She lives with her family in Minnesota
and loves the four seasons, even if one of them
lasts six months and can be colder than a deep-
freeze. You can find out more about her at www.
michelehauf.com.

To Mary Schultz, Lois Greiman and Susan
Sizemore, friends who know just how
much chocolate is required to celebrate the
good times, and to double that amount
for the not-so-good times.

Acknowledgements
Thanks to Julie Barrett for some incredible
plotting sessions. Special cyber-wave to
Thomas A Ross, a jeweller I found online. I
was a little wary of asking him questions about
encoding diamonds with secrets that assassins
might kill for. Imagine my surprise, and incredible luck, when Tom happened to also be
a writer *and* a former Special Forces officer.
He answered my questions without a single
cyber-smirk, and I am grateful to him for
that. (Of course, any mistakes made or liberties taken with the ion-beam process and the
scientific references are entirely my own.) And
a click of my spike heels goes to my fellow
It Girls—Erica Orloff, Nancy Bartholomew,
Sylvie Kurtz, Natalie Dunbar and
Vicki Hinze.

Prologue

How had a Turkish prince discovered his secret research in bioluminescent polymers? And think he could buy it so easily?

Uther Magnusson inserted a ten-carat diamond into the rubber aperture and locked it securely in place.

"He didn't sound Turkish," Uther muttered as he turned to his computer and brought up a classified file. A file he feared might lure in hackers and thieves if he didn't dispose of it immediately.

No private party was going to buy his research. Uther wasn't sure he even wanted to sell it to the U.S. government. They'd been keeping an eye on him—he felt it. And he could deal with that.

But suspicious men wearing obnoxious gold jewelry and claiming to be something they were not—and escorted by burly bodyguards—made Uther nervous. Time to get out of town for a while.

But first, he had to save the formula. He would hide it in a remarkably ingenious place. Easily concealed, yet if found, who would guess what secrets lay within?

"You are so clever," he said to himself, and nodded in agreement.

He'd make two—no, three—copies. Hide two elsewhere, offsite. The third, he'd keep close, but out of sight. A backup copy, if you will.

Amandus Magnusson stared at the two ten-carat diamonds his son had frantically pleaded for him to hide. The boy was up to no good. He could feel it.

Now he expected his old man to face whatever dangers these rocks would lure?

Not in a million years.

Hell, the best method of hiding was to place the thing in plain sight.

Chapter 1

Green and crimson fire escaped myriad facets of the diamond. It was cut in the asscher style—a stepped square cut with cropped corners—and each slight tilt of the jeweler's tweezers released another scintillating wink of color. Even beneath the harsh fluorescent lights of a Scotland Yard interrogation room, the rock put on a show.

Measurement with a digital jeweler's caliper verified that the diamond was a healthy ten carats. Study with the triplex loupe could not identify any remarkable flaws. Of course, a high-powered microscope was required to detect minute inclusions, but the diamond gave no clue that any were present.

If this was a D grade transparent stone... Such a rarity, a flawless diamond of such size, seemed impossible.

There must be a flaw. Nothing in this world was perfect.

Whistling in the corridor distracted Becca Whitmore from her thoughts. Symphony No. 8 in B minor? That one of the Scotland Yard inspectors would cruise down the hallway whistling Schubert made her smile.

Her mood lightened, she glanced over the chipped Formica table, expecting to spy the GIA report amid the few pieces of evidence. Such a report was issued by the Gemological Institute of America, and accompanied all stones.

"Miss Whitmore, I am told?"

Thoroughly startled by the male voice, Becca dropped the diamond. It clinked onto the table and then bounced onto the creased ultrawhite card she always used to lay out gemstones.

A whistle acknowledged her jumpiness. "Sorry," the man said. "Will dropping it damage the thing?"

Tucking her wavy brown hair behind her ear, Becca let out a breath. "No."

Why had she been so jumpy about dropping the gem? Likely because it was 8:00 a.m. in London, and she was still on New York time.

"Diamond is one of the hardest substances found in nature, Mr...."

"Agent Dane."

A slender, six-foot-tall advertisement for laid-back leaned in the doorway to the interrogation room, wearing a presumptuous smile and a pale blue turtleneck sweater. Tufted blond hair warred for some semblance of order, and lost. A hand cocked at his hip pushed back a black tailored suit coat to reveal sculpted pecs beneath a snug sweater. The Brits had a thing for close-to-body tailoring, as if they still clung to '60s-era styles.

Swank, Becca thought.

Swank, who knew the Unfinished Symphony. Score one point for him on the impressive scale.

The man tugged out a leather badge wallet from inside his coat pocket and flashed it quickly. "Agent Aston Dane. MI-6."

The wallet snapped shut as Becca stood and offered her hand. "Becca Whitmore."

Grasping it with both of his, Agent Dane pumped twice. A simple band circled his right thumb. Silver? He was cool, relaxed. Ring on his thumb? He was open. She had a knack for judging people by the jewelry they wore. Men, most particularly, offered intriguing analyses merely for the subtleties their choices uncovered.

"Nice to meet you. Could I see that badge again?"

Still holding her hand, he winked. "You show me yours, I'll show you mine."

Becca tugged her hand from his grip, lifting her right eyebrow in mock challenge. "I don't need a little slice of plastic to prove my credentials."

"Oh? So who the bloody hell *is* Becca Whitmore?"

"I'm the gemologist."

"Ah! Yes, the expert in gems imported from the good old U.S. of A. I was told an American was making the trek. From the JAG?"

He referred to the FBI's Jewelry and Gem program,

which only worked thefts in the United States. This case had begun in New York, but had quickly gone international with last evening's theft in London. The CIA had been the group to contact Becca. She had worked with Zeek, her CIA contact, previously, investigating a conflict-diamond smuggling ring based in Africa. Obviously she'd made an impression.

The New York theft had involved a request for a specific ten-carat diamond—the very one sitting on the white card, Becca presumed. The New York gems dealer had told the thief she'd sold the stone, and then he'd shot her in the head.

The victim? One MaryEllen Sommerfield. Becca knew the woman from the occasional purchase or meeting at a gems convention. MaryEllen was still alive, with a bullet lodged in her frontal lobe like a ticking time bomb. Surprisingly, she remained coherent, and had been able to give a few details to the investigating officers. The suspect—male, tall and wearing a black face mask and clothing—had sounded foreign, but MaryEllen couldn't place the accent.

She'd told the officers she'd sold one ten-carat stone to a London jeweler who had plans to create a necklace for a Transylvanian countess, and another to a Paris dealer. Had the thief been aware there were *two* stones? He hadn't made such knowledge apparent to MaryEllen.

Zeek had been pleased to find Becca, a freelance agent, available to hop a flight to London. Her cover was more than a story; she actually was a gemologist. But she was much more.

Recruited into the Gotham Roses four years earlier

at the age of twenty-two by Renee Dalton-Sinclair, Becca served as an agent in an undercover operation that concentrated on crimes committed by the rich and untouchable. Those "good ole boys" who lived above the law and could get by with nearly anything—yes, even murder—merely by flashing their cash or the incredible power of political connections. The Roses often partnered with the FBI or CIA, as well as local authorities, as inside operatives who could easily assume the disguise of the rich, young and unassuming.

On the surface, the Gotham Roses were a New York City women's club made up of two hundred young socialites who focused on charity and giving back to the community. Hardly the sort criminals would expect to be hot on their trail. Less than two dozen of those exceptional young women had been recruited for the covert branch of the Roses.

Fate had placed Becca in the path of a fleeing purse snatcher four years earlier. Reacting to instincts she'd never known she possessed, she'd swung her Fendi bag, catching the thief in the face and laying him out flat. Renee Dalton-Sinclair had witnessed the scene from the back seat of her limo. Several days later—after a background check that included her famous family lineage and wealth, Becca now knew—Renee had invited her to join not just the Gotham Roses society club for women, but also the underground spy agency.

Becca's expertise with gemstones put her at the top of the Gotham Rose list when stolen bling—as fellow Gotham Rose agent Vanessa Dawson would voice—was involved. Becca had recently assisted the JAG to bring down an organization of thieves who stole from traveling jewel sales reps. The thieves were all former law enforcement, with connections to police databases, and had easily tracked the salespeople from city to city merely by bringing up a DMV search. Then they'd sell the stolen jewels to wealthy, but bargain-minded, no-questions-asked clients that had included big-name senators and businessmen.

When invited to work for the agency, Becca's main physical skills had been yoga and dance, thanks to her mother's training as a professional dancer. Not that Becca's obsessive attention to detail didn't come in handy. Jimmy Valentine, the Roses' sexy trainer, had run her through an intense course of physical training, espionage skills and weapons handling.

Thanks to a strict language teacher in boarding school, Becca's fluency in Spanish, Russian, French and Italian frequently saw her working international cases.

Renee Dalton-Sinclair was a gorgeous and powerful woman married to Preston Sinclair, a noted businessman who had been incarcerated for embezzlement at his own family's financial company. The rumor was that the scandal had been the motivating force behind Renee's creating the Gotham Roses. Renee felt her husband had been framed by greedy family members, used as a scapegoat for their own financial misdealings.

Becca found it fascinating that Renee herself answered to a mysterious woman the Roses knew only as the Governess. Becca often wondered if she were CIA or FBI, or someone higher.

No matter, the Governess had made it clear she wanted intel on this gem case—and hard evidence. Suspicious unnamed sources suggested there was something different about these two diamonds. Something worth attempting murder.

Turning her attention back to the MI-6 agent, Becca said, "I'm not at liberty to discuss my orders." The usual excuse. Scotland Yard knew the CIA had sent her here. "You said you're with MI-6? Wasn't it an MI-5 agent who showed me to this room?"

"Five jumped on the case, as usual—bloody stealing magpies—but as soon as we learned the connections to New York, Six took over."

"Do I detect glee in your tone, Agent Dane?"

He smoothed his palm down the front of his thin blue sweater. Summoning the truth or concocting a lie? It was the kind of pause Becca was familiar with, and used herself, when needed. "Five is domestic. We're international—the obvious match for this case."

"I see."

Yes, he was pleased. Rivalries between the two organizations were well known, even to civilians. Because of their international reach, MI-6 agents considered themselves superior.

"As well, MI-6 tends to jump in when organized crime is involved," he explained.

"Oh? What makes you believe it's organized crime?"

The agent stepped backward and slapped a hand over the wall next to a large picture window. The expanse of glass changed from an opaque white to reveal it was actually a two-way window.

"Exhibit A," he offered, crossing his arms and ankles to pose beside the scene.

Inside the room sat a thin man in black sweats. Blood trickled down his stubble-darkened jaw. A vivid purple bruise marred the left side of his forehead. His hands were secured behind his back, his head hung forward and his shaved scalp revealed a scar that curved around his ear. At the door stood an armed guard, looking nearly asleep.

"Is that the thief?"

"You'd bloody better believe it. Picked him up as a lovely bonus prize along with the diamond. Sergei the Dog, a middle tier thief."

"Middle tier?"

"Sure. You've got your scummy low-class blokes who do smash-and-grabs and tilt over little old ladies on street corners." He ticked off his fingers as he explained. "You've got your upper tiers who do exquisitely planned heists. Gotta admire those types. And then there's the middle, basically all the rest. They work in groups, or are hired by the big blokes who haven't the time or motivation to delegate the upper tier heists."

"I see."

"Good on you, Miss Whitmore. I like a woman who picks up the ball without fumbling. There's also a notation on Sergei's record he's snitched for the SVR. Er, that's the—"

"I know what the SVR is." Thanks to a run-in with them last year in Africa.

"Stupid Violent Russians."

Becca compressed her lips and crossed her arms.

"What is it about the Russians you don't like, Agent Dane?"

"Besides the Cold War?" He shrugged. "It's a joke. You know, humor?" He sighed and punched a fist into his opposite palm. "Okay, tough room. SVR, *Sluzhba Vneshney Razvedki,* Russian Federal Intelligence Service," he said. "But isn't that an oxymoron? Russian and intelligent?"

Despite her reservations, Becca had to smile at his audacity. Ah hell, she let out a chuckle.

"Whew. The room is finally starting to warm up."

Agent Dane's smile was easy and it piqued Becca's attention. Yes, definitely an open man. Direct opposition to her need to keep things close to the vest.

"So, the CIA has flown you all the way to London for that pretty little rock?"

Nodding and exhaling a sigh, she said, "Don't remind me of the flight."

"Don't like to fly in aeroplanes?"

"I fly well enough, it's over water that makes me, um—" she tilted her palm up and down "—nervous."

"Hydrophobic?"

"Yes." And this was far too much information to reveal to a perfect stranger.

He gestured to the diamond. "A nice piece. Ten carats, I believe. Snatched from a gems dealer on Liverpool Street last night as he closed up shop. I don't understand why the entire store was not ransacked. There were other gems of equal size, yet this bit of sparkle was the only thing taken."

"Are you the arresting officer?"

"No, it was—"

"MI-5?"

"Scotland Yard, actually." He winked again. "Five stepped in after the arrest."

Smoothing a palm over her camel-colored Cynthia Rowley tweed slacks, Becca eyed the man. How she did admire a man in a turtleneck. The sweater matched his eyes, which were ice-blue, like translucent aquamarine. Yet the effect was warm, like bonfires in the evening in the Hamptons in fall.

"Um…" Snapping back to the here and now, Becca pulled her gaze from the flash of silver at Agent Dane's hip—that ring. "If you don't mind, I'd like to finish examining the diamond and determine what would make it worth chasing cross-country."

"You don't think the healthy chunk of dosh would do it?"

Dosh? The Brits were difficult at times to decipher. Ah—money, cash.

"Yes, but to murder someone who didn't even have the stone?"

"Attempted murder. The jeweler survived," he said accusingly.

Becca flashed him a condemning look.

Dane shrugged. Typical agent, unconcerned for the emotional aspects of a case.

"It is curious nothing else was stolen," she agreed. "There was no sign of a forced break-in at the New York store. The dealer said the thief specifically asked for this stone. As if he knew she had it. And yet she had only purchased it three days earlier."

"Headquarters is running through the victim's sales

receipts as we speak. If we can discover who sold the diamond—or diamonds, as is the case—perhaps that will give us a clue who's after them and why."

"The CIA is currently tracking stone number two somewhere in Paris."

"So is Six. Sounds as if the two of us will be working together, Miss Whitmore. It'll be a boon to have a dab hand at my side. I couldn't tell a diamond from one of those synthetic bits—what do you call them?"

"Cubic zirconia?"

"That's the ticket."

"You planning to interrogate the suspect?"

"Most definitely," he said. "But first, I'm waiting on a report regarding his SVR connections. Don't let me interrupt you further, Miss Whitmore. Do have a look. I'm eager to watch a gemologist in action."

Tucking her shoulder-length hair behind her left ear, Becca drew in a deep, cleansing breath. She didn't care to be watched. And she wasn't keen on working with a partner. They got in the way, and liked to chat and get to know you.

But in order to gain access to his information source, she'd smile and play nice. If some MI-6 agent wanted to bounce around on her Burberry coattails, he'd better be able to keep up the pace.

Becca again seated herself before the table. An old beige PC sat at the end of the stretch of Formica, tangled cords snaking down to the rubber-streaked linoleum floor. The distinct odor of burned wiring made her wonder if it was more a conversation piece than an actual working computer.

Picking up the diamond, she redirected her focus. Hefty. Solid. The asscher cut was rather ugly. Herself, she preferred the classic round-brilliant cut stones.

But it was an extraordinary showpiece. A stone this size would likely be utilized as the key setting in a necklace or brooch. Only the wealthiest of wealthy could touch so fine a piece. She knew because she belonged to this exclusive, but often troubled social sect.

So she held a cool bit of cash in her palm, but didn't feel the least bit giddy.

What bothered Becca was that someone had tried to kill for this diamond. Murder didn't seem necessary. Had the London theft been foiled by the arrival of Scotland Yard? Or had the thief's MO changed? Was this even the same thief who had struck in New York? Or had that man alerted another in his gang to the sale?

If it was organized crime, as Agent Dane had alluded, the scenario seemed likely.

Mentally, Becca reminded herself that her task wasn't to bemoan the method, but to study the gem. Her expertise was not homicide. Which was why she intended to play nice with MI-6.

"Big as my thumb," Dane noted over her shoulder. "Cat burglars always go for the flash."

"Can he still be considered a mere burglar once a homicide has been attempted?"

"You're right. A proper murderer, with a taste for sparklers."

"A stone this size," she said, "could fetch over a million American dollars—maybe two—depending on its characteristics."

Dane whistled appreciatively. "And I work a fifty-hour week to make my bloody rent."

He assumed his casual pose again in the open door frame, hands shoved in the pockets of his loose-fitting black trousers of indefinable label. Curiosity flashed from his blues, accompanied by a satisfied kitten-in-the-cream smile. For the next few seconds he simply held that Cheshire cat expression, which managed to make Becca wonder.

"What are you looking at?" she asked.

A tilt of his head surveyed her from heel to crown. "You."

"Oooh-kay. Don't you have an interrogation to begin?"

"Soon, love. Just doing a bit of surveillance."

"On me?"

"Indeed. Since when can a CIA agent afford the pretty stuff?"

"I'm not CIA. I'm a gemologist assisting the CIA."

"Right." He winked. "So what have we got? Tweed and silk. Cashmere scarf and Burberry coat." He made a show of peeking under the table at her calfskin shoes. "Ferragamos, yes?"

"Yes," she answered, utterly stunned the man would know something so trivial as the brand of shoes barely revealed beneath her slacks.

"So, you've a bit of dosh," he deduced. "And you get your hair done at the best salons, to judge from its don't-touch-me sheen and delicious fragrance of frangipani."

Reduced to a gape at that correct deduction, Becca lifted a brow.

"I do love that word *frangipani*. Such a treat for the lips. But what the hell does it mean?" he asked.

"How would you recognize the scent if you don't even know what it is from?"

"I'm quite the expert on female perfumes, Miss Whitmore."

"I can imagine."

"Meow." He paced to the two-way window, glanced at the suspect still sitting at the table, and walked back to the doorway. A whistle preceded his announcement. "Look out, blokes, we've another strong woman in our midst."

"You have something against strong women?"

"Not at all," he answered quickly. Then he shrugged, hands still in his pants pockets. "Maybe. No."

"Which is it?"

"Ah hell, I like to be a man. To protect, you understand?"

"Well, you needn't waste your protection skills on me, Agent Dane."

"Duly warned." He punched a fist into his palm once again.

If that little exchange had been an example of his flirtation skills, Becca had little to worry about.

The Louis Vuitton valise on the table held tools of Becca's trade: viewing loupes, refractometer, dichroscope, a calibration scale and a few measurement charts. Her laptop sat in a Gucci bag on the floor.

Dane tapped the alligator leather valise with his finger. "Nice."

Ignoring his continued implications of her wealth, she

picked up the diamond with a tweezers and again searched the square girdle for a lasered ID number or origin name. This was the part she liked best, investigation.

Hours spent picking and perusing rocks as a child during her summers at the Hamptons had led to a passion for gemstones. Mere rocks, yet cut and polished to breathtaking beauty, at least in the eyes of a child. To her, rocks held secrets, some revealed, some forever hidden in their depths. A lot like herself, she often mused. Becca had her secrets, and like a rock with more facets than met the eye, she wasn't about to reveal them all.

Aware of Dane's soft breathing and faint cologne, Becca tried to concentrate. She turned the stone around twice, seeking its secrets. It was completely unmarked. Which was either a good thing or a very bad thing. Unmarked stones were generally sold in lots of much smaller carat size. The single ones should cause suspicion.

"Divulge your findings, oh, strong, wise one."

Tilting her head to look up, Becca nearly banged foreheads with him. Ole blue eyes didn't flinch, but stared at the stone, silently inquiring.

"Do you mind? You're in my light."

"Sorry. Though I must say, a woman so remarkable as you tends to give off her own light."

"Agent Dane." Becca dug about in the valise. "Your blatant flirtations may prove effective in procuring company in your bed every night, but I am not interested. I'm here to do a job, and I'll ask you not to interfere."

"You find my sparkling personality interferes with your concentration?"

"Please." She leaned against the hard metal chair

back and stretched her right leg under the table. Without even looking she could *feel* those perfect blue eyes trained on her movement. It wasn't a bad feeling, but it was interfering with her concentration. "I just…" she sighed "…haven't entirely woken up yet. I slept only half the flight. Is there coffee in this place?"

"Sure you won't have a cup of tea?"

"Just coffee."

"Cream or sugar?"

"Both please."

"Back in a twink." He spun out of the room with an enthusiastic, "Ta!"

Closing her eyes, Becca rubbed her palms over her face. The British Airways 747 had landed at Heathrow Airport an hour earlier. She had glimpsed the rising sun glinting gold on the eastern face of Big Ben as they'd circled the city during their descent.

Sitting up, she fished out a disk light from her valise. A little larger than a quarter, the snappy little device had been designed for her by Alan Burke. Alan was the gadget guru for the Gotham Roses, and he never encountered a challenge he couldn't meet or a foreign movie he didn't like.

A squeeze of the rubber case produced ultraviolet light on one side and white light on the other side. Leaning over the table to block some of the unnatural overhead light, Becca beamed the white light across the diamond. "That's odd." She tilted the diamond to redirect the blocks of prismatic color being beamed across the white card. There was something…

Startled at her discovery, she turned the crown of the

diamond toward the tabletop. Beaming the white light through the lower pavilion of the gem produced a kaleidoscopic dance of light on the pale gray Formica. Within the glow, small, dark spots littered the colors…in a pattern.

Letters?

She couldn't be seeing right.

She squinted at a few of the larger but blurry color blocks. Her breathing grew faster. Thinking to try the UV light, she flipped the disk.

As expected, the diamond fluoresced. But wow, it fluoresced pink! Most diamonds fluoresced blue, and fluorescence wasn't necessarily favorable when pricing a stone. More fluorescence tended to make the diamond murky, sometimes oily in color when viewed in daylight. As an attribute, the fluorescence was prized only if it cut the yellow in the stone to produce a blue-white color.

But this stone wasn't yellow; in fact, in was quite clear.

The door to her left opened and in came Agent Dane, whistling.

"Coffee swimming in cream and dazzled with sugar." He set a cup of extremely pale brew before her. "The man does know how to pour up a cup."

"Did you manage to get a few drops of coffee in my cream?" she asked. A sip proved it the perfect temperature, and very coffeelike, but smooth as her favorite indulgence, a Godiva chocolate martini. "Delicious."

"My personal blend," he stated, while seating himself next to her. Stealing her elbow room, he slid the squeaky metal chair up to the table. His dark suit coat brushed the sleeve of her white silk blouse in a hiss of couture battling bargain basement. "So, did our way-ward American germologist find anything?"

"Gemologist." She couldn't stop a smile, followed by a laugh. Cocky Brit. Becca jiggled the diamond on the white card before her. "Strangely…yes."

"Divulge."

Another sip of caffeine glided down her throat. "There's something on the table of this diamond. An ion beam brand?" She spoke her suspicions out loud.

Ion beam branding served as a means to place iden-tification information, even coded matrixes, upon the table of a gemstone. It was rarely used by any but De-Beers, the industry's leading diamond retailer, though Becca had seen such markings on more than a few oc-casions. But it was impossible to read the nano-size brand with the naked eye. And *should* be impossible to view with anything but a high-powered electron microscope.

Dane stretched his right arm across the table, slouch-ing like a bored student. "There's something inside the diamond?"

"I'm not sure." Becca held up the stone before him. "There is a method jewelers use to mark diamonds in a minute manner. It's completely invisible to the naked eye, unlike the oft-used laser engraving etched into the girdle. This is the girdle." She ran a finger around the edge of the diamond. "Ion beam branding deposits identification codes or matrixes on the table of a dia-mond. They're only viewable with a high-powered microscope."

"And where is yours?"

"Not here. The 200x microscope required is too large to lug about in my little case. But what makes the discovery strange is that I didn't need it."

Grabbing up the light disk, she clicked it on the UV side and flashed it over the crown of the diamond. Again a faint pink glowed within the stone.

"Brilliant."

"Yes, but check this out." She flashed the white light across the stone.

This time, Becca didn't see anything. No letters or branded matrix. In fact, the marks she had seen were now completely gone. "This isn't right—"

"Oh, blighted bollocks!" In a clatter of metal, Dane's chair collapsed as he sprung to his feet and dashed from the room.

Becca spun to the two-way window, then jumped up herself and rushed to it, slapping her palms to the glass. The suspect was convulsing on his chair, the guard talking frantically into his two-way radio.

Dane appeared and grabbed the suspect by the throat. White spittle oozed over the man's tightly clamped lips. Dane pounded a fist against the bound man's chest, then released him with a thrust. Still strapped to the chair, the man fell backward, landing on the floor, his feet in the air. He didn't move.

Dane shouted, "Sod me!"

He flung his arms out and turned to approach the two-way window, giving the glass a blow with his fist. A tight grimace stretched his mouth.

He kicked the chair leg, and exited the room.

Becca rushed to the open door and peeked around another posted guard to find Agent Dane standing in the hallway, hands on his hips and head shaking. He looked at her and clenched his fists. "Bastard killed himself."

Chapter 2

"Cyanide?" Becca asked.

She watched as two officers unstrapped the suspect from the chair and dragged him out of the interrogation room.

Agent Dane paced a trench across the hallway, pounding the opposite wall each time he made a pass. "I shouldn't have left him alone."

"We were right in the next room. And there was a guard! There's nothing you could have done even if you'd been standing directly over him."

Dane stared daggers at her.

She didn't back down. "They can hide those damn pills in a popped-out filling. They're very small. Undetectable."

Coming to a standstill, Dane cocked his head to one

side, then the other, snapping his neck in frustration. "Right."

Spreading an arm across her shoulders, he led her back to the adjoining room. "Didn't need the suss, anyway. We've got the rock." He smoothed that beringed thumb down the front of his suit jacket. "So you claim to have seen something in that diamond?"

A little disturbed at his abrupt personality change, Becca picked up the diamond and her light disk. One more scan with the white light proved what she'd realized before the suspect had committed suicide.

"I thought I did. But now the markings are gone. Something was on the crown. I know it." She tilted the light, then rotated the diamond and looked at it through the side of the pavilion and back through the crown. "I don't understand."

"Would you tell me if you saw something?"

Snapping her gaze up to Dane, she searched his face. All business, signaled by the tight corners of his mouth. His smile was long gone.

"Are you accusing me of something?"

He shrugged. "Accusation is a harsh word."

"So is asshole."

He whistled and snatched for the diamond. "Watch it, Miss Whitmore. You want to play tough guy, I can match you punch for punch."

"I thought you didn't mind strong women?"

"Right. Strong, but not bitchy."

Resisting a snappy riposte, Becca compressed her lips. Why were strong women always labeled "bitch"?

Moving the diamond like a magician manipulating a

coin, Dane finally clasped it between his first and second fingers so the crown of the stone sat like a ring. "Maybe I should have forensics check it out."

"I'm here for a reason, Agent Dane. Forensics won't know the first thing about gemstones."

Becca nabbed the rock, redirecting her rising ire with a heavy exhalation. How easily she'd assumed the agent's peevishness, merely by breathing the same air as Austin Powers here. She wasn't sure her sanity was safe.

"I think I need some breakfast," she decided. She packaged the diamond in its plastic evidence bag. "I'm going to need to do some more work with the diamond."

"So *many* needs," he said, with a dramatic gesture of his arms. "*I* need answers."

"Which you will have. But not right now. I don't have the advanced equipment to view the stone."

Instantly, Becca knew who could assist her. She had worked with Lester Price a year ago on a case that had tracked a dirty gems dealer from New York to the seedy back alleys of London. Rubies and sapphires were being transferred in live geese by an Irish cartel. Extracting the gems? Not a pretty picture.

"May I take this with me?"

Agent Dane gave a wry chuckle, which soon segued to straight-faced disbelief. "You want to tote a ten-carat diamond out of here, just like a bit of all right?"

She nodded.

He swiped long fingers over his clean-shaven chin. Glee glittered in his eyes. "You are bold, Miss Whitmore. Now I do like a bold woman, but they have protocols here at Scotland Yard. As well, I'm taking that hunk of carbon into evidence on behalf of MI-6."

Becca countered with an authoritative stance, arms crossed and feet spread. "I need to borrow it for a few hours. If you can't approve such a loan, Agent Dane, you'll have to let me speak to your superior."

"No need to get all ballsy on me, love."

"One of us had better use them."

"Oh ho?" He made a grab for the plastic evidence bag, but Becca was quicker. "Fine. I'll see what I can arrange. I'm sure you are trustworthy?"

"I am, Agent—"

"Could we make it Dane? And I'll call you Becca."

She was about to correct with a "Ms. Whitmore" to his retreating back, but she held her tongue.

He'd gone to see if she could borrow the stone? Not a likely outcome. That gave her just enough time to get the hell out of Dodge.

There was a goodly amount of paperwork involved in borrowing a priceless diamond from evidence. Exactly what was required to dissuade the woman.

Dane smiled to himself as he shuffled the stack of forms and carbons. Cheeky woman. To ask such a favor? Pretty bit of New York, that one.

He liked New York, the skyscrapers flashing like steel robots stalking through a kitschy sci-fi movie, the raucous nightlife that mixed all levels of human society, the models on virtually every corner. Or were they prostitutes? Either way, a bit of all right, that.

But Becca Whitmore had class. Soft, pretty-smelling

wavy hair that looked like the sun had streaked it—
Dane knew better—it was an expensive salon treatment,
likely. Ferragamos, tweed and Burberry. Stuffy class—
a one-eighty change from the women he was accustomed to keeping on his arm.

As far as female agents partnering on the job, he preferred them in the past tense. Went. Gone. It was too difficult to work with a woman, especially one who fancied
herself so professional and able to do anything the big
boys could do. Doubtful New York could manage a foot
chase in those heels.

Though an expert in gemstones wouldn't hurt this investigation. He'd meant it when he'd said he couldn't
recognize the real thing from a fake. Who could without the proper training? He'd keep her around for a bit
of all right.

British military intelligence wanted what was inside
the diamond. And MI-6 had been charged to get it—at
any price, and before the U.S. snatched it. Intel had
been intercepted during a routine tap of SVR communications. Of course, objectives could be…embellished.
And if the trail of bread crumbs led where he hoped, the
end result would see Dane supremely satisfied.

He thought of the chunk of carbon the woman had
handled like a toy. Something inside and then…noth-
ing? What game was she playing?

Dane paused in the open doorway to the interrogation room where he'd left Miss Whitmore. The table had
been cleared of her tools and fancy leather valise. New
York had left the room.

And so had the diamond.

* * * * *

Cell phone pressed to her ear, Becca walked swiftly down the block, the blue oval Scotland Yard sign fading behind her. The morning had not gotten any warmer. Her breath condensed before her and she swore she could almost hear it crackle.

Ten steps to her right a boy sat on a city bench, his head buried in a book.

She wondered which direction it was to Liverpool, and if there was a place along the way that served tea and raspberry scones like the delicious ones she used to get at the Plaza in New York. She missed Jake's poached eggs and caviar. Her butler-cum-chauffeur pampered her. She deserved it.

She waited on hold as Zeek checked her files. The GIA report on the diamond should have been obtained from MaryEllen Sommerfield's shop by now.

She'd worked closely with Zeek on the African conflict case last year, but had never met her in person. She didn't even know the CIA handler's last name, or if Zeek was her real name, for that matter. But it wasn't important. The Gotham Roses were assigned to various contacts at the CIA, FBI, Homeland Security, or whatever authority the Governess had them working with on a particular case.

"Becca?"

"I'm here, Zeek. What did you find? Did you get the GIA report?"

"Negative." A loud snap cracked the phone line. "I can't imagine what the report would provide beyond— what is it?—cut, color, clarity?"

"Yes, those things. Plus original seller's name, possibly. I've got the diamond in hand, by the way."

"Excellent. I'll arrange for a pickup."

"Hold off, will you? I'm taking it to a friend who has the proper equipment so I can really get a good look at it. It's either incredibly flawed or, well…I'm not sure." Becca toed the curb, where a black rubber skid mark curled high.

"Cool. I'll give you a few hours." Snaps crackled across the phone lines—Zeek had a serious gum habit. Becca assumed Zeek was her age, maybe even younger. Zeek must have been a child genius to have been recruited by the CIA and assigned such high-profile cases. "I do have a tag on the second stone. It's been traced to a Parisian dealer who is holding an auction this evening. I'll want you on a flight to Paris as soon as possible."

"Three countries in one day? Why not."

"You meet the MI-6 agent?"

"Yes. And you neglected to tell me I'd have a partner."

"Couldn't be prevented. It was arranged while you were flying across the ocean, after a bit of to-do, of course, with MI-5. The U.S. and the Brits tend to graciously accept each other's interference. It's goodwill, Becca. Play along for now."

"Right."

"I'll be in contact soon."

"Thanks." She clicked off.

Goodwill? Joy.

Becca had learned over the four years she'd been working covertly for the Roses that people in the government and justice system could be bought for a price.

And while she'd had the pleasure of busting some high-ranking law enforcement officials and rich old corporate bastards, the biggest thrill was in knowing she had busted the men who considered her a piece of arm candy. Oh yeah, she could spread around the goodwill.

She and her sister agents often joked how they should be called the Gotham Thorns, for they were a real thorn in the sides for the big boys of high-society crime. Specialized agents, they were as comfortable handling a semiautomatic as they were sashaying through Saks in their Jimmy Choos and Fred Leighton jewels.

Becca touched the thin gold choker about her neck. It didn't hook in the back, which made it easy to remove. Despite her social status, she wasn't much for flashy accessories. An inch-long heart dangled from the band.

Shuffling her feet to fight off the chill, she cursed the need to wear the calfskin sling-backs. They weren't at all warm, but the heels were chunky, good for movement.

To her right sat the boy reading the comic book. Looking about thirteen years old, he huddled on a stone bench. His legs were covered with a tartan blanket and he was bundled against the cold with earmuffs, mittens, scarf, you name it.

Odd place to sit and relax with a book. Was he waiting for someone inside the station? Was he homeless? The blanket seemed in nice shape, as was his clothing.

Becca inched to the side, keeping one eye peeled for a taxi and the other for Agent Dane.

"Oh, Batman," she said, glancing down at the comic book the boy clutched in his hands.

He didn't look up.

"Is that the issue where Batman gets berated by the women of Gotham City for not treating the opposite sex fairly?"

The boy's head spun around. "How'd you know stuff like that, lady?"

She shrugged. "I'm a big fan of Batman. I've read them all."

"Really? Fancy-looking lady like you?"

"I guess so. I feel as if we've led the same lives."

"You and Batman?"

"Uh-huh."

The boy made a chuffing sound. Freckles danced on his wrinkling nose. "You know Bruce Wayne is a millionaire, don't you, lady?"

"I do. So are you here alone?"

"Me mum's inside paying her parking tickets." He peered through strands of long dark hair. "So you're saying you're like Bruce Wayne. A man so rich he could buy all of the British Isles if he wanted. A man who wears a bat costume and fights crime?" His chuckle dismissed Becca to the rank of fool.

All she could think was...exactly. She related so much with Bruce Wayne, living the high life in the eyes of the public, concealing his dark secret from friends and family. Chasing bad guys under the guise of secrecy, fearing discovery would bring danger to her family. She even had an Alfred who looked after her secret and kept her home: Jake.

"You're a loony, lady."

"Maybe. Oh!"

She was grabbed from behind, gently, but it was a

surprise all the same. Then the metallic bite of cold steel encircled her left wrist.

"What are you—?" She lifted the valise, now attached to her arm with chain links. "Handcuffs?"

The boy's attention was suddenly keen. "Mister, did you put the cuffs to the lady?"

"Safety precaution," he whispered in her ear. "Shouldn't have let you vacate the building without it." To the boy he announced, "Indeed I did, kiddywink. And now I've plans to take the lady home with me and make her my naughty sex slave."

"Wicked!" the boy said.

"No, I'm—" Becca was utterly horrified the man would say such a thing to a kid. Becca was prepared to tell the truth. She carried a valuable gemstone in a mere combination-dial-locked valise, which could be easily accessed by even the stupidest of thieves.

On the other hand…

With a surrendering sigh, she offered to the boy, "What he said."

The boy giggled, then became engrossed in his comic book again.

"Have something you were going to tell me?" Dane asked.

"I should ask you the same."

"Need to know, love. Need to know."

"Of all the… Look, Agent Dane, if we're going to work together on this case I'll need access to all your intel."

"I'll ask for the same."

"Very well, there are two diamonds."

"I know that."

"Do you also know the second has been placed up for auction this evening in Paris?"

"So, off to Paris?"

"Yes, but only after I've made a stop by a friend's. I want him to take a look at this diamond. After which I will return it to evidence here at Scotland Yard."

"From your lips, love. I'll believe it when I see it." He paused, thinking. "Come along, my pampered American pretty, I'll not let you out of my sight. My car is right across the street. I wouldn't dream of allowing you to endure the tortures of London cab drivers."

"Now he's suddenly dashing," she muttered.

With a wave to the boy on the bench, Becca followed Dane across the cobbled street. While the man had the remarkable ability to say the wrong thing, his breezy manner and gregarious posture tempted like the Pied Piper.

He didn't drive a fancy sports car. In fact, Becca wasn't sure what model or make the tiny white-and-black vehicle was, only that it was half the size of a Volkswagen. It wasn't so much parked as placed at the curb, as if a toy in an oversize children's play scene.

"What the hell is it?"

"A fortwo." He gave the back wheel a kick. "You don't like it?"

"It's only half a car!"

"This is a proper car. Not a lumbering behemoth like your Yank tanks. What do they call them? Humvees?"

"Hummers."

"No thanks, I hardly know you." His wink neutralized her sudden urge to slap British face. "But I wager a guess you are accustomed to limousines filled with champagne and caviar. Tough bit of luck, Becky."

Enough. Becca gripped Dane's collar and tugged him into her space. "Becca. Or better yet, Miss Whitmore, if you please."

"Sure thing, love." He liked to wink at her. "Buck up. It'll be an adventure."

The silver iPod attached to Dane's car radio pumped American pop music from the eighties through the speakers. Becca winced as each tune reminded her of her childhood. She was so glad to be finished with boarding school. Conformity had never been her forte.

"Here it is—Price's shop," Dane announced. "This is one of the nicer neighborhoods, I must admit. But still a dive. This your suss?"

"He's not a suss—er, suspect. Lester Price is a technical wizard. And he owns practically every electronic device known to man, one of which should be a high-powered microscope."

"So let's go in."

Becca eyed the doughnut store across the street from Lester's place. "Still haven't had breakfast," she murmured longingly.

Dane saw her glance at the shop. "Is that a hint?"

She batted her eyelashes.

"Ah, sign language. Very good, love. What do you want?"

Biting back an "I am not your love," Becca reminded herself that playing nice was key to accessing this agent's secrets. "A scone, please. No sugar, no frosting. Just plain."

"Sounds proper unsatisfying."

"I don't do sugar."

"Ah. I bet you're a joy over dinner. Are you as high maintenance as I suspect?"

She swung her legs out to the slushy pavement and retorted, "I am."

"Scone, no sugar, ban the frosting. Coming right up!"

She dismissed him with a wave of her hand and crossed the street to the glass-fronted shop. As Dane entered the doughnut store, she called, "Take your time!"

"Haste, my love," Dane replied. "I cannot part from the pretty stone for too long."

After placing his order, Dane stepped to the store window and peered across the street.

He trusted Lester Price. The über-geek had once assisted on a racketeering case that had resulted in bringing down a minor betting scam, which had then led to information on one of London's most notorious gambling dens.

No, it wasn't Price Dane was worried about.

He pulled out his mobile phone and called headquarters. "Silver Fox. Location—London. Got a name I want you to check out."

"Go ahead, Agent Dane."

"Becca Whitmore of New York City. CIA…maybe. Get back to me with everything you can find."

Chapter 3

Lester's computer repair shop was legit. Besides being a cyber whiz, he also indulged in reverse-engineering simple electronics, role playing games and microbrewery—he made his own ale.

Becca had liked him instantly, for he'd not looked at her exterior, but into her. They had become instant friends while working together last year on the Irish gem-smuggling case. It was odd to her, but she found it much easier to relate to people not in her social class. Lester didn't judge and there were no subtle meanings to every word he spoke. He couldn't care less about how many zeroes appeared in her checkbook.

"Lester." Becca backed away when he moved to hug her. He wasn't offended; he was keen on her quirks. "It's been a year," she said as they awkwardly shook hands. "You're still looking tough."

"And you are still as gorgeous as a newly minted Pentium chip." He gestured for her to sit on a wooden stool before a stainless steel counter.

Almost six feet tall but with the hunched shoulders and rounded spine of someone who spent too much time leaning over a computer keyboard, Lester wore his red hair long, tucked beneath a wool cap with the tabs flapping over his ears. Long wool strings dangled from each tab, a pale blue pompom hanging at each of his shoulders.

Starting to take off her coat, Becca paused when she got the first shoulder off. "Yikes, it's freezing in here." She buttoned it up again with her free hand and considered putting her gloves on. "I know you like to keep the shop cool for all the electronics, but this is taking it a bit far."

"Is a bit nippy, isn't it?" He smiled and then whispered, "Haven't paid the utilities for a few months."

"Really? Yet you have power."

"Heat I can do without. Electricity? Not on your nadgers. So, what brings you to the drippy nose of the world? I thought you did Paris during the winter. Isn't fashion week coming up?"

"I did Paris for Christmas."

Shoving aside a scattering of motherboards and a soldering gun dripping solidified silver, Becca set the valise on the counter.

Still cuffed, she wished Agent Dane had set her free before taking off.

"You're kidding me," he said, lifting the handle to

examine the cuffs. "This is the least secure setup I've ever seen."

"I know. It's not my doing."

"Oh?"

"No questions."

"Right, I know the drill."

Entering the four-digit code snapped open the valise lock. Becca then laid the plastic bag on the counter. "What brings me to London? This pretty girl."

"Brill." Lester tapped out the diamond onto his palm, then held it before him. His pale green eyes crossed comically. "How many carats?"

"Ten. But I can't determine if there are inclusions."

"My guess is you need a high-powered microscope?"

"Pretty please? There's something inside the stone. It fluoresces pink."

"I thought diamonds only fluoresced blue."

"They can fluoresce any color, but blue is most common. Pink, I have never seen." She dug out the light disk from the valise. "Here. It's a UV light on this side."

"Nice. Where'd you score this?"

"I have my sources."

"Sources I'd love to infiltrate."

Which was exactly why her lips were sealed.

"I flashed it across the crown and thought I saw…writing…or a code?" The notion hadn't occurred to her until now. Had someone implanted a code within the diamond? Why? And how would the gem have ended up in a New York dealer's store?

"You're surprised?"

"Just thinking on my feet."

And why not a code? It might explain why people were willing to kill—and die—for the stone.

Lester swept the white light over the diamond. Rainbow blocks danced on the walls, which were stashed floor to ceiling with computer parts, old televisions, all sorts of electronic equipment and his mascot stuffed pig which sported a tuft of red fur on its noggin.

"Where'd you get this?"

"Can't tell you. Sealed lips, remember?" She glanced out the window, stretching her neck to insure her babysitter was nowhere in sight. "Agent Dane would never forgive me."

"You working with Dane?" Lester chuckled, but his attention remained on the diamond. "Guy's a proper character."

"No kidding."

"But keen, Becca. He's one of the smartest at Scotland Yard."

"I thought he was MI-6?"

"Oh, right. He was promoted last summer, though I hadn't known it was to Six. A right proper bloke, even if the Yard was trying to bust his arse. You'll appreciate working with him."

"You know why they were trying to bust his arse—er, ass?"

Lester shrugged. "Dane never goes by the book. He's all intuition and spur-of-the-moment kind of thinking. If he's after something, he'll let nothing stand in his way. I don't think he fit in with the tighty-whitey code of Scotland Yard—probably why they rushed through his app to MI-6. Course, could have had something to do with his father's death."

Interesting. Becca filed that information away for further perusal.

She leaned in to study the diamond, nudging shoulders with Lester. "Flash it across the crown. I could swear I saw words embedded within. Maybe in a matrixlike design."

"Ion beam?"

"Good, you know your stuff."

"I've read about the process online but have never seen the actual markings before. Access to sparkly bits of this size doesn't come easily. Ion beam branding is high-tech stuff, Becca. We're talking nanotechnology."

"Yes, but it's a much better process than lasers for marking a diamond," she said. "Doesn't damage the integrity of the stone. Nor does it decrease the value. Of course, it should be impossible to view with the naked eye."

"Not if you have an electron microscope." The prismatic light beamed through the stone and onto the pocked plaster wall. "Sticky sweet, that's gorgeous!"

Becca smiled at Lester's wonder, but tilted his wrist to beam it on the steel counter. "The laser or microscope should reflect the dark matrix in the center." She moved his hand up to spread the width of the light across a white calendar pad.

"I'm not seeing anything," he said.

"But something was there. I know it. Have you anything more powerful than this little disk?"

"Somewhere in this disaster." He got up and shuffled

to the shelves behind his desk. Metal parts crashed and the pig landed on its snout with a squeak.

While he traversed the hardware forest, Becca studied the diamond with her naked eye, using the pale winter light beaming through the window. Lester's store sat on a corner; one wall was entirely window. Couldn't waste all the natural light. Or obviously, the natural chill.

"You hungry?"

She looked up from her study to see the package of cherry licorice nubs Lester offered, and shook her head. He tossed it over his shoulder to the floor.

"Here we go." A moment later he emerged from the darkness at the far wall, pushing a wobbly utility cart through a cavalcade of empty boxes that spewed white packing peanuts in his wake.

Becca moved aside to allow him to set up the microscope and plug it into a strip of outlets longer than her arm. Talk about taking your life into your own hands merely by plugging in one more electronic device. It was a miracle he even had electricity.

Seconds later he leaned over the scope's lens, searching, but seeing absolutely nothing inside the facets of the asscher stone.

Had she thought she'd seen something that wasn't there?

"Do *you* see anything, Lester?"

"Well… It's so fine. It's not a code. More like… dust."

"Dust?" She leaned over his shoulder, but could not see what he saw.

"Nanodust."

"Okay, now you've lost me."

"Very small, incredibly minute dust. Like…residue of something that was once there. Wait. A. Minute."

"You see something?"

"Oh yeah. This is—well, nothing is impossible. The technology to do something like this…"

"Talk to me, Lester."

He sat up straight and flipped one pompom over his shoulder. Furrowing one red brow, he tilted his head. "Do you hear that?"

Beyond the hum produced by dozens of computers?

"What is it, Lester?"

The man's eyes widened.

Becca spun around as the grille of a Mercedes soared toward Lester's window.

Chapter 4

Glass sprayed toward them as the car charged through the window.

Instincts kicking in like a mother lion protecting her young, Becca twisted at the waist, hooked Lester across the chest with her arm and sprang into flight. They landed on the stainless steel cart and rolled to the far wall, the rubber wheels crushing cardboard boxes as they went. Packing peanuts flew everywhere.

The microscope sailed over their heads and beat them to the wall with a metallic splat.

Becca's shoulder impacted with the plaster wall. The cart wobbled, then tilted. Lester's weight rolled over hers as the two fell to the floor. Shattered glass and white foam bits showered around them.

She crawled over Lester and lay on top of him,

spreading her arms up to protect his head. Pressing her face to his chest, she felt a woolly pompom smush into her cheek.

A sharp metal track, previously supporting the ceiling tiles, stabbed the wall near Becca's face. Amazingly, the cart blocked them from being impaled.

Becca pushed up onto her elbows. Lester lay immobile. Blood streaked from his temple to his jaw. She choked on the dust of Sheetrock and debris. Shivering with fear, she suddenly…relaxed. Her senses shut down.

And then it all flooded back in a mix of terror and confusion. She must have briefly passed out.

Pushing away from Lester's body, Becca looked toward the gaping hole in the corner of the building. A black Mercedes had decided to park in Lester's shop.

Becca released the tight hold on what she gripped in her left hand. The diamond's pointed pavilion had impressed a dent into her palm. Smiling at the pain of it— because that meant nothing else was hurt more severely—she shifted off Lester and nudged his arm.

He flipped onto his back and moaned, then let out a swear word.

Becca pressed his shoulder firmly. "Just wait. It might not be safe to move yet. Give it a few minutes to let the debris settle."

He nodded and rubbed his elbow.

"You all right? You're bleeding."

Lester tongued his lower lip. "Bit it when you flung me to the floor."

"Sorry."

"Sorry? You saved my life, you perfectly wonderful bit of action heroine."

"So you owe me one." Becca twisted and squatted to scan the vehicle.

The front right tire spun. The hood had crinkled and bulged open to reveal a hissing engine. The car horn sounded continuously. There was a splash of blood on the cracked windshield.

"You expecting company, Lester?"

"Just the pizza boy, but he usually comes on bicycle."

Standing and brushing aside a broken bit of plastered wall, Becca reached down to help Lester up.

He yanked off his wool cap and looked around. "Sod it all!"

Slapping a palm on the dented Mercedes's trunk, Becca stepped carefully through the broken glass and shattered wood around to the driver's side. The window had not been safety glass, and so it had broken in long sharp shards. Impulsively slipping a hand down her side—no gun; customs would never have allowed her to pass through—she wished calling for backup was an option.

Where was Dane?

Now she realized there was not a valise dangling from her wrist. She held up her left hand and swung the handcuffs before her. The handle must have been ripped off during her flying trip to the wall. Her wrist hurt, but she could bend it, so it wasn't broken.

She reached through the shattered car window and gripped the back of the driver's head. The steering wheel had crushed his nose back into his skull. Blood drooled from his nose, eyes and mouth. Dead? Incapacitated, at the very least.

The smell of gasoline panicked her momentarily. Becca knew better; the car would not blow unless there was something to ignite a blaze. No gas heat, no flame. But she couldn't take a chance; she had to get Lester out—

"Becca!"

Agent Dane stood before what was once the entrance, waving over the mountain of debris.

"We're all right!" she called. Releasing the door of the car, she stumbled backward, settling less than gracefully onto a heap of crumbled brick.

"I leave you for five minutes and look at the trouble you find. You all right?"

"Peachy."

Ten minutes later the emergency crew had arrived— two green-and-white ambulances and a police car. Dane had helped Becca and Lester out of the rubble and on to the street. As soon as Dane had reached her, she'd demanded he remove her handcuffs. No need to raise suspicion from the local authorities.

The ambulance crew had determined she was sound, no broken bones, just scratches. Thankfully, her wrist wasn't even sprained. But her shoulder muscles would ache for days and she would have plenty of bruises.

The driver was dead. Dane had done a search of his pockets and the glove box—no ID. A crane was on its way to pull the Mercedes from the shop. The license plates were missing.

Gasoline fumes and dust still hung heavily in the chilly air.

"Suicide mission," Dane noted. He leaned against the trunk of his car—if you could call it a trunk. The Brits called it a boot, and it didn't appear as if it could hold much more than a pair of them.

Becca joined him and rubbed her aching shoulder. "What makes you think it wasn't an accident?"

"Because I was standing across the street. The road was empty. Life was all sugar doughnuts and fat-free scones. All of a sudden a Mercedes guns it and takes a sharp swerve to the left."

"Maybe the driver was drunk?"

"At eleven in the morning? A drunk could not have been so precise. Nor would he be driving a car without plates. Someone wanted you dead."

"Impossible that someone could have known I was in Lester's shop," Becca argued. "I just decided to come here thirty minutes earlier. I didn't call Lester to tell him I was coming, either. If it was preplanned, the target had to have been Lester."

They glanced to the back of one of the open ambulances, where Lester flirted with two female techs. One of them toyed with the pompom on his hat.

"Pity." Dane crossed his ankles and sighed. "We lost the stone."

Becca dug into her coat pocket and handed him the diamond.

"You hung on to it? *And* rescued Lester from becoming a piece of squish? Pure dead brilliant, New York."

"It was more like self-preservation. I just took

Lester along for the ride." She glanced at the diamond. "Don't get too attached to that baby. I'm not ready to turn it back into evidence. Lester found traces of dust on the crown. I need equipment that is not scattered all over an accident site, and preferably, a steel-walled lab."

"Dust? It's evidence." Dane tossed the stone and caught it in his palm.

If he was going to start that again… "That will sit in a storage safe when it could be utilized to help me solve this crime."

"Me?"

"What?"

"You said me, as in, *you* are trying to solve this one. You're just the gemologist, right?" He bent before her, a curious glint in his aquamarine eyes. "What's your objective? You want to take this beauty back to the States?"

"I'm…I thought we were playing the need-to-know game? You show me your objective, I'll show you mine."

"Well. That's peachy." He straightened. "But you're simply a glorified jeweler, love. MI-6 will get this. And I'm not required to provide you any evidence."

And this mission was supposed to breed goodwill?

"The CIA will have a problem with that."

"The diamond stays with me until I can check it into evidence, which is what I should have done in the first place."

Becca huffed out her growing anger. Cocky British jerk.

"What if there is something inside the diamond that can help me—er, *us*—solve the case?"

"What could possibly be *inside* a rock, Miss Whitmore?"

Becca winced at the ache in her right shoulder. She'd fallen hard.

"You sure you're all right?"

She flinched violently when Dane touched her shoulder.

"You've hurt something, love."

"I don't like to be touched." That confession came out a little too bluntly. Her family had never been the touchy-feely sort.

Dane twisted his lips wryly. Now, besides a strong-willed bitch, he surely also thought her a prude.

"Just…the standard bruises following having a building fall down around me. I'm tired. I ache all over. I was almost killed. And now I'm frustrated. Please, Agent Dane, I need that diamond."

"Again with her needs."

If he only knew. Needs, wants, requirements. And everything in her wake was imperfect and based on lies. "Your life will become a lie." Becca recalled Renee Dalton-Sinclair telling her that when she'd decided to join the Gotham Roses spy club. "Can you live with that? Lying to friends, family and even lovers? Your needs will change. You will crave what you have always ignored—emotion."

Growing up in a family of old money and zealous ambition, Becca found that emotion fell to the wayside in favor of putting on a good face for the public. The rare bit of human contact Becca cherished was the music she shared with her father.

Sure, there had been minor emotional casualties because of the choices she had made. But she loved what she did. The covert lifestyle? It fitted her like a glove.

As for needs? Oh, she had them. Right now a steam room and hot-rock massage would feel perfect.

Dane joggled the diamond in his palm. "Something inside, eh?" The cold winter sun glinted in the facets.

Becca couldn't find the strength to argue her case for keeping the diamond. She needed to rest for a few minutes. And where was that scone?

Lester walked over and leaned on the trunk next to her, forcing her to slide closer to Dane.

"How are you, Lester?" she asked with as much interest as she could muster. "All in one piece?"

"They want to take me to Casualty for some X-rays. I can tell them already it's just a fractured rib or two. You've still got it? Brill. I know what I saw, Becca."

Dane sent him a curious glance. "First name basis, eh?"

"We've worked together previously," Becca said. "I already told you that. Now talk to me, Lester."

"Agent Dane…" Lester murmured.

"Yes, Agent Dane can hear what you've got to say," Dane said, obviously miffed.

"Well, Becca said she saw something in the rock earlier, and now it's gone."

She nodded in confirmation. They all three watched as Dane manipulated the stone across his fingers.

"So, I've been postulating," Lester continued, "and this is a bold speculation—but it might be an EPROM."

"Speak English, boy," Dane said. "The queen's English, if you please."

"You know what I mean when I say ROM? Like the CDs and computer data?"

"Yes," Becca said.

"Well, an EPROM is programmable read-only memory that can ultimately be erased. I think there's a chip in this diamond."

"Impossible," Becca said immediately. "You cannot put something like a computer chip inside a diamond." She caught Dane's nod of agreement. "Unless it's a synthetic stone, and I know it's not. It's too perfect."

"Save the nanodust."

"You think the dust is actually some sort of microscopic computer chip?"

Lester shrugged. "I'm no scientist."

"I'll never believe it, Lester."

"Nanotechnology can do amazing things, Becca. Don't think of the chip as a piece of metal or even anything tangible. It's nanosize, maybe even organic or biological in nature."

She sighed.

"I've got another theory," Lester added. "It could be photoreflective polymers, which would explain the odd-colored fluorescence. They can be viewed by shining different colored light on them, like the UV disk."

"Again, how would these polymers get inside the stone?"

"You said you knew the ion beam branding process?"

"Yes."

"Same way those markings get onto the stone. Ultraprecise nanolaser. And they aren't exactly inside, but on the surface."

"All this from a glance?" Dane queried. There was no belief whatsoever in his voice. "The lady was in your shop less than five minutes."

"Of course, it's all theory. I'll need to do further study of the stone," Lester said.

Dane again tossed the diamond and snatched it out of the air. "Evidence."

"Stop that," Becca said to him, and then added, "If Lester is right, this could help our—*your* investigation."

"You believe him? You, the expert on gemstones, believes someone embedded a tiny computer chip into an object that is one of the hardest substances known to man?"

Well, there was such a thing as flaws. Natural inclusions in rocks. If flaws could get into a stone, then… It was an incredible leap to make, Becca thought.

"It's just a hunk of carbon," Lester said with a sigh. "Carbon can easily be altered at the molecular level. I could go into fullerenes and buckyballs, but then I'd really see your eyes glaze. Unfortunately, my equipment is trashed."

"And why is that?" Dane walked up to Lester. The agent was a full head taller, and seemed to loom over his stooped figure. "You get a look at the driver?"

Lester shrugged.

"Why would someone drive a bloody Mercedes through your shop window? You in for a bit with any dark sorts, Lester?"

"No! I mean, I haven't a clue, Agent Dane. Maybe someone knew Becca was carrying the diamond?" he suggested.

"Impossible," Dane countered. "Besides, why com-mit a suicide mission and leave the stone untouched? That's two suicides in less than two hours."

Both men glared at each other. Becca could feel the testosterone oozing from Dane. Lester looked even punier and weaker.

"He's hurt. He needs medical attention," she said to break the standoff. "We'll question him later at the hospital. *After* he's had a thorough look at the diamond."

"I'm sorry, Becca, I'd need the right stuff," Lester said. "You know that."

"What about the hospital?"

"St. Mary's? What about it?" Lester met Becca's gaze, and within two blinks, he nodded. "They've got electron microscopes. And I am going that way...."

"Give me the stone," she said to Dane. He shook his head, like a petulant child not about to hand over his stash.

Becca lowered her head, looked up at Dane through her lashes and licked her lower lip. "Agent..."

"Oh, don't even try."

"Try what?"

"You think batting those thick dark lashes and licking those full lips will get you the diamond?" He bristled and gave a tug to his turtleneck. "I am impervious."

Becca fluttered her lashes, all innocence.

Behind her Lester chuckled.

"No," Dane said. A bit less defensively he added, "Abso-sodding-lutely not."

"What if you send an MI-6 agent to babysit Lester?"

Dane huffed through his nose, obviously not about to back down so easily.

Becca ran her fingers over her ear and tucked in her

hair. It hurt like hell to make such a move, but she had to try. How difficult could it be to seduce Agent Swank?

"Rot it." Dane grabbed Becca's hand and slapped the diamond onto her palm. "But you realize you just made me a silent promise?"

To what, she could guess. She'd worry about that later. At the moment, all that mattered was her mission. She twisted and palmed the stone to Lester.

To Dane she said, "Call up your watchdogs."

"Already doing so," he said with a flip of his phone.

"You've got my cell number, Lester? Call me as soon as you've had a look."

"Will do." Lester waved to the ambulance techs waiting for him. "Becca. Agent Dane."

Five minutes later a plainclothes agent arrived. With an acknowledging wink to Dane, the man climbed into the back of the ambulance. They watched it roll off, leaving thick clouds of exhaust hanging above the tarmac in its wake.

Becca absently curled her fingers around the gold heart at her neck. The gold was still warm despite the weather.

"No jewels for the gemologist?"

"Hmm? I prefer gold."

"Interesting."

"Don't get me wrong, gemstones are a passion."

"You don't strike me as the passionate sort."

That comment punched her in the gut. Did he mean sexually? Certainly, she liked to put distance between herself and new acquaintances. One had to be leery in her line of work. But she wasn't cold. Was she?

Not about to let on that he had wounded her, Becca turned and looked around to the passenger side of his buglike car.

"The auction is this evening. Much as you'd like it to be a singular operation, we are in this together. And—" she delivered an admonishing slash of her finger toward him "—if you're keeping anything from me, evidence, intel, information, anything—I promise you will regret it."

"I love a woman who can make a threat with a smile."

"I won't be smiling if I discover you're holding out on me."

"Me, keep secrets from you? You're too gorgeous to want to upset, love. Just stay one step behind me, and try to keep up."

"I never stand behind any man."

Chapter 5

Dane had suggested they take the Chunnel train to Paris. While the travel time wasn't any shorter than a flight, the ticketing, boarding and waiting time was greatly decreased.

It was fifteen minutes until boarding. While Dane toddled off to the coffee shop to buy tea and hot chocolate, Becca parked her aching body on a stool before a curved blue plastic table.

She patted her Gucci bag with her laptop in it, glad it hadn't been damaged.

Her kit of loupes and gem-gauging aids was a total loss. She would need replacements, and so phoned ahead to a friend in Paris. Vincent would hook her up, and leave the supplies at the hotel for her. He was one of her more shady connections—she suspected he was a jewel thief—but she didn't question him. Nor had she been overly interrogative the one night following a gemstone auction when they had danced until dawn. As far as Frenchmen went, Vincent was classic. Refined yet raw. Stark yet soft. Seductive but cold. A panoply of opposites that had thrilled her, literally, into bed with him. Pity his aspirations appeared criminal.

She wasn't a hedonist; rather refined, actually. But it was much easier to have affairs than relationships. She didn't like to take names, and so rarely did, with the exception of Vincent and Zen.

Becca indulged in regular Zen sessions. He was tall, dark and able to spend an entire evening without taking more than one break from sex. Zen was not Becca Whitmore's lover. He had sex with her lusty alter ego, who kept an apartment in the Village especially for those nights when she faltered from society's rigid expectations and the all-seeing eyes of the paparazzi.

Lately, her work with her charity Grace Notes and her constant assignments for the Gotham Roses kept her far too busy to even think about a relationship.

A year devoted to one man—her ex-fiancé—had been a big chunk of her life. God knows she was entirely to blame for the breakup with David Chester, of Chester Jewelers fame, a year earlier. It was impossible to live a double life and expect to keep The Secret from someone you loved. When faced with the dilemma, instead of choosing to reveal her secret life with the Gotham Roses, she'd dumped her fiancé. Why? He would have never been able to handle the truth.

At least, that was her story, and she planned to stick to it.

After speaking to Vincent, Becca dialed up her favorite Paris hotel and made a reservation under her name. It was the one where the auction was to be held this evening. The staff knew her as a New York socialite who often visited the Place Vendôme to purchase gemstones. The truth. As a gemologist she was frequently hired by wealthy clients to attend auctions to verify rare gemstones, ensure they were not fake. Perfect cover.

A woman joined her at the curved table. "Batman?"

The silly code name she had chosen to identify herself to a fellow agent. Who said she didn't have a sense of humor?

Becca surreptitiously took in the woman's profile without turning to look at her directly. A dark scarf concealed the back of her head and her ear. Her jawline was sharp and her lips parted as if in wait of a cigarette. Dark sunglasses sat on a small face with little makeup, but a flawless olive complexion.

"Gotham City's finest." Becca gave the expected verification.

A simple nod. "Becca Whitmore, I'm Agent Arlowe. Zeek sent me. I've come to make the exchange."

Becca kept her head forward, avoiding eye contact. Just a casual conversation between two strangers. Zeek had said she'd send someone to pick up the diamond.

"I don't have it in hand."

Arlowe's lips compressed.

"It's with Lester Price. He's been admitted to St. Mary's Hospital."

"Zeek mentioned Price. But we assumed you'd not leave him alone."

"MI-6 is babysitting. Price is trustworthy—a cyber genius I've worked with before. I sent the diamond along with him—best place to find an electron microscope. You should have no problem obtaining the evidence."

"Right. If MI-6 is in a cooperative mood." The agent tapped a clear-polished nail on the plastic countertop, paused in thought, then murmured, "Agent Dane's intel is of value.… But I caution you against a full-out partnership with MI-6. Use him for his intel, then dump him."

Becca nodded. No skin off her back. The sooner she got rid of her partner, the better.

Arlowe looked directly at Becca for a few seconds, with a flash of pretty gold eyes, before looking away. "I have info about your Paris stop. You're authorized to bid, but not win."

"Why not close down the auction, or obtain the stone beforehand?"

"Much as we'd like to acquire the second diamond, what is of prime import is to draw out the thieves. I wish you luck."

Seconds after Arlowe had left, Dane arrived with cardboard cups of steaming tea and hot chocolate. Pressed between his thumbs was a sack of salted nuts.

"Who was that gorgeous bit of duck?"

"I don't know." Becca sipped the hot chocolate carefully.

Dane shook out a handful of salted nuts. "You were chatting her up like you knew her."

And here she thought she'd been so discreet.

"She liked my coat. I gave her directions to Burberry on Bond Street."

"Uh-huh. Right. Even though there's a big slash in the back of it?"

"There is?" Becca tugged off her coat to discover she, indeed, wore a tattered coat.

Dane eyed Arlowe's retreating figure. He chewed slowly, thoughtfully. "Funny."

Becca folded her coat in half and laid it on the stool. "What?"

"Duck is wearing Doc Martens and camo pants. Doesn't look the sort to shop at Burberry."

"Well, you obviously know her better than I do, because I just met her." And that was the truth. If the CIA wasn't keen on MI-6, then she could hold her intel as tight as Dane held his. "I'm going to need a new coat."

"That one looks fine. From the front." He smirked behind his tea.

"Ah. Humor. Not funny. I'll meet you on the train," Becca said.

Hooking her laptop bag over her left shoulder, because the right still hurt like a mother, she walked across the aisle for distance, dialing her phone as she did. The contacts the Gotham Roses used across the nation changed frequently, so she always went through base in New York with gadget and wardrobe requests. "Kristi?"

Kristi Burke designed all the costumes and managed wardrobes for the Gotham Roses. She was gadget guru Alan Burke's sister.

"Becca, good to hear your voice. So you're in London?"

"Dashing off to Paris in a few minutes. Can I ask a big favor?"

"Is it about fashion?"

"Always."

"Then shoot."

"I'll need a gown for a gemstone auction tonight, a change of clothing, and a nice warm coat to see me through the Paris chill and rain."

"Shoes or boots?"

"Both."

"I'll get in touch with my Paris connections. Alan is working on arranging some gadgets for you. You'll need to communicate during the auction. Everything should be waiting upon your arrival."

"You know where I'm staying?"

"Your hotel credit reservation just popped up on the grid."

"Of course." The strangest part of her life was the constant surveillance, be it by the paparazzi seeking the rich and famous, or the Gotham Roses. She couldn't make a move without someone noticing.

And now she had a handsome Brit watching her every move.

No one had ever said this job didn't have a few perks.

Chapter 6

France—Paris

The Place Vendôme was a small city square of bankers, jewelers and shops that offered Paris's most densely concentrated area of diamonds. Becca always passed up the Hotel Ritz for her favorite, the Hotel Regina, which was down the street from the Vendôme.

The Regina was not as opulent as the Ritz, which was why Becca liked it. It was homey in a rococo-trashes-art-deco kind of way. A huge fan of the deco period, she never missed an auction that offered an Alphonse Mucha original.

Tonight's auction was actually being held at the hotel, with a festival of lights in the Vendôme following.

Dane hung back in the lobby, iPod and earbuds in place, picking through the pamphlets while Becca registered. She was greeted at the front desk with the usual élan.

"Ah, Mademoiselle Whitmore! So lovely to see you in our modest home again."

"*Bonsoir,* Jean Paul. It is very good to see you again." The boy-size senior ran the front desk, and was renowned for his work ethic. He was in his early nineties, but didn't look a day over eighty. "Is madame feeling better?" Becca asked.

"Ah, *très bien. Merci* for asking. She settles into melancholy on occasion, but I have bought her one of those fancy bright lights to make her happy. You know of what I speak?"

"I do. The winter months can be bleak. I wish her much happiness." Becca laid her Centurion card on the counter and he discreetly swiped it for her. "Were there any packages left for me, Jean Paul?"

Perusing his thoughts with a rolling of his eyes, he then tapped the air with a long finger. "But of course!" He turned to sort through the wooden files behind him.

Jean Paul returned with a breadbasket-size package wrapped in brown paper and twine. Inside would be all the tools a jeweler would need, plus there was a note from Vincent attached, which Becca discreetly tucked in her coat pocket.

"There was also a delivery to your room not an hour ago, Mademoiselle Whitmore. A tailor's dress bag and a smaller box. Will you be attending the auction this evening…? But of course!"

"You know me well, Jean Paul. I'll ring for room service as soon as I've settled in. *Merci!*"

As she and Dane walked up two flights to their hotel room, Becca's cell phone rang, and she clicked on. "Yes?"

Lester's whispers were barely audible. She plugged her other ear to better hear. "You're where?"

"In the laboratory at the hospital. I can't talk loud. I've snuck in here."

"Where's the MI-6 agent?"

"Getting a coffee. He's a prick. I had to take a chance."

"Does that chance include taking a look at the diamond?"

That got Dane's attention. Walking the hallway toward their room, he turned and studied her.

"It's remarkable, Becca. There was definitely something inside. *Was* being the key word. The structural integrity of the diamond has been faintly altered. Never would anyone pick up on it—the stone could be sold as flawless."

"Go on."

"It is the ion beam branding, but a completely new process. It's got to be. I can detect a ten-micron line—that's a tenth the width of a human hair. It's part of something greater that was once there. You know? The ion beam process etches the nanolines into the diamond table, but it is permanent. You can't erase it unless you grind it off. I think someone found a way to undo the permanence."

"You think it was erased? *Without* grinding it off?"

Dane stopped at the door to their room. The tilt of his head told Becca he hung on her every word.

"It's possible. Nanotechnology does some amazing stuff with different colored light sources. Whatever was originally on this stone—organic, is what I think— could have been excited by the UV light you shined on it, which may have led it to self-destruct."

What Lester said made little sense. It was unbelievable. But she knew nothing of nanotechnology. Who was she to question?

"You said there was another diamond?"

"Yes." Had she told him that?

"You need to get your hands on it," Lester whispered. "And don't shine the UV light on it until you've had opportunity to look at it under a high-powered microscope. Like I said, you might have inadvertently excited the nanodata, caused it to move, and erased it. Oh shit, I think someone's coming."

"I've arranged for a courier to pick up the diamond at the hospital. Maybe that's her—Lester?"

"It's not safe, Becca." Static crackled in her ear. "I've got to go," he murmured.

"Wait, Lester. It could be Agent Ar—"

The connection clicked off. Becca stared at the small platinum cell phone. What was Lester up to? He knew the danger in going against protocol. She couldn't lose that stone.

"What's up?"

She slid in the keycard and entered the room. "Lester."

"Don't tell me he lost the stone."

"No, it's safe." Maybe. "He's just checking in with me."

Earbuds still in place, Dane followed Becca into her room and slouched into the Louis XVI chair next to an ornate mahogany secretary that might have felt the weighty decisions and royal palms of past kings.

Decorated in warm red-tapestried wallpaper and painted a soft cream, the room felt luminous and safe. Heavy red drapes, drawn back by thick tasseled ties, separated a sleeping alcove with twin beds from the living area. A marble-topped table held a bouquet of striped red lilies and fragrant white roses. The scent reminded Becca of Renee Dalton-Sinclair's sitting room. White tea roses were her favorite.

In her bag Becca carried a Powerbook, which she slipped out and set on the secretary. She massaged her right shoulder. The ache would get worse if she didn't take an aspirin or put something on it. A call to a pharmacy might become necessity, but a hot shower, and a session of deep breathing and focus, should dispel most of the pain.

She patted the smooth metallic laptop. The auction began at 8:00 p.m.—three hours from now. Contacting Zeek about Lester was first on the list.

"Nice digs," Dane said, tugging out one earbud.

Guessing he wasn't as far ahead of the curve as she, Becca thought to play with him.

"This is our room," she said, setting the package from Vincent on the marble table. "They're fully booked, but they always save a room or two for regulars or celebrities."

Dane looked about. "I must see if I can get me one of those black credit cards. What's the limit on that thing? Isn't it a cool million?"

"If you have to ask…" She breezed about the room, checking the curtains and the corners of the ceilings with an eye for any sort of listening device. Lifting the phone, she inspected the underside. It looked tamper-free. She didn't expect bugs, but one could never be sure.

"I know who you are," Dane chanted in a singsong.

"We've already done the introductions, Agent Dane. You going batty on me?"

"Becca *Whitmore*," he said, as if putting emphasis on her last name meant all the difference in the world. When she didn't react, he tugged the earbud from his other ear and handed them to her.

She shook her head emphatically.

"Just give a listen."

"Agent Dane, I don't care to put whatever you've had in your ears in mine."

"You *are* a stiff one." He rubbed the white earbuds over his blue sweater, then, clasping the iPod, handed the whole thing to her. Apparently he wasn't about to give up until she'd listened.

Becca took the tiny silver music player and surreptitiously rubbed the earbuds over her pant leg. Then she touched one earbud to her ear.

A luscious symphony in D minor filled her brain. She smiled, knowing the melody instantly, a childhood lullaby that she'd heard over and over.

"The *Midsummer Serenade*," she said. It had been

composed in her honor. Strange, how visceral one's re-actions could be to memory.

"Your father?"

"Yes. He wrote this when I was six. I used to perform the violin solo in the second movement."

Which was long before she'd decided a career in music wasn't for her. The memory made her chuckle. She'd been so precocious in her early teens.

She handed the iPod back. "You like this kind of music?"

"Love it. I like most music, even some country. I hadn't picked up on your name until I started listening to this. So your father is the twentieth century Mozart?"

She shrugged at the name the world had coined for her genius parent. Reinhardt Whitmore had been born with music in his veins. And quite a lot of cash, thanks to his grandfather's investments in Arctic oil. "Guess so."

"I thought I once read or heard something about his daughter being equally as talented?"

"I can play any instrument you put in my hands." But that didn't mean she enjoyed it. Reading and perform-ing music was vastly different from *feeling* the music.

Gemstones, now those she felt in her very soul.

"Really?" Dane twisted on the chair. Both wrists dan-gled over the arm, the iPod forgotten in his lap. "A flute?"

"Doesn't every high school girl know how to play the flute?"

"Drums?"

"Keeping the beat comes naturally to me." She tapped out a mock drumroll on her legs. "I think it's def-initely something I got from my father's genes."

"Electric guitar?"

"Plug it in." She assumed her best rocker sneer. "And I can rock the house."

"Well, well." He nodded, impressed, tapping his finger to his chin and thoughtfully pursing his lips. "How about a harmonica?"

"I'd give it a try."

"So…you'll try anything once?" A waggle of his eyebrows clued her to his double meaning.

"So long as it performs to my standards."

He took that retort with silent glee, cupping his palm under his chin and looking at her as if for the first time. "You're quite the dichotomy, New York. Can't imagine Daddy's little girl chasing after the bad guys for a living. Especially when she doesn't have to make a living. Daddy's filthy rich, if I remember correctly."

She offered a shrug as she finished her scan of the room. It was true; she didn't have to work. But from early on her father had instilled a sense of self-productivity in her.

"We've got a few hours to make ourselves look auction-ready. You should ring up the front desk and have the concierge order you a tuxedo."

"Joy. I like togging up. What about yourself? There's no time to…ah."

She followed Dane's gaze.

A white gauze dress bag hung on a silver hook next to the bathroom door. Kristi Burke could work a miracle, even from three thousand miles away. Likely it would be couture.

Becca tingled with anticipation. It would be like opening a really good Christmas present.

The soft jingle of her cell phone prompted Becca to dig it out of her coat pocket. Caller ID flashed the name: Lucy. Becca's personal assistant.

Lucy had worked for her two years, having been referred by a close friend who'd met her at a fall harvest charity event. Young, bubbly and overflowing with energy, the sassy redhead was like an extra limb to Becca. She was savvy when it came to planning events for Grace Notes, Becca's charity, and thrilled to be given control—and Becca had no problem doing so, especially when a case took her out of town. Lucy had no clue to Becca's alter ego as crime fighter.

Mentally mourning the plaid Burberry, she shrugged off her ripped coat as she listened.

Lucy started right in, as usual, forgoing even a friendly hello. "I've got the approval for the musicians. The building code doesn't allow for candles. The tablecloth fiasco has been taken care of. I've found a dry cleaner to come directly to the hotel and steam them for me. The feathers have been shipped, half white and half red. They sound absolutely divine! The Krug arrived less than an hour ago. Will you want to check that out?"

"Lucy, hi, er…" Becca worked at the brown paper package, tearing it open and peeking inside the box.

"And Samantha Kyle's mom called. She has to cancel her daughter's music lesson tonight."

Damn. Becca had missed only two lessons in the years she'd been working covertly—each time because she was out of the country chasing bad guys.

But she'd always remembered to cancel, or managed a phone call at least a day before the student was to arrive.

"Did she reschedule?"

"Her mother said it would be fine to wait for next week's lesson. Samantha isn't feeling well and she didn't want her to pass anything nasty along to you. Whew! I wouldn't have been able to go near you if you caught a bug, Becca. Not that I've been near you lately. Could you imagine if I got sick before the gala? If we were both sick? No, I'm not even going there. Everything will be great. Right? I hope so, because—"

"Lucy, stop. Just…chill. The gala is going to be gorgeous and spectacular, and come off without a hitch."

Every Gotham Roses club member was required to do fund-raising and charity work, and the undercover agents were no exception. Becca volunteered through Grace Notes by teaching music lessons to schoolchildren a few times a week.

She'd developed Grace Notes to introduce music to those children who would never have a chance to hear a live symphony orchestra perform. Twice a year, they'd fund field trips to Carnegie Hall for local schools. In September, the charity distributed instruments to the schools in all the boroughs. Entire bands had been formed in some schools thanks to donations and fund-raising they did at their annual charity gala in February, an event that was, unfortunately, this weekend.

"I'm sorry, I'm a bit tied up this week, Lucy. Fittings for the gala. Last minute invites to send out. Contributions to secure."

Becca smiled at Dane, who watched her with fascination, his fingers propped in a steeple to his lips.

"Oh, Becca, I forget you are always so busy. You don't need me bothering you with this minor stuff."

"No, it's perfectly fine, Lucy. You're doing my job as it is. So keep bugging me. I'll see you as soon as possible, okay?"

"Before tomorrow night?"

Who could make a promise like that? It was already Friday. If all went well with the auction, Becca could be on the next flight to New York. She glanced at Dane. He waggled a brow.

If all went well.

"I'll call you, Lucy."

"Thanks, Becca!"

Clicking off, Becca laid the cell phone on the table by the laptop. The spicy roses seeped into her senses on stealthy waves, but did not dispel her anxiety. "I completely forgot about that lesson."

"What lesson?"

"I teach music to a few students twice a week."

"A gemologist, as well as a music teacher?"

"It's part of my charity foundation, Grace Notes."

"Impressive."

"No time for accolades. We've got work to do and I've got somewhere to be Saturday night. So, your tux?"

"Can't I run across the street and buy myself a dinner jacket?" Dane asked, looking physically pained.

"The auction is a glamorous event. It's followed by a full-dress ball at the Palais Royal, black tie and diamonds."

"Got to love all those Kermits dressed to the nines."

"Kermits? Ah." Frogs. Frenchmen. He certainly was not PC. Stodgy Brit. "Do you think you can pull this off?"

"You want me to pull something off you?" He shot upright. "Just tell me which bit of clothing, love. I aim to please."

She rolled her eyes and he slouched back down in the chair.

"Yes, I can pull it off. I shall watch my tongue, most uptight one."

About to snap back with a protest, Becca kept quiet. Yes, she was uptight. And yes, she worried this evening wouldn't go well. That was what she did. Worry, and then work her buns off—and Lucy's—to achieve perfection. Becca Whitmore strove to be as flawless as a D grade colorless diamond. Only through her alter ego could she let her hair down. Let loose. Just…be.

"I think I'll nose around," Dane said. "Check out this auction room beforehand."

Use him for his intel, then dump him.

"Strange that MI-6 doesn't close it down and take the diamond into hand," she stated, seeking a clue from him.

"We want to draw out the thief, love." Nothing she didn't already know. "But you wouldn't know about that sort of covert action. You're just here to look at the pretty stones for the CIA."

"Sure. But you are going to sit tight while I order you a tux. I may not know about covert activities, but I do know it is important to look the part. I think I can guess your measurements. Stand up."

"You just told me to sit tight."

"Please? You're about my ex-fiancé's size."

Dane stood and slipped off his coat, tossing it to the foot of one of the beds. "Fiancé?"

"Ex."

"Interesting development in the saga of the heiress's adventures across the sea as a secret agent."

"I am a gemologist contracted by the CIA. I hope you'll keep my connection to the spy business to yourself."

"Just joshing, love. You do have a good cover story."

"And what's yours?"

"Cocky Brit."

"Mastered," she declared. "Lift your arms, will you? I'm going to check your height."

Standing before him, she awkwardly curled her arms around his back and clasped her hands. He drew in a barely audible gasp. Face-to-face, Becca inhaled his warm scent—Burberry Brit cologne in the flesh.

His aquamarine eyes glinted with amusement and…curiosity? His mouth parted. Becca felt her heartbeat race. If this wasn't the perfect moment for a kiss.

Don't even go there.

If she wanted a kiss. Which she didn't.

Yep, he was about the same hug-er size as David Chester. Both were trim, tall and…cocky. Both took ownership of said cockiness and wielded it like a samurai's katana.

But the mistake of her engagement had taught her something. Men would never get it. A woman didn't need a man to make her way in this world.

Not that she intended to forge through life single. The ideal mate would accept her as a partner and not a project to be improved upon. The ideal man would have the compassion of Reinhardt Whitmore, yet the self-assurance of, well…Batman. He would be someone she could trust completely. Someone she could bring into her secret world—

Hell. The ideal man might not exist. And if he did? Who was she to endanger him with her secrets?

Dane's breath fluttered at her hair. "I've never had such a pathetic hug in my life, love."

"I'm not hugging you, I'm measuring."

"Step any closer and you'll have plenty to measure."

It was difficult not to slide her eyes down to his trousers, where she guessed said measurements were increasing. Such a move would sink her in this little competition.

Dane caught her in that moment of wondering. "What *are* you thinking, Ms. Whitmore?"

She stepped back and, toying with the gold choker, pretended she needed to do a visual study of him from shoulder to hem. "About the same height, too, I'd guess. Six feet two inches. Forty-inch chest and thirty-four inch waist?"

"Impressive." He plunked back down into the chair, but this time dangled a leg over the arm. A swanky brat prince.

Becca scribbled the measurements on the pad of paper next to the phone.

"So why is that?" he asked her.

"Why is what?" She picked up the phone, prepared to dial the concierge and have him connect her to a tailor.

"The ex an ex?"

She and David had been all set to call the wedding

planner. Until the night David almost discovered her secret. Why he'd been at the trendy new restaurant Cream by himself still bothered her. Becca, wearing a red wig and so close to getting the dirt from a local snitch, had excused herself to go to the bathroom at the sight of her fiancé's curious gaze.

It was a moment later, while sneaking out the bathroom window, that Becca had decided to call it off. Love didn't make sense when you couldn't be totally honest with someone.

"Goodness, you've really got a lot on your pretty little mind. Tuppence for your thoughts?"

"A mere tuppence?" She smiled at the notion her thoughts could be worth so little. And yet she appreciated the token gesture. "I'm worth a little more, Agent Dane."

Chapter 7

While Dane showered, Becca found a penlight that had a high-powered magnification disk on one end. Nice little piece. Vincent had sent lock picks as well, which she stuffed into her other pocket, along with gloves. She'd have to thank Vincent some night soon.

She decided to take a walk down to the auction room.

Dane's observation had been a good one. The layout of the area must be studied before the event. And why wait for Mr. Need-to-Know to finish primping?

The brochure Dane had picked up in the lobby stated the viewing for the auction had been yesterday in the Salon de Flore. The auction was to be held in the Salon de Marsan, which was connected to the de Flore room. No admittance would be granted to the salon until seven this evening, an hour before the auction. Until then,

Becca assumed, the gemstones and art to be auctioned must be kept in a secure on-site location.

Nodding to a maroon-liveried hotel employee toting towels, she paused to take in the foyer near the salons. Soft yellow paint and minimal decorations opposed the extravagance of the rooms.

An auction implied someone would *buy* the diamond. But didn't thieves steal?

She had to take a chance on finding the stone before anyone—especially a thief—could buy or steal it. If the storage method was secure she could rest assured the heist would not go down until the auction.

As she turned to stroll down the Galerie Adélaïde she felt a strain at the backs of her calves. From the car crash or from the high heels? She'd changed out of the Ferragamos, finding a prettier pair had caught her eye. When in Paris, Christian Louboutins were de rigueur.

The Galerie Adélaïde was a long stretch of hallway that looked out onto the Rue de Rivoli. Though it was usually used as a dining hall, this afternoon the pale yellow walls and marble floors were clear of tables.

Becca wandered casually, faking her best I'm-a-lost-visitor look, but she took in everything. The faint odor of lavender, also de rigueur in French hotels. The Gauguin secured to the wall, motion sensors blipping red beneath.

A posterboard sign advertising the auction was set on a wooden tripod outside the first of three double doors to the Marsan salon.

A man in a black suit stood at the end of the hallway by the final entrance. He looked Polynesian, and was about the size of a truck. Definitely security.

Behind his broad shoulders Becca made out another less obvious door, likely an office.

"Bingo," she murmured, and strode forward, tucking a wave of hair behind her ear as she did. "Here goes nothing."

He'd abandoned his plan to shower the moment he heard the door to the room click shut. Dane had slipped his shirt back on and peered out of the bathroom, to find he'd been ditched.

"What is New York up to?"

He peeked outside and saw Becca walking down the hallway, and decided to follow her to the main floor, trying not to look too obvious as he trailed her down two flights. He stepped back into a doorway when she approached the massive bodyguard stationed at the end of the hall.

"Oh, you sit back and wait for your tux," he mocked. "Right. Sneaky bit of designer leather pumps."

New York was hiding something from him. Not that he'd expect a foreign agent to be forthright. He wasn't playing straight with her, either. Why should he? This case was too important to risk a cock-up.

It was apparent she did not have all the intel, and her focus was much narrower than his. She merely sought the diamonds and the information inside them. But if she thought to sneak in and nab the stones for her team...

Dane made a fist and quietly punched his palm. If she had asked, he might have been able to swing a look for her by flashing his credentials.

That's right, credentials. And what had she to show?

Nothing, save that smart little black Centurion card. Credentials, he had to admit, but the wrong kind for this game.

Money did not buy the kind of revenge he was chasing.

Was she a real CIA agent or just a gemologist, as she claimed? His query in London had yet to uncover anything on her besides the obvious, that she was Reinhardt Whitmore's daughter, and her net worth pushed the billion mark.

A billion. Brilliant.

Strange to find an heiress working the covert life. Her main expertise was gemology, not espionage. Unless she got her kicks by playing secret agent. Not a wise choice. Sooner or later, the bad guys took down all but the most serious of operatives.

If the Russians were involved in this one, little Miss Billion Dollars would be in over her head. No gung-ho heiress was going to mess up his case. Even if she did smell like fruit and had soft, pink lips. And that laugh. She liked to laugh, and did it with gusto. Liked to tease, too.

But laugh or no, the pampered princess was going to have to learn to play by his rules.

Snaking his fingers around the edge of the doorway, Dane peered carefully down the hall.

New York was gone. And so was the guard.

Dragging a three hundred pound ox more than a few feet was plain impossible. But all she need do was get him inside the office.

Just a few…more…inches!

Becca closed the door and stepped carefully over the

fallen bruiser. A Vulcan nerve pinch to the carotid in his neck had taken him down in eight seconds. She wasn't a fan of the sci-fi television series herself; it had been her trainer, Jimmy Valentine, who'd taught her the oddly named nerve squeeze. Call it what you may, Becca figured she might have five to ten minutes now, depending on how completely Large Wide Guy succumbed to her persuasion.

Flashing the penlight around the room, Becca saw she stood in little more than a supply closet. Orderly steel shelves holding towels and cleaning products lined the south wall. File cabinets stood in metal columns to the north. Down the center were two long tables cluttered with items that sparkled and winked at her as the beam passed over them. White cloth streamed to the floor. On the tables were neat lot numbers, the items to be auctioned ready to be plucked up and placed on the auction block.

Hardly high security. An easy take for a thief. The urge to turn and race out to find the manager struck her. What was he thinking, leaving such a precious cache guarded by one man? With nothing more than an easily pickable mushroom-pin lock securing the door?

In the next second, Becca realized *she* was the thief in this scenario. She'd already committed breaking and entering. No one was going to alert anyone until she'd had her five minutes.

Of which she'd just wasted one minute.

Looking up, she beamed her light across the base of a small black camera. Bingo. Counting the seconds, she determined it had a ten-second sweep. No problem.

Stepping quickly along the first table, she didn't give more than a glance to the vases, the crystal decanters or even the smaller-carat set stones that glittered upon black velvet display boards.

Once at the end of the first table, she flashed her light toward the door. Large Wide Guy actually snored. Ducking behind the end of the table, she avoided the camera's tracking eye.

From her position, she eyed the next table. Sitting inside the glass cube was the stone. A round brilliant ten-carat diamond rested on four silver prongs set upon a mirror to enhance the stunning show of refracted light.

Would anyone be so idiotic as to make it easy? Not in this neighborhood. It was the Parisian equivalent of the New York diamond district.

Becca perused her options. She could lift the glass top and risk setting off an alarm. Not keen on that option.

Then she recalled a robbery months earlier in a small underground salon north of the Louvre. The thieves had made off with three million dollars in set stones merely by lifting up the unsecured glass cases and slipping out the jewels. While there had been guards present during the exhibition, the classic use of diversion had served well.

Was it possible?

You're not here to steal it; you're supposed to catch whoever wants it.

True.

Heartbeat racing, Becca lunged across the aisle. Still out of view of the camera she knelt at the end of the table, but a reach from the diamond. She had ten seconds to make her move.

Closing her eyes tightly, she sucked in a huge breath. Take the chance or not? As a free agent, should she be caught, the Gotham Roses would disavow any connections. And Zeek would have to jump through high hoops to straighten up the mess.

Fear simmered in Becca's veins. Her heart pounded. Oh, but she loved the feeling.

A click signaled a change in camera position as it swept back the opposite way. With a decisive nod and an irrepressible smile, Becca swung up and pushed on the glass cube, tilting it back on the far panel.

The seal had been broken. No alarms. At least, no alarms she could hear.

She had to work fast.

Slipping her hand up under the case, she grabbed the diamond, then ducked out of camera view.

Lester had warned her not to use a UV light, but this simple white light would do no harm. Beaming it over the crown of the stone, she initially saw nothing. Prismatic color blocks danced on the concrete walls. The pen had a microscope view at the opposite end. Time to test it.

The creak of the door made her pause.

Chapter 8

Becca fumbled with the stone, which bounced onto her thigh. She slapped a palm over it, catching it on her knee.

The guard? No, he was already inside. Had his snoring body tilted against the door?

She had forgotten to relock it.

Ducking beneath the white tablecloth, she took cover in one fluid movement.

Whoever had entered was not using a flashlight and didn't flick on a light switch. Save for the soft tread of shoes on concrete, tracing the path Becca had taken down the first aisle, the intruder was absolutely silent.

A rumble of snores alerted her. Was the guard waking up? Why would someone walk in and *not* wake the guard? Must have ulterior motives.

"Hmm, pink silk rimmed with Swarovski crystal."

Becca tugged the toe of her shoe under the cloth.

"Uh-uh, I saw that. The soles are red, which can only be—" with a shimmy, the white linen rose before her to reveal his Cheshire cat smirk "—Christian Louboutin. Got ya, love."

"What are you doing?" she whispered, more forcefully than she should have. Dane knelt before her. "And what…how?" She leaned forward and gripped Dane by the shoulders. Nice, strong… "You have this absolutely freakish ability to identify women's designer footwear. How is that?"

"Money laundering case last year—which ended in multiple homicides. One victim was an old biddy who had Imelda's fetish for shoes. Blood everywhere, even on the Manolo Blahniks."

"Right. Do you happen to notice the camera?"

"Yes, but I've got a nice shiny badge as an excuse to be here. What's yours?"

An interrupted snore indicated Large Wide Guy had woken.

"Sit tight, love. Time to let the big boys handle this."

"Big boys?" she mouthed as Dane rose and walked away.

She liked playing with the big boys. Becca liked to tell them what to do, and then watch them scramble to try to please her. But let them handle the job? For now…

"Agent Aston Dane."

…she'd sit tight, out of camera range.

Crouched beneath the table, Becca listened intently as Dane spoke to the guard. As she did so, she leaned forward, forming a cocoon with her arms around her knees, pressed the penlight on and flashed the beam over the diamond in her palm.

"You were sleeping on the job," Agent Dane stated. "I was able to simply walk through an unlocked door— and over your large body, I might add."

"The door was locked. I checked it myself, *monsieur*—"

"I could have absconded with millions of euros worth of gemstones and art pieces. Explain that to me."

"There was a woman, *monsieur.*"

"A woman?"

Dane's laughter concealed Becca's fumble. The diamond fell on the hard concrete floor. Her hands were actually shaking!

"And what did she do to you, *monsieur,* give you a Vulcan nerve pinch?"

Becca winced. If he only knew.

"A large man like you? Don't you know the big boys never let a little girl get the better of them?"

Little girl? Oh yeah?

"I'm going to have to call this one in."

She heard Dane flip open his phone.

"Please, *monsieur,* it is my first job. I…"

"Well…" there was a dramatic pause "…you're a lucky bloke. I've scanned the room. There's no one in here. Nor does there appear to be anything missing. But we must have the auction manager take a look."

"There's a manifest of the items in a room across the hall. I could go get it. *Mon Dieu,* I cannot lose this assignment, *monsieur,* I have bills to pay. A girlfriend with a baby!"

"And whose fault is that? Don't you believe in the sanctity of marriage, *monsieur?*"

Oh, but he was laying it on thick.

There. The microscope zoomed in on… Definitely letters. But they didn't make sense. Letters and symbols and pluses—an equation or a formula? The first line was short. Tugging out the notepad, Becca copied it.

"Fine," Dane conceded. "You run and get the manifest. I'll stand guard outside the door."

The door creaked open.

"Time to move, love. I'll mark your exit as soon as the camera switches—now!"

Becca snaked her body up to look over the table. She could see Dane's hand frantically motioning. Tilting up the glass case, she slipped the diamond back into its steel-pronged nest, and then scrambled for the door.

Stopping her abruptly, Dane put both hands to the sides of her head. "When you get home, young lady…!" A smirk covered his false anger. "Skedaddle," he said.

And skedaddle she did.

Mackerel on toast and black caviar arrived ten minutes after Becca's return to the room, along with the promise a tuxedo was on its way. Dane had returned minutes ago. Without a word he'd excused himself to take the shower he had somehow gotten sidetracked from earlier.

His anger was evident in the icy look he'd flashed her way. Had he been listening? Waiting for her to slip out? Obviously.

He'd saved her butt back there.

Score one point for the big boy.

Attacking the mackerel toast with vigor—because no one was looking—Becca didn't even taste the first slice. Scooping up a spoon of caviar, she downed the second piece just as quickly. It was a far cry from a full meal. On the other hand, it would keep her tummy flat for whatever gown Kristi had sent. Speaking of which…

The auction started in an hour, so Becca shimmied into the black strapless Emanuel Ungaro gown she found hanging in the garment bag. It had a wicked slit up the right leg she could adjust with a toothless plastic zipper. A small diamond-studded black ribbon bow topped the slit and concealed the zipper. Right now she set it to just above the knee. A higher slit might be required later; she'd play that hand if needed.

A glance to the shoe trolley below the dress hook landed on steel-spiked heels. Black patent leather Manolos. Nummy.

Padding barefoot across the room, shoes hooked on her thumbs, Becca powered up her laptop. After typing in the few letters she'd scribbled down while under the table, she saved the file: [d_code.doc.]

She did a mental tally of the time difference as she dialed up Alan Burke through iChat. No problem; she wouldn't be waking anyone in New York. Alan should be in his secret basement office at the Gotham Roses brownstone on 68th Street.

"Alan."

"Becca! I was disappointed not to send you off from New York." On the laptop screen his words were just ahead of his facial movements.

"Couldn't be helped. I had to hop right onto the plane to England. I'm in Paris now."

"*Mais oui,* I recognize the decor in your room—the Hotel Regina. Adore it. Did you get the room they used in *La Femme Nikita*?"

"A movie?"

"Girl, you so need to study popular culture. Does the bathroom have a stained glass window?"

"Yes."

"That's the one! Cool. So, I can't see you...."

"Sorry." Becca leaned toward the laptop's small optical lens. "Haven't much time. I'm dressing as we speak. Agent Dane is in the shower—"

"Who is?" Kristi Burke's auburn curls and curious smile appeared on the computer screen, nudging out Alan. "Did you just say you have a man in your shower?"

"Yes, but it's not what you think. He's with MI-6."

"Oh. Well then, that explains everything. Not!"

"I'm working with him on the case."

"Oh, you bet." Alan winked. "I've been in contact with Zeek. She wanted me to send you the essentials. Your bidding number is somewhere in the room." Alan appeared to look to the left of the screen, as if he could see around her room. "Ah, there, over by the vase of flowers."

Becca paused and leaned over the monitor. "How'd you do that? Are there cameras in here?"

"I wish. It was a guess. Kristi sent the roses, along with the dress."

"Thank you, Kristi. It fits perfectly."

"You've such a gorgeous figure to work with, Becca. It's not stick-straight like a model, but has some curves to make it interesting."

"Oh la la," Alan sang. "Gotta love those curves."

"As if you notice." Kristi shoved Alan's face out of the range of the camera.

Becca turned and spied the auction number sitting below the massive vase of flowers. "The number is here."

"You told Zeek you thought there was a code in the diamond?"

She nodded. "I no longer think there is, I *know* there is, and I've had opportunity to write down a few lines. It makes no sense. I checked out the diamond. Just in case something goes wrong tonight."

"Smart."

"It's some sort of mathematical equation. Maybe. I only got part of it. I've typed it into a document and am sending you and Zeek the file right now." She attached the file to an e-mail and hit Send.

"I'm getting it," Alan replied. "Together, Zeek and I should be able to figure it out and let you know exactly what it is, as well as who you're chasing."

"Did you get the earrings? They should have arrived by courier express," Kristi stated.

"Let me check." As far as Becca knew, only the clothing had been delivered to her room— Ah. There, sitting bedside, as if placed there by a thoughtful valet, sat a shiny black jewelry box. Jean Paul had mentioned a smaller box.

Retrieving it, Becca eyed the monstrosities of platinum and diamond it held as she returned to sit before the computer. They were diamond sprays that when worn looked as if they'd curl into her ear.

"I'll take that awkward silence as a yes." Alan grimaced.

"They are a bit gaudy," Becca said. She knew Alan hadn't designed them. One of his contacts in Paris had.

"But not for this ball. It's all about the carats, darling. Who has them, who can wear the big ones."

"And he likes to wear the big ones." Kristi's voice sounded right behind Alan's.

"At least I date, Miss Hausfrau." It looked as if he pushed Kristi aside with a playful shove. "Put them on."

"Putting them on," Becca said as she secured the clip earrings. "Now what?"

"Tap the largest diamond on your right ear," Alan instructed.

Becca did. "Okay."

"Just wait…I'm sequencing…there it is."

The image of her laptop featuring Alan's face appeared in a new iChat window. "It's a camera."

"Snap everyone's mug, darling. Zeek will be your contact tonight. She will run stats on every face you record. The range is about ten feet. There's a microphone in the other earring, with a receiver that'll pick up your voice and anything within an eight-inch range."

"Perfect. Thanks, Alan."

"Talk to you soon. I may tune in later to listen."

"Oh? So how do I turn these things off?"

"Why? Have you a wet Englishman you want to keep all to yourself?"

"He's not your type, Alan. He's moody and cocky. And he's definitely a ladies' man."

"Ah well, had to try. The clip on the back of the earring adjusts the volume. Once you exit your room, keep it on high."

Lowering the volume, she thanked them both.

Becca caught Alan's blown kiss as she shut off the laptop and turned to pick up the Manolos. The heels were steel spikes that would serve as a deliciously deadly weapon should she need one.

Standing and turning before the cheval mirror, she admired the costume. Becca Whitmore would never be seen in public in such a thigh-baring number. The socialite side of her was more refined, a charitable hostess who always wore a smile and knew the names of all the trendsetters, and was famous for getting things done right. She could raise millions without breaking a sweat, and converse on a variety of topics from culture to books to fashion.

But her alter ego? She could so work these shoes.

The thought that she might meet up with Large Wide Guy later stirred her to investigate the remainder of clothing and accessories provided in the black nylon sports bag.

As she dug out a blond bobbed wig, Becca complimented the Gotham Roses' wardrobe mistress. "Good girl. All the essentials."

She tugged on the wig. Perfect fit. Turning before the mirror again, she decided she looked a little bit punk with lots of sass. Very chic.

Big boys, look out.

The shower stopped and it suddenly occurred to Becca she wasn't prepared to face a wet Englishman who might emerge from the bathroom in a towel.

For a moment she indulged herself in the image of a hasty fling, clothes falling to the floor and body parts twining as the two of them landed on the bed in a flurry of passionate kisses.

Becca shook her head. The blond bob swung sharply.

"Don't go there, girl. Not when you need to be on your toes."

A knock at the door redirected her straying libido.

Letting in the valet, Becca nodded in approval. Room service and a Christian LaCroix tuxedo. She tipped the young man and he left.

Becca strode to the bathroom door and, before knocking on it, listened. Dane was whistling again, but not a symphony. This tune sounded jazzy. A man of many musical flavors… Chalk up another point for Agent Dane.

With a smile, Becca knocked, and then announced, "I'm going down to the auction, Dane. It's in the Salons de Marsan and de Flore. Your tux arrived. I'll meet you there?"

"Give me ten minutes!"

"Great. Do eat some of the mackerel toast before you come down."

"Yes, mum."

Smirking, Becca left the big boy to his jazz.

Chapter 9

"Zeek?" Becca tested communications as she strode down the narrow hallway from her room.

"Hello, Becca. We all set for this evening?"

"Should be. So tell me what happened with Lester. Did the field agent pick up the diamond?"

"I haven't heard from Agent Arlowe yet. But I'm making a call right now. Knock 'em dead, Becca. I'll be close."

The Regina staff directed Becca to the connected salons. The Flore salon served as a cocktail room. Grand Cru appellation Alsace bubbled over, and silver trays with chocolate truffles set alongside caviar beckoned as she strode by lingering couples and a sea of black tuxedos and red-lipsticked smiles. These were her people.

Giving a corrective tug to her wig, she sashayed

through the Adélaïde gallery, where murmured conversation filled the air. The wig had been a necessity, Becca decided. Large Wide Guy had seen her this afternoon, and she couldn't risk being identified tonight. Besides, any chance to don a disguise could not be missed. Dressing up made spying all the more exciting.

Just as she was ready to enter the Salon de Marsan, a British voice called to her. Becca turned.

She couldn't hold back an ear-to-ear grin.

Well, her "partner" certainly did clean up nicely. All togged up, as he would put it, in the fitted black LaCroix tuxedo, with a sporting black bow tie and thin tailored sleeves.

A corrective tug to his tie appeared a practiced move, à la James Bond. Dane plied his seduction skills on many a female, Becca surmised. Let him sharpen them on her and see how dull his blade would become. On the other hand, a friendly duel stirred her blood.

That caddish smirk quickly changed to an expression of dismay.

"Are you in pain?" Becca asked, at Dane's gape. "Is it the couture? You must be breaking out in a rash or something."

"Woman." He huffed out a laugh, smoothing a hand down the lapel of his jacket. "I clean up with the best of them, but you…"

Becca worked the Ungaro gown by tilting a hip and assuming not so much a pose as a natural position. It was the heels. They made her feel provocative. A little bit wicked. Powerful.

And powerful was a good feeling to own.

"Wow."

That remark stymied her. "Wow?"

"You're familiar with the vernacular."

"Not pure dead brilliant?"

"Wow goes one step beyond, love. That…hair?"

She cupped the saucy, swinging locks and gave them a shake. "I've been seen in a compromising position as a brunette, so I figured I'd better go blond."

"Well. And do they have more fun?"

"That has yet to be determined."

"I can help you find out." Curving an arm about her waist, he slid his hand down her hip to dangerous territory. "Hmm, someone's not wearing underwear."

"Really, Agent Dane, you feel compelled to announce your fetish?"

"I meant you, love."

She smirked and said, "I know," and entered the auction room a stride ahead of him.

The salon's decor was subtle, with a few touches of art deco on the frescoes above the doorways and on the carved wood chair backs. There were approximately forty people seated before the movable wood dais, where a pair of tuxedoed auctioneers exchanged whispered conversation. Another dozen people milled about.

Expensive perfume mingled with cigar smoke. Feminine laughter eddied like champagne bubbles. Bids had already started. A red crystal Lalique vase currently glittered on the block.

Touching the camera in her earring, Becca snapped a few shots of a couple walking toward her.

Zeek spoke in her left ear. "He's a bit of a rogue, eh?"

"Who's a rogue?"

"Your MI-6 agent. Snap a picture of him for me, will you?"

"I will not."

"Ah, the punishment of working a desk job."

Zeek's pouty tone made Becca laugh.

"There she goes with the sexy laughter again," Dane commented as he followed her around the bank of chairs. "I love those little bursts. They just sort of explode out of you."

Becca murmured noncommittally. When she stopped walking, he put his arm around her again. She reached back to readjust Dane's hand to *above* hip level. "Don't go any lower," she warned.

"But if you know about my fetish, then you should learn to accept it," he teased.

"Oh, he's a real charmer," Zeek interjected.

"Isn't he?" Becca answered.

"Who are you talking to?" Dane leaned close to whisper in her ear. "Are you wired? Where is it?" His breath fanned across her mouth. Blue eyes traveled over her breasts, nicely revealed by the low, strapless neckline. "Nestled between these lovelies?"

She tilted up his chin with a stern finger. "It's in my earrings, pervert. What about you? Can I leer?"

"All you like, love."

She'd never win an argument with Dane by playing the prudish princess.

Before he could move away, she gripped him by the arm and pulled him close so he had a bird's-eye view of her cleavage. "Watch yourself, Agent. You know what they say about women who don't wear underwear? They're insatiable. Now, let's get to work."

She left him standing with an utterly lost look in his aquamarine eyes.

Becca scanned the room for a prospective diamond buyer among the sea of black-and-white tuxes and brilliant red, emerald and multicolored gowns. Whatever was in that code had been important enough to justify murder. She'd learned over the years it was impossible to pick out a cold-blooded killer from exterior clues alone. Evil was much more subtle.

She paused to greet Jacques Mauboussin, who owned a sixth-generation boutique in the Place Vendôme. Jacques was from old money, like her. He was impeccable in his manner and words, a rare attribute in men. Not a suspect.

Becca moved to the far wall to stand beneath a pair of red-tasseled gold candelabra.

"First photos have been verified," Zeek relayed. "Monsieur and Madame de Veux. Paris residents. Private citizens. Richer than God. They check out."

"I don't think God is rich," Becca answered wryly.

"Gotcha. Richer than Trump then."

Becca glanced toward Dane, who was loitering behind a pair of whispering, elderly women. He caught her eye and shrugged. He was out of the loop. Secretly, Becca liked that she had a bit of leverage over the man, because she suspected he was still playing his need-to-know card.

And why was he out of the loop? Shouldn't he be wired, as well? He'd had little contact with MI-6 since they'd joined forces this morning. Hmm...

Drawing the tip of her tongue along her upper lip, Becca watched as Dane made his way through the crowd. Halfway across the room he commandeered a flute of champagne and started making small talk with a woman corseted in pink satin and a river of rubies. Rubies were a passionate choice and, set in silver, made the wearer unpredictable. Young and blonde, she lingered, smiling readily at Dane's comments. Fake boobs, Becca guessed, as well as plumped lips, dyed hair and a fake laugh.

Rolling her eyes, she snapped a shot of Pink, then moved on to survey the remaining bidders.

An elegant woman in her fifties wore Prada and a skinny strand of sapphires. Wise and reserved.

A burst of amethysts on the shoulder of a fresh-faced young beauty revealed her attention to detail.

A huge yellow diamond cocktail ring called out for notice. Validation.

The value of the gems glittering around the necks of women in this salon alone must be pushing the double-digit millions, Becca estimated. A thief could have his or her pick of a priceless gem—for nothing more than a five-finger discount.

So why bid on *and pay for* a diamond that should by rights sell for over a million dollars?

It was all in the code. Whatever it contained must be worth paying big bucks for.

Now more than ever, Becca felt certain the diamonds were not the real prize, but instead it was the information they contained.

Something was recorded inside the stones. In a small

computer chip? No, she wasn't ready to go that far. But the ion beam branding was very possible. Erasable? Maybe. But why was that even necessary? If someone went to all the trouble to put information inside a diamond, why would they want to erase it?

And had the thief the proper equipment to read the code? Maybe there was to be a handoff, and the ultimate buyer relied on the fact that the thief wouldn't have the technology to read the contents.

But who wanted that information? The government? Terrorists?

What about the CIA and MI-6's positions in this subterfuge? She knew the CIA and Dane wouldn't tell her even if she asked, but she was starting to feel like a pawn in a very high-stakes game.

"Zeek?" she whispered, turning to inspect a tassel dangling from a gold sconce on the wall behind her. "Can you check something out for me?"

"Go ahead."

"Did we ever get the name of the original seller? The party who sold the diamonds to MaryEllen Sommerfield?"

"Yes," Zeek said, "the stones were sold by a private citizen. Amandus Magnusson."

Why did that name sound familiar?

Catching a wink from Dane, Becca nodded back. He seemed to be watching her with as much attention as he paid to the rest of the room. Cheeky Brit.

"And his history?"

"I'll get back to you on that."

Wait, she knew the Magnusson family. Uther, Amandus's son, had taken lessons from her father—

"Mademoiselle Whitmore!"

Becca turned to find Madame Elisha DuCharme standing with arms outspread, waiting for a hug. Gray chinchilla clung to her shoulders and garish pink diamonds twinkled at her décolletage. She was the equivalent to the Palm Beach grande dame socialite, Fluffy Peters. Never would the woman be caught in anything but the latest LaCroix couture.

Becca moved in to buss the woman's cheeks, and was pulled into a vigorous hug.

"I didn't recognize you at first in the new hair color. Oh, but it's smashing!"

Ignoring Elisha's enthusiastic verve, Becca nodded cheerfully and pushed her way out from the gregarious hug. Hugs, especially surprise ones, always made her skin crawl. The woman spoke rather loudly. Now was no time to blow her cover.

"Madame DuCharme, it's been a few months. You look lovely. Pink diamonds are your stone. They bring all attention to your, well…" Her eyes landed on the woman's generous bosom.

Stick your foot in it?

"You're a *petite amour, mademoiselle*. What are you doing in Paris? I thought you returned to New York after the holidays?"

The truth offered an easy alibi. "I'm buying, of course. Can't keep me away from an auction."

"I should have guessed. But I noticed you entered with the sexy blonde across the room. A Brit, yes? *Très bien!*"

"He's a friend."

"Ah-huh." Utter disbelief.

Thankful when the woman didn't press, Becca exchanged a few more pleasantries, and then excused herself to listen to the auction.

Lot twelve arrived on the block. The dazzling ten-carat, round brilliant stone stirred up more than a few oohs and aahs. It was difficult not to drool over it.

Becca allowed a few initial bids. She jumped in at one hundred thousand, knowing it was futile, but playing the role. She bid against a man in the back of the salon who wore a goatee. The bidder looked Mediterranean, with his olive skin and dark hair. His square jaw gave him a thuggish appearance.

Becca snapped a picture.

The next bid came from the front of the room. A young socialite seated in the first row—the woman Dane had spoken to earlier, dressed in a shiny pink satin gown—LaCroix winter couture, so last year—nudged the gray-haired man next to her for each bid. A sugar daddy?

Catching Dane's eye from across the room, Becca flicked her gaze to the man in back. Dane nodded and began to move to the rear of the salon. As a partner, he took suggestions remarkably well. A trainable man? Score another point for the cocky Brit.

At two hundred thousand, Becca raised her bid card. Pink speared her with a pouting sneer. Another nudge prompted the man next to her to match the three hundred thousand mark.

The man in the back shook his head to decline when prompted to raise the bid. Couldn't be the thief—if he had given up so easily?

"Any possibles?" Zeek asked.

"Not sure. Any info on Pink?"

"The woman with the blond hair and fake tits? I can't match her in two databases."

"That's odd."

"She look like a suspect?"

"Who can say? She's with a gray-haired man. Early sixties, I'd guess. Sunken cheeks, silver cuffs with a big fat pearl in each one. He's secretive. I'll provide details once they turn around and I can get a good look. What about the Mediterranean?"

"Still sequencing."

"He's dropped out of bidding."

"May be a play. Keep your eye on him."

"One million two hundred thousand euros." The auctioneer announced a winner with a solid *thunk* of his gavel.

Becca scanned the rows of bidders to spy the pouting blonde. She hadn't won? Then who had?

Dane caught her eye and nodded to her right, where a wide marble column blocked her view. Becca stepped around it, on the pretense of reaching for a glass of champagne from a passing tray, and spied a tall man nodding acknowledgment to his bid. His sleek wave of dark brown hair was tugged back tightly and secured at the base of his neck in a tail that streamed to the center of his shoulder blades. He backed away and turned to leave.

Becca followed him, knowing claims could be made immediately. As she passed Dane, she said, "I'm on him."

He gripped her upper arm. It was difficult to resist tugging away, but she didn't want to cause a scene. He was just lucky he hadn't grabbed her sore right arm.

"Look at you, Miss Action Adventure," he said in an undertone. "Don't worry, I've got the suss. You toddle along and—"

"Toddle? Dane—"

"This is big boy territory, love. Remember? Let the professional handle it."

"I've every right… Let go of me."

"That's right, the woman doesn't like to be touched." He released her.

"Believe it or not, I am authorized," she hissed.

For a moment their eyes danced the duel she had previously considered. Tension. Challenge. Edged with a glint of desire.

"Fine." He tapped the ribbon at the top of her thigh. "But play this cool. I'm on your heels."

"Yeah? Well, just don't step on my Manolos. The winning bidder is collecting the diamond. I'm going to talk to him before he arranges delivery. Maybe he'll let me take a peek, as a fascinated onlooker."

Dane nodded, submitting to her suggestion. "If you smile real pretty, I'm sure you can get him to let you look at whatever you want, love."

"Back me up."

"I'll be on you like mackerel on toast."

Chapter 10

Becca followed the ponytailed man to the Flore salon, where he produced a signature card to identify himself to the cashier. She couldn't get close enough to snap a picture.

Bank account information was entered into a laptop computer and within five minutes the transaction was complete. He refused the proffered security escort—not the burly Polynesian, thank goodness—and insisting he hadn't the time for delivery, took the stone immediately into possession. He slipped the diamond into his suit pocket.

"Idiot," Becca muttered. But most definitely their man.

Had they expected the stone to leave immediately, the CIA would surely have posted more agents. This was not a good surprise. "He's on the move with the diamond," Becca communicated to Zeek.

Walking out into the hallway that led to the salon foyer, the winner headed toward the stairway descending to the Place des Pyramides outside.

His path was suddenly blocked by the blonde. He stepped back, spreading his arms in question as Pink moved in closer. She was coming on strong to him and soon maneuvered them both against the wall by the stairs.

Did they know one another? The man seemed to flinch when she touched his arm.

"We've got interference," Becca communicated to Zeek. "The blonde. She's miffed about not winning. I'll wait it out. Any details on her yet?"

"Nope. But I'll search the international databases. I should get some help if I drop Agent Dane's name. Don't let the diamond out of your sight."

Feeling the brush of a hand across her back, Becca did not turn. "Dane, you toddling up behind?"

"It's your lack of underwear, love. Compels me like a magnet. You got the mark?"

She nodded across the foyer. "He's talking to the woman who lost the bid. Pink. She's working her charms on him. I suppose if she couldn't convince her sugar daddy to buy a treat for her she'll just come on to the next idiot."

"If she thinks she can flirt that stone off him…" Dane whistled under his breath. He was close enough to Becca that their shoulders touched.

She whispered, "Maybe she's making him promises that can only be kept in the dark?"

Dane's fingers slid across her back; it seemed an absentminded move as he kept an eye to the mark. "Something occurred to me while I was watching the rich suck back their champagne and the old buzzards fondle their young trophies."

"That you're one trophy short?"

"You're getting better, love. Huzzah to you." He leaned in, resting one palm on the white-painted chair rail behind her and pointing to her earring with his other hand. Receiving a confirming nod that yes, their conversation was being recorded, he spoke in a low tone. "What puzzles me is why the thief would pay so much for what doesn't seem to be the ultimate prize."

"I had the same thought."

"Thinking alike? We've been spending far too much time together. Maybe the thief has the same idea as us. He or she isn't going to pay for any information that can simply be taken. He *is* a thief, after all."

"Which means it's likely the winner is not our target?"

"And the real target is currently seducing the winner?"

Dane leaned in close and looked down her body. His eyes touched her more profoundly than a finger could. "You think you can run in those heels?"

"*Now* you want my help?"

"I don't think it's possible. What are they, three inches high? Manolo Blahniks, black patent leather. Sexy, but not track shoes."

"They're four inches, with a reinforced steel heel. And I can outrun anyone who tries to take them from me."

From the corner of her eye Becca noticed a change to the scenario. The man who had won the bid suddenly collapsed. His palms slid down the yellow wall. He sprawled on the floor as the blonde turned and scampered toward the stairway.

"She's got it," Dane said as he started across the foyer.

"What's going on?" Zeek asked calmly. "Becca?"

Becca rushed after Dane. "Wrong target. The diamond has changed hands."

Chapter 11

"Pink is fleeing the building. I'll go west," she said to Dane, who nodded. "There's a parking garage below ground."

"I'll take the lift down," he called, heading along the hallway. "Try to cut her off."

Taking off at full speed, Becca grinned, thinking about what Dane had said about her spike heels. She'd been wearing high heels since she was a teenager. It was all in where you placed the weight of your body, preferably on the balls of your feet. So long as she didn't try to run a marathon, she would do just fine, thank you.

LaCroix couture swished around the corner at the base of the stairs. Pink wore more sensible shoes, the heels appearing less than an inch high. She had obviously planned to do a bit of running this evening.

"You ID her yet, Zeek?"

"Pink. I've found her right now and am running a sequence."

Running a sequence. It was a statement Becca often heard from Alan, but she never really knew what the techno-babble term meant. A sequence of what? Whatever, it had better go quickly.

Heels clicking down the tight, twisting stairway to the parking garage, Becca entered chilling darkness. There were no lights. Someone must have killed them. Pink?

Stretching out both arms, Becca swept her palms across the walls. No switches.

In the distance she could see the shimmer of streetlights through what must be the exit ramp to the Place des Pyramides. She heard the repeated swish of cars driving by, and the flash of their headlights jittered intermittently across the concrete walls.

Stepping forward slowly, she paused and listened, her breath frozen in her throat. Chill February air touched bare skin revealed by her slinky gown, and goose bumps formed upon goose bumps. As a tried and true New Yorker, she should be acclimated to the cold, but the slide of silk against her skin jacked up the chill to a shiver.

Moving on her toes made her steps shorter. Using her left hand, she touched the trunks of parked cars to guide her in the darkness. Exhaust fumes mixed with the sweet scent of winter rain.

Something was not right. With a shake of her head, she realized the diamond earring with the microphone had slipped from her ear. If Zeek found info on Pink, Becca wouldn't have access to it.

"Shoot."

Where was Dane? In the dimness she couldn't get a handle on the elevator location.

Deciding to seek out an unlocked car to turn on the headlights, Becca spun suddenly. There, across the expanse of the parking garage, near the ramp, she saw a small beam of light. A female figure, her face highlighted by the brightness, stood next to a column. And then it blinked out.

Becca ran across the concrete as Pink's dark shadow moved toward the exit ramp.

The ding of the elevator announced its arrival. Dane stepped out, scanning the darkness.

"This way!" Becca hissed as she dashed toward the exit. "She's headed up the ramp to the street!"

Topside, a gilded statue of Jeanne d'Arc dominated the courtyard, lit from below by four spotlights.

Dane jogged up beside Becca, his huffs of breath visible in the icy air.

"Getaway car waiting," Becca reported. "A midnight-blue Audi, plate 702 CHL 38. Damn! She's getting away!"

Dane waved an arm, but the two cabs parked down the street didn't budge.

Becca whistled and one of them pulled up promptly. "Get in! We can't lose them." She gave directions to the cabbie as Dane slid onto the seat beside her.

He shrugged off his jacket. "It's colder than Iceland out there. Put this on."

Grateful for the gesture, Becca tugged it about her shoulders and tapped on the plastic screen between them and the driver. *"Ne les perdez pas!"*

The cabbie nodded and stepped on the gas.

"Call in the license number," she directed Dane.

"Doing so right now, mum." He clicked on his cell phone and reported the car to his sources. Becca had to rely on his cooperation because she'd lost the link to Zeek. "They'll locate the car via satellite should we lose them. Buck up, love, this isn't a cock-up yet."

"If he would only drive a little faster... *Allez-vous en!*"

Dane reported the plate number, then turned to her and said, "Pretty impressive, love."

"What?"

"Your speed in those killer heels. And on slippery concrete?"

"Told you I could take care of myself."

"I've new respect for Mr. Blahnik."

"Good on you. I like a man who appreciates a pretty shoe—"

Dane put up a finger as a musical jingle echoed from his phone. "Hold that thought."

After a brief exchange he hung up. "The plates trace to a rental service on the Île de la Cité. The place was robbed earlier this evening. Trying to make a global fix right now, but it's more difficult at night."

Becca nodded. She had been so close to grabbing Pink. But she wouldn't give up hope. The Audi was still in sight.

Five minutes later the vehicle stopped in a dark neighborhood somewhere in the Ninth Arrondisement, not far from the Moulin Rouge, and let out Pink.

Becca told the cab driver to slow down a few blocks up and let them out. She surveyed the dark, quiet street.

Cobbled and wide, it was a newer one, having been built sometime this century. Four-story buildings lined the street; most appeared residential. The one their suspect walked into looked to be abandoned, judging by the broken window next to the entrance. But Becca knew better. Real estate in Paris was prime; nothing was left vacant.

"What do you think?" Dane asked. He peered over her shoulder, breathing on her neck. "A private exchange?"

Another car pulled up behind the departing Audi and let off a quartet of women dressed in party wear.

"Might be an underground club," Becca suggested.

Invitations were unnecessary in such clubs, because of the elite and secretive sights. Which meant if you could find the place you had been previously invited. Becca knew of a few such spots in New York; they moved often, but clubs of the sort offered a venue where someone who did not want to be seen or recognized could go.

Tugging off the wig and giving a shake to her hair, she smiled wickedly. "Let's check it out."

Chapter 12

Shivering as they walked through what had become a sprinkling of fine snowflakes, Becca handed back Dane's jacket. If she'd guessed right, her sexy black dress and spike heels would fit right in at this place.

"You'll freeze your tits off, love."

"They're already frozen. And aren't you the king of suave?"

"They are? Mind if I have a look?"

"Is that part of your investigation?"

"It could be a perk. And speaking of perky…"

Becca chuckled and strode ahead of him.

Another well-dressed couple filed in behind them as they approached a simple, unlocked entry door of dented metal painted lime-green.

Becca stepped in, with Dane in tow. It appeared to

be an old apartment building, with a lobby, high ceilings and a dusty iron chandelier. The scent of tobacco smoke filled the air. The foyer and a hallway to the right were lined at the baseboards with strip lighting that flashed green to violet, back and forth.

The pulse of distant music revved Becca's heartbeat before she could even make out sound. Vibrations shivered in the dusty floorboards, some kind of heavy trance beat.

Following the lights down a series of steps, they arrived at a door that featured a small sign the size of Becca's palm. The neon-green, lowercase italic read *verte*.

Hmm…

"Green?" Dane said over her shoulder.

On a wild guess, Becca suspected she knew what the bar served—and it hadn't been legal for almost a century.

She pushed open the door. Techno music washed over her, setting her senses on ultra-alert and then, as quickly, numbing her to all but the steady bass beat. A DJ suspended high above the dance floor in a green metallic cage shifted to the beat, in shades of green and gold.

The thick-necked bouncer looked her over and nodded. As she had suspected, if you could find the place and didn't appear to be a threat, you were in.

She blew a kiss to the man and sashayed in with her best sexy stride as the techno music shimmied over her. Bodies clad in skin-baring strips of fabric gyrated. The dance floor begged serious movement so she hung back along the edge.

Someone clasped her upper arm. Ready to protest, she turned.

"Stay close," Dane said. "We are partners, remember?"

"Now he wants to work together." But he didn't hear.

The club stretched four stories high, the vast cathedral ceiling topped with long rectangular skylights. Gothic sculptures of gargoyles and naked bodies twined and twisted up and down the walls. Green damask upholstered chaises littered the floor and violet-cushioned stools queued about the bar. The Plexiglass dance floor eddied from green to violet. Green smoke hissed out from small vents concealed under tables and beneath the stage.

The atmosphere channeled Quasimodo meets *Dangerous Liaisons* meets *The Matrix*.

A waitress dressed in slinky green lamé, with fluttering green fairy wings hooked at her back, smiled as she wheeled past a large oxygen tank on a steel dolly.

Becca spied more oxygen tanks—smaller and portable—sitting along the bar and in the center of each table. The tanks were about ten inches high and featured a vaporizer tube for breathing in alcoholic fumes.

"AWOL," she said.

"Alcohol Without Liquid," Dane verified, a note of fascination in his voice. "Nasty stuff."

"Really?" She had heard about the European rage of inhaling oxygen infused with alcohol. It was slowly making a showing in the States, the no-calorie part being its biggest draw for the diet-obsessed nation. "I thought it was safe."

"Not on your life. Initial reports advertised it as a chic new way to get your alcohol without all the calories or the hangover. But rapid ingestion into the lungs and bloodstream can really rough a person up."

"Don't they have the tanks gauged?"

"Supposedly. If properly—and legally—adjusted, they should allow a shot to be inhaled over a twenty-minute period. But idiots have begun shortening the time. Just like binge drinking without the messy liquid. Bloody hell. Do you think that's absinthe?"

Another fairy, bewinged in fluttery violet silk, walked by with a silver rack full of clanking vials glittering with green liquid.

"I guess that's the *verte,* eh?" Becca raked her eyes over the room and up the stairway to the second floor. She still wore the earring with the camera. It could come in handy yet. "Follow me. I see Pink."

Becca moved through the crowd toward the iron stairway spiraling up to the second floor balcony. The mindless, unending rhythm was impossible to ignore. And why should she? The best cover was in blending with the crowd. Gyrating, Becca grabbed the beat and started working her hips.

Sayonara, stuffy socialite.

This was the part of the lie that felt most real to her. A free spirit who could run with the punches and conform to any scenario. No one here cared what she did.

"That's her," Dane whispered in her ear.

Becca kept up a hip dance, but followed Dane's nod. Pink had topped the stairs. A man whose shaved head bore an intricate pattern of black tribal tattoos greeted Pink with a sloppy openmouthed kiss. Large rough hands snaked up her dress, exposing her thigh-high stockings and garters. She pushed him off and, hand in hand, they walked out of Becca's line of sight.

"Let's move." She mounted the stairs, surveying the room as she did. Now Becca noticed the smell wafting up in the tendrils of fog. Sweet and cloying. Sage.

Crossing through a beam of violet light, she turned and reached for Dane's hand as they reached the top. "Come on. She's across the room at the far table," Becca said. "Impossible to lose that bright pink silk."

Turning to embrace Dane, she situated them against the wall beneath the lascivious grin of a cat-faced serpent sculpture. "I'm making it look good."

"You won't get any arguments from me. Neither should you complain when I do this." His hand slid down her waist and over her derriere. The touch compelled her forward, into his personal space. An invasion she knew he was equipped to handle.

But was she? This sexual play teased at her sense of right and wrong. A line must always be drawn when on a case. But she'd never before had to draw one because of a partner. So where did the demarcation begin?

Becca moved closer, nuzzling her nose to Dane's cheek. All for show, she reminded herself. Keep it that way. "See who she's talking to?"

Dane brushed his cheek against hers as he glanced across the room. "The guy in the purple suit? I can't get a good look at his face."

"I believe it's aubergine."

"What?"

"The color... Never mind." Slipping her fingers through Dane's, Becca stepped back. Tossing her hair, she did a sexy spin, landing with her back against his chest and wrapping his arms across her stomach so they could both watch. "Mind your hands," she warned sweetly.

"You put them there, Miss I'm-Just-Making-This-Look-Good. Wait—you see that?"

Pink handed the man in the aubergine suit a small black pouch. One guess what was inside.

The suit opened the pouch. The bar was dark, but when the violet lights flashed over their table the diamond sent out a laserlike beam to the ceiling.

"Bloody idiot."

"It's dark," Becca said. "And he's probably high."

The suit clasped hands with Pink and yanked her to him to seal the deal with a kiss. A hard one, but Pink responded by wrapping her arms about the man's shoulders. Both pulled away, smiled and nodded.

The tattooed man dragged Pink off into the darkness. Exchange complete. Pink had not looked disappointed.

Dane spun Becca and pressed a palm to her cheek. "They're coming this way."

She studied the hard blue of Dane's eyes as he followed the suspects. Those eyes could turn serious or sexy in a flash. Beguiling.

"Headed down to the dance floor," he reported.

Snuggling her head against Dane's neck, Becca glanced sideways across the room. The suit was studying the diamond. Then he gave it a toss, caught it smartly, and shoved it back into the pouch and into his right pants pocket.

Swiping a palm over his goatee, he grinned. Green light highlighted an angular face, made even harsher by the exact lines of his dark beard, as he took in the crowd on the balcony.

Becca stilled. "He looks familiar."

It was a startling realization. Did she recognize him? From where?

"Who? Dimitri?"

Becca's heartbeat thudded to a halt. Wrenching her head up, she speared Dane with her gaze. "You *know* him?"

He had the audacity to shrug.

"The man in the purple suit. You just called him Dimitri."

"I believe it's aubergine."

"Don't fuck with me." She slid her hand up to his neck, squeezing.

"Chill, woman, this dinner jacket is a rental. Where have *you* seen him?

"Somewhere. I just…" Was completely floored how Dane had pulled a name out of the atmosphere like that. "He's…" She searched her memory for an exact event, but nothing jumped out at her. "That prince… Dimitri…I think that was his name. He's been in town for about a month. He's prince of some Turkish place."

"Turks don't have princes."

"Sure they do. I just don't recall…"

"Have you spoken to him?"

"No. Have *you* spoken to him?"

"Never met him before."

"Yet you know his name." She studied Dane's eyes, seeking the truth. This was a need-to-know moment and she wasn't going to back down. "Talk to me, Dane."

"I read Pink's lips."

"You're kidding me. Lipreading?"

"It's a skill oft used by our sort. You telling me you've never heard of it?"

Becca held her tongue. She'd heard of lipreading. Had tried it herself—unsuccessfully.

But she wasn't buying Dane's excuse. "I'm moving in for a closer look," she stated.

Dane tightened his grip about her waist. His palms molded to her hipbones with surprising heat. He knew how to touch a woman and exert minute control. And those eyes always commanded the attention he required.

Becca adjusted her weight to the other foot, tilting one hip against Dane's. Defiance held her there as she silently challenged him.

"Let's think this through," he said. "We can follow him out of here."

"Or we can take the diamond from him, call the Paris police to make an arrest, and be done with this chase. Let me go."

"I can't lose this guy."

"You won't. I'll have a finger on him the whole time."

"New York, you haven't a clue—"

"And are you going to give me one? Care to divulge all you know about the man?" She waited; Dane remained stone-faced. "Just as I thought. Cover me."

"Don't cock this up, love."

Becca laughed. "Isn't that the point?" She smirked. "Getting a cock up?"

Dane rubbed a hand over his tense jaw, fighting some urge to stall her, no doubt. "Watch yourself."

"If anyone is going to be doing any watching…" She trailed a finger under Dane's chin, and with a glance to the suit, who was still scanning the room, she leaned in and kissed Dane. A real, openmouthed, deep and delving kiss. Caught unaware, Dane gasped into her mouth, but didn't push her away. Instead, he fed into the passion, the hunger.

It actually hurt her chest to end it, as if an electric shock were tweaking her heart. "Don't take your eyes off me. Got it?"

Becca licked her lower lip. Her glance to the side caught the suspect's eye. He'd seen their kiss.

"Don't look away," she chided as she walked off, working the rhythm for all it was worth.

"Don't look away," Dane murmured mockingly to himself as Becca left.

A bombshell strode away from him, hips swinging and Thoroughbred gams prancing. Oh, but the beat belonged right there, in the confident steps of a dangerous woman.

But dangerous to her own detriment?

New York's plan could backfire and be detrimental to them both.

"Fine. I'm watching."

Because it was easier than revealing everything he knew. And Dane figured if he tried to tug her out of here it would only create a scene.

"And what a show we have tonight, ladies and gentleman," he muttered to himself. "Look at that sweet, tight arse. Shake it, love. What's that?"

Becca's hand slid up the side of her slinky black dress, to the small bow he'd noticed earlier. She moved the zipper higher, until it stopped at her thigh, just below her bottom.

"Careful, love." Dane crossed his arms and assumed a defensive stance.

From what he knew of the man in the purple suit, this was one encounter he should have tried to prevent. It was too soon. He hadn't expected to make contact. And not in such a bloody crowded place. That Dimitri was here defied all logic. Wasn't he supposed to be in New York?

"Contact with suss," he reluctantly narrated.

To stand by and watch made Dane itchy to pick a fight. But he'd invested too much time to jump the gun now. He trusted Becca wouldn't learn anything yet. And so long as she was happy chasing after her diamonds, he could concentrate on his own objective. Sure, MI-6 wanted the stones, but he wanted Dimitri.

"He's interested. Bloody arsehole's stretching his eyes from tit to toe and back up again. Work them, New York. He knows what he wants. Oh! The killer hair swing. That got him. That's right, chat him up. Lick those lips I just kissed—"

Dane licked his own lips. A remnant of something fine and expensive, like a droplet of Krug, clung to his mouth. Bloody brilliant, that kiss. But the untouchable bit of dosh fired all his caution buttons.

If only it hadn't been *this* case, and *this* Russian, he'd consider investing a lot more time in Miss Billion Dollars.

Who was currently feeling up *his* suss. Dane had tracked Dimitri too long. She'd better not mess things up.

Her last words, *Don't look away,* rang sexily in his head.

It was all a game of dress-up to her. Did she think she was one of those superheroines who pranced across the movie screen, always looking gorgeous, yet never getting more than a broken fingernail?

With a shake of his head, Dane focused.

"That's right, I'm watching. What the hell?"

Dimitri turned and looked right at Dane. He raised the vaporizer to him in a toast, and nodded.

Sodding—had she blown his cover?

No, the man couldn't ID him. Dane had not made contact with Dimitri. He'd been very careful this past year.

He gave a sheepish wave in acknowledgment and muttered, "What are you up to, New York?"

He was about to find out.

Dimitri and Becca were headed toward him. The bastard draped a hand at Becca's waist and she couldn't get any closer to the man unless she was wearing his clothes. He was not Turkish. And far from a prince. Dane didn't need to read lips to know that.

When they reached Dane's side, the man, who was very tall, with shoulders as broad as a rugby player's, said, "Is good," and nodded for Dane to follow.

Definitely Russian.

"It's all right, baby." Becca threaded her fingers through Dane's. She'd assumed a soft, lilting accent, as if she were an idiot blonde. "I told him you like to watch."

Chapter 13

The balcony was lined with doors, each covered with yards of the hideous green damask. Each door led to a small room, outfitted with a vaporizer bar that included ice water for those less adventurous, a chaise, and a two-way window, so occupants could watch the frenzy on the dance floor below, yet still get it on by themselves.

Dimitri slashed a green card through the lock and invited Becca inside. He didn't wait for Dane; neither did she.

"You like *verte?*" Dimitri called to Becca as he went to the dry bar and cracked open an ampoule of absinthe to insert into the portable oxygen tank.

"We both do." She drew a finger from Dane's shoulder to his elbow, feeling tension in his pulsing muscles even through the tux.

Get into the act, she wanted to yell at him.

Dane accepted a draw of absinthe-laced oxygen from Dimitri. He winced at the initial hit.

The thujone contained within the absinthe was an active ingredient found in marijuana. A fast hit would go right to the brain and have a person trancing in no time. Becca guessed the dosage had been increased. Dane probably got a good hit.

Dimitri clapped Dane on the shoulder. He had to shout because the music was piped into the room from speakers in every corner. "You like to watch?"

Dane made a "cheers" gesture and handed the vaporizer back to Dimitri, who offered it to Becca, but she refused.

"You said you liked?" Dimitri, mocking a pout at her refusal, set the vaporizer aside, then pulled her to him. "We will have a show then? You and I, is good?"

Dimitri's breath smelled of the anise contained in the absinthe. Becca liked the sweet flavor and pushed her mouth to his, mining the lingering taste of the tantalizing alcoholic fumes. It was a sneaky way to snatch the buzz without endangering her morals. She didn't do illicit substances.

Dimitri smelled of all things forbidden. He felt rough, from the stubble on his jaw to the firm palm he pressed against her spine. Every part of him was hard, demanding and dangerous.

Over his crop of dark curls she spied Dane. He signaled with his hand, pointing to her, digging into his pocket and then wiggling two fingers.

Right. The diamond.

All in good time.

Shimmying to the beat, Becca lifted her arms high in Dimitri's grasp. She lowered a hand in the shape of a gun and shot at Dane well out of Dimitri's line of sight. Bull's-eye. Blowing away the imaginary smoke, she winked and gave him a thumbs-up.

Dane reciprocated, but his aim was definitely targeted toward Dimitri.

"I like sexy American women," Dimitri announced eagerly. "What is your name?"

"Becky," she said, laughing loudly at Dane's reaction to her choice of moniker.

Dimitri released her, bussing her chin with a kiss, then bounced with the beat over to the bar to take another long hit.

When he offered Dane the vaporizer a second time, Becca intervened. She glided in front of Dimitri, distracting his attention. Music crept under the thin silk dress and invaded her pores. It felt natural to dance. With his dark eyes eating her every move, she slid into Dimitri's strong, muscular arms. His mouth tripped along her neck. With every beat of the heavy, trance-inducing music, Dimitri pumped his cock against her groin. Nice and hard. He was primed.

The two of them moved as one, taking, stealing the rhythm from one another. Only the beat.

Repetitive.

Intoxicating.

A girl could close her eyes and lose herself in a moment like this. A strong man intent on giving and taking pleasure. And another man who couldn't remove his steely aquamarine eyes from her.

And everything that could destroy her upper-crust status.

Tilting back her head, Becca slid down to squat before Dimitri.

Dimitri reached to the bar to grab the vaporizer and suck in another long inhalation. Eyes closed and mouth shut tight, he held the fumes in his lungs, until a mischievous smile curved his mouth.

He moaned as Becca ran her palms up his thighs, rising, bracketing his hard-on through his clothes.

"American women know what men want," he growled, and glanced over his shoulder to grin at Dane.

Becca caught a glimpse of her audience. Arms crossed over his chest. Jaw set. Dane averted his gaze to the madness on the dance floor. Because he didn't want to watch *her* madness?

Come on, Dane, see me.

She was playing. Pushing the edge. Living the lie.

It's not a lie. This is you. You know it is.

So why did that thought disturb her so much?

Sliding her hands up the aubergine silk, Becca rose. Grinding her hips from side to side, she rocked them against Dimitri's erection. He reached for his fly, but she stopped him, her fingernails tapping the solid core of him.

"Let's play awhile," she mouthed, knowing he couldn't hear her. But he understood.

The beat changed and she gyrated for him and unbuttoned his shirt. Hard abs and pecs. Faint curls of dark hair around each nipple and a promising bit disappearing into his pants. He worked out. Likely, he knew how to fight. But despite his size, she could hold her own. She favored Shen Ku, an ancient form of Chinese street fighting.

Becca couldn't resist. And why should she? She pressed her mouth to Dimitri's flesh and licked a trail from his neck to one nipple and then the other. His moan spurred her on. Spinning about, she raised her arms and wiggled her derriere into his groin.

She was face-to-face with Dane, only a few feet away.

With his head lowered, his eyes focused directly on hers, he communicated some form of silent criticism.

Too bad the music was so loud. And she was working.

Closing her eyes, Becca followed Dimitri's roaming hands with her own. His fingers were long and smooth. Obviously hadn't worked a day of manual labor in his life. But what *did* he do?

"You look so familiar," she called, fighting the music's volume, and spinning to face Dimitri. "Have I seen you before?

"Do you come here many times?"

"My first. You've such a remarkable face." She caressed his cheek. The rough stubble tickled her wrist; his goatee was thick and smooth. "Almost like…royalty."

He winced.

That verified her suspicions. She *had* seen this man before.

But if she had seen him, then he—

"I don't like all this talk," Dimitri said with a bored sneer. "Do you want to talk or do you want to fuck?"

Neither.

"Oh, I do." She ran her hand down the front of his pants. "Oh! So hard."

"You want to see?"

"What's in your pocket?"

"Not my pocket, pretty one."

Smooth and searching hands glided over her cleavage.

She glanced at Dane. Watch me, she thought. Feel this, you British tease.

"So hot," Dimitri groaned. He skated a hand beneath the black silk and cupped her breast. "Is good. We will all fuck. Yes?" he called to Dane.

Becca coaxed up her dress. "Slow, baby," she cooed into Dimitri's ear. "We've got all the time in the world! Loverboy over there likes it that way," she declared boldly so Dane could hear. "Right, lover?"

Dane poked his chest with his thumb. "Slow? Oh yeah…" He worked hard to summon the words and spit them out. "'Cause that's the way I *like it*."

Becca shot him daggers. Dane was more strung than a Tyburn dangler.

Why did men always have to be the ones in charge? If the reins of control slipped from their greedy fingers, they always started pouting. Stiff, not at all relaxed, utterly pissed. Little boys in need of a time-out.

Hell, this wasn't working. And if Dimitri went any further, she'd have to stick around for the fireworks. Becca never crossed that line.

"Baby, I think I need something to drink."

"Take a hit," Dimitri cooed. "Loosen up, sexy woman."

Loosen up? What the hell did he think she was

doing? "Just some water, please. My mouth is so dry," she exclaimed.

Dimitri reluctantly pulled away with a helpless blink.

"Pretty please?" She landed on the chaise with a kick of her leg, and stretched her arms across the plush damask.

Dimitri obliged and went to pour water into one of the glass tumblers kept in a drawer of the dry bar.

While he did so, Dane moved in, kneeling on the chaise over her. He swept Becca's hair back with a glide of his hand and a possessive tug. She wrapped her legs around his and toppled him forward.

Knees straddling her thighs, he whispered in her ear, "Are you finished playing games, New York?"

"Why? Can't take the heat?"

"It's not mere heat you're playing with, love. This bastard is fire."

The tinkle of ice cubes sounded near Becca's ear. She reached for the tumbler and pushed against the aggressive male in her space. Dane sprang upright.

Dimitri smiled and smoothed his hand over Dane's ass. "We can do a threesome. Is good?"

Dane stepped back and raised his hands. "I just like to watch, buddy."

"Buddy?" Dimitri looked to her, then back to Dane. "Do you not like? You let me touch your woman, but you are so angry."

"You'd better believe it. She's not yours—"

Dimitri curved a fist into his palm.

Dane reacted in kind.

Two bulls snorted in the middle of the ring.

Time to send in the cavalry.

Becca swept up her tumbler, delivering the heavy weighted bottom directly to Dimitri's jaw. Underneath, where a direct hit should knock out his lights.

A splatter of spit and ice misted her face. Arms flailing, Dimitri dropped like a boulder onto the chaise.

There were two bulges in Dimitri's pants. Becca reached for the one she was interested in. The velvet pouch fitted into her palm. Drawing it out, she turned and stood and found herself in Dane's arms.

Flashing green light flickered across his tense jaw. "You know you frustrate me, love?"

"Nothing a million dollar rock can't cure, eh?"

"You forget that the exchange rate sucks." He angrily snatched the pouch. "Come on, let's get the hell out of Dodge before he wakes."

"We can't leave. Call in reinforcements for an arrest."

"I will."

Gripping the earring she still wore, Becca snapped a shot of the sprawled pseudo-Turk.

Dane waited in the doorway. "What are you doing?" He tossed the pouch once and caught it. "This is all we came for." He slipped down the hallway. "Come on!"

Becca started to follow him, but slapped her palm against the door frame. Dane was in a hurry. He didn't even turn to see if she followed.

She frowned. Should they leave this guy? Was he the high man on the ladder? And what about Pink? Dimitri could answer questions. They needed to interrogate him. Call in backup for an arrest. The CIA would want him in hand.

Why was Dane so eager to leave when, for all purposes, the job was only half-done?

A burning coiled in Becca's gut, making it almost impossible to take a step forward. Something wasn't right.

Dane and his need-to-know bullshit. Well, she'd show him all he needed to know. Starting with the heel of her Manolos.

She was just dashing out the doorway when she was suddenly grabbed from behind.

Lifted from the floor and flung across the room, she landed on the chaise, heels pointing to the ceiling. Her jaw clacked and she almost bit her tongue.

"Who are you?"

The plush cushions made righting herself a struggle. She wasn't able to get to her feet before Dimitri pounced, caging her thighs with his knees.

He grabbed her around the throat, choking her. "Bitch! Your lover steal the prize and leave? Not good for you."

A toe to his thigh did little more than aggravate. Dimitri sneered. Spittle sprayed her face.

Choking and gagging, she dragged her fingernails down the underside of his wrist, and he momentarily released her.

Pulling the thin gold choker from around her neck, Becca manipulated the heart charm to fit between her first two fingers. A wicked slash drew a red line across Dimitri's forehead with the sharpened tip.

He jumped back, clutching his forehead. Checked his fingers.

"Yes, asshole, it's called blood."

Becca sprang to her feet, gave a moment's thought

to where the hell Dane had disappeared to, then lifted her foot and, turning on the ball of her opposite foot, drilled her heel into Dimitri's groin. She felt resistance as the metal spike pierced the aubergine fabric.

Dimitri went down with little more than a squeak. Blood spotted his trousers.

Gasping out a breath, Becca replaced her choker and tugged down her skirt. It had torn, breaking the zipper and exposing her thigh to her hip.

"This is couture!"

Gripping the slashed fabric, she stepped over Dimitri, then scanned the balcony to see if anyone had been alerted by the debacle. Zombie-eyed revelers danced below.

Moving swiftly, she descended to the main floor.

Dane waited at the bottom of the stairs.

"Derzhi vora!" Stop the thief.

Becca didn't turn around. Remarkably, Dimitri had risen.

Dane grasped her hand and they ran toward the entrance door of the club.

"Taking a Sunday stroll, love? What happened to you—"

"I've been busy trying to keep up with my partner, who left me behind," she snapped.

"I thought you were right— Sod me, it's too loud!"

They reached the street and ran down the block toward the distant glimmer of a traffic light. Chill air swept down Becca's aching throat. Her gasps turned to coughs. Stalking up behind Dane, she gripped him by the shoulder and spun him about.

He summoned a protest, but her fist beat him to it.

Head snapping back from the impact, Dane recovered from her punch by rubbing his palm over his jaw. "What the sodding hell?"

"We should have waited for backup."

Becca spied a taxi half a block down. She flagged it. Headlights flashed in confirmation.

Turning abruptly, she wrapped her hand around Dane's neck and slammed him against the brick wall of a garden enclosure. "Until you can get over your need-to-know attitude, I don't need you, asshole."

The cab stopped with a screech. Becca slipped into the back seat and slammed the door. "Place Vendôme," she told the cabbie.

As they pulled from the curb she spied Dimitri's thugs barreling down the sidewalk toward Dane. He hadn't noticed them, so stunned he was that she'd left him.

But he now held the diamond. *Fuck.*

"Back up," she directed the cabbie.

Seconds before Dane got trampled by thugs, she opened the back door and he dived inside the cab. Dimitri's men pounded the trunk as the cab peeled off again.

Dane pulled himself upright in the seat. With a jut of his chin, he regained his composure but kept his distance. "Why'd you come back? I thought I was an arsehole?"

"You are." She patted down his jacket. A flick of her wrist produced the velvet pouch. "But you're an arsehole with a priceless jewel."

When they returned to the room, Dane picked over the mackerel toast. The thin slices of fish had begun to dry and turn gray around the edges.

   Tossing the velvet pouch to the bed, Becca then powered up her laptop and sent Zeek the photo she'd
snapped of Dimitri. Then she began an online search designed to keep her from strangling Dane with her bare
hands. She decided to cool down, let her anger dissipate,
before approaching him about what had just happened.

   Hell, she was tense. Her typing fingers moved stiffly.
She felt betrayed on so many levels. A moment of peace
was required.

   But not until she relieved her curiosity about Dimitri.
Where had she seen him before?

   Thinking through the usual sources, she accessed
the Internet and did a search for "Dimitri" and "Turkish" in the *New York Times* for the past few months.
Nothing.

   "What. The. Bloody—"

   Becca spun toward the alcove. Dane stood at the end
of one of the twin beds. The black velvet pouch dangled
from his fingers, then dropped. She got up to inspect.

   "Wow." And that was all she could say.

Chapter 14

Two diamonds lay on the red-and-cream toile de Jouy counterpane. The round brilliant Pink had nabbed from the auction, and the asscher diamond they had left in London with Lester. The diamond Agent Arlowe had supposedly secured for the CIA.

"What's going on?"

Becca eased a hand over her aching right shoulder. "Beats me."

How had the asscher stone followed them to Paris? Had Pink known Lester? Why would he give it to her knowing it was evidence that belonged to Scotland Yard?

Had Agent Arlowe gotten to him too late? Of course. But why hadn't she contacted Zeek about not finding the diamond?

Dane said, "Is that—"

"It's the stone Scotland Yard nabbed in London."

"The one you gave to your very trustworthy friend, Lester Price?"

Becca rubbed her palms up her arms, chasing a chill. "I don't know what the hell is going on. If Pink took that diamond from Lester it means she's been on our tail since London. Or we've been following her."

"Unless another contact took the diamond from Lester and handed it over to Pink?"

"Well, Zeek…"

"Your CIA handler?"

"You make me sound like a monkey on a leash."

He smirked, but the lack of comment raised her ire.

"We sent an agent to pick up the stone."

"Need to know, eh?"

Sucking in her lower lip, Becca winced. She'd been playing the need-to-know card, too. And getting caught felt so wrong.

Had she handed the diamond over to the enemy? No. Lester had to have been robbed.

Are you going to be that naive?

Lester could have been working against her. But Arlowe's silence troubled her the most. The CIA had dropped the ball.

"All that matters is it's back in our hands," Dane stated.

"Did you say 'our'? As in, we're sharing this one?"

"Slip of the tongue, love."

Of course.

Dane blasted out a tremendous sigh and scrubbed the back of his neck with a palm. "So we've got both stones."

"Looks like our mission here is complete. Evidence in hand." Becca wandered to the serving tray and popped a sliver of cracker into her mouth. "Except there's still Dimitri."

Reminded of her search, she returned to the laptop.

"I thought you were charged to get the stone? Just that."

"You don't want to know who that bastard was in *verte?*"

"I'll leave it to headquarters."

"Well, I don't like to rely on others if I can do it myself."

"I've noticed."

"You were never going to call for an arrest, were you?"

"I did."

"Didn't."

"Doesn't matter now."

"It should."

"Love, you're stepping in over your head. Germologists don't—"

"Stop!" She held up a hand to silence him. Closing her eyes, Becca silently counted to five and then let out a breath. He just didn't get it.

Ignoring Dane's heavy and troubling presence, she tapped out the URL for the *New York Social Diary*. It listed a daily diary of happenings, parties and galas, along with pictures of the lavish events. "The List" featured a veritable gallery of who's who. She skipped that, knowing it was only residents, and instead paged through the events she had been to of late. Pictures of celebrities and heiresses and foreign billionaires scrolled before her.

"I think you love that computer more than me."

She smirked. "Love is not a part of this equation."

"Right." He slouched in his favorite chair. "I suspect you haven't a clue what love is."

"I do, too. Asshole."

"Such talk is not becoming of a lady."

"So now I'm a lady?"

"Well. Not after that lap dance you gave the Turk."

"I—"

"I was stunned that you, a woman who has made it crystal clear she doesn't like to be touched, descended to such—"

"Why do you insist on calling him Turkish?"

"You're the one who first said it. You're also changing the subject."

"Yes, and for good reason. We both talked to him. He spoke Russian, idiot."

"Oh, idiot. Much better than arsehole."

Becca caught her forehead in a palm.

It was well past midnight. She needed to sleep. This day might be the longest in her life. It had started with her boarding a plane to London, and now here she sat in Paris, exchanging barbs with a strange man who wasn't so much strange as…frustrating. In ways that challenged her every need for truth and human contact.

"Wait. A. Minute."

The photo that unscrolled before her featured one Dimitri, aka Aubergine Suit, with his arms wrapped around two young socialites. The caption below the photo read: *Sally Devereaux, Dimitri Boratav, Turkish prince, and Molly von Hutchins enjoy the festivities.*

"You found him?"

She leaned back to allow Dane to look over her shoulder at the screen.

"That's him," he said. "Turkish prince?"

"This picture is one of dozens taken at a cocktail reception given by the American Turkish Society held at the Metropolitan Museum of Art. I knew I'd seen him somewhere."

"Copy that and I'll forward it to headquarters."

"Right. Like you called for an arrest? I'll do you one better and send it on to the CIA."

"Love."

"I'm not your love, and this is not your computer, so back off and just chill."

She forwarded the picture to Zeek and Alan. Suspicions running the gamut, Becca hoped Zeek would get back to her soon. She had questions that needed answers.

Aware when Dane stalked off and stretched out on the bed, Becca held back a smile. While he seemed capable enough, he didn't make a lot of contact with his own people. Which didn't score him any points on the trustworthy scale.

The click of diamond against diamond punctuated Becca's keystrokes as she signed off.

"I'm going to shower." She stood and headed toward the bathroom.

"Thought you were hydrophobic?"

"Please. The shower?"

Dane held up a diamond to each of his eyes. "Go for it."

Becca wondered if she could trust the man while she

bathed. Not for a New York minute. "Toss me those, will you?"

"What, these lovely bits?"

She curled her fingers in a "gimmee" gesture.

Dane jumped from the bed and approached, the diamonds clicking in one palm. "You don't trust me?"

"You know I don't."

"Fair enough. I'll give you this one." He offered the asscher, but any data that may have been encoded on the crown had been erased.

"I want the other." She snatched for it, but he retracted.

"Ah, ah. For a price."

Becca blustered. If he was going to ask for another kiss… "Look, Dane—"

"I want the truth. A confession."

Frankly, a kiss would have been easier.

"Like what?"

"Did you enjoy it?"

"What?"

"Dancing with Dimitri. His hands all over you." The distance between them lessened. Dane's breath grazed her neck and chin. "And me standing there in the shadows, watching you play the bad girl."

She moved in and slipped her tongue across her lips, then slid her fingers over the diamonds. "Every bloody moment."

Grasping the brilliant, she dodged into the bathroom and slammed the door behind her. Listening, she waited. Dane rapped on the door once, then walked away.

She set the diamond on a plush white hand towel. The stained glass window, in turquoise and red art deco curves, scattered colored beams of moonlight across the shower stall.

Becca quickly shed the clingy Ungaro gown and stepped beneath the water. It was merely a stream; the water pressure in most European hotels stunk. But the lavender soap the hotel provided seeped into her pores and relaxed her.

As far as her superiors were concerned, the mission had been a success. She'd obtained both diamonds and figured out who wanted them. Or had she?

The fact that Dimitri Whoever-He-Was roamed free bothered her. Why had he wanted the diamonds? Obviously for whatever was inside. Shouldn't that cause both the CIA and MI-6 more concern than they were showing?

Alan had yet to report on the code she had sent to him, and Zeek hadn't given her further info on Amandus Magnusson or Pink. It was as if a puzzle lay scattered upon the table. She had all the pieces and now just needed to assemble them.

She ran a soapy hand over her shoulder, massaging her sore muscles. No Parisian shower was going to beat away the pulsing pain of bruised flesh.

Did you enjoy it?

That Dane had even asked proved he was more bothered by her display than she had been. Good. The Brit needed to have his world rocked.

Turning off the water, Becca stepped out and wrapped a towel around her torso. She missed having warm towels at the ready, and Jake nearby with a chocolate martini in hand after a long day.

Staring at her steam-fogged reflection, Becca grimaced at how tired she appeared. Jet lag aside, she felt as hellish as she looked. Inspecting her shoulder, she traced a thin purple line from her armpit to the top of her shoulder. And now she noticed a huge purple bruise on her left thigh. Yikes, when had that happened?

"You so need a massage," she said to her reflection. And not the strenuous Thai massage she indulged in every Wednesday morning, which was more like an assisted yoga session. Right now she needed gentle fingers and soft music. Release.

A Zen session would be perfect. Zen never wasted words when his mouth could be put to better use. Hell, she needed to have sex and come wildly. That usually settled her anxieties and made her sleep like a baby.

An angry knock sounded repeatedly on the bathroom door.

"What?" she muttered, so tired she didn't even have the energy to muster annoyance for Mr. Need-to-Know. Likely, because she'd come to realize she was engaged in the same game.

Dane's voice seeped through the wood door. "Are you going to be in the loo all night?"

"Not *all* night." But if it bothered him, she'd find something to do to waste more time.

"Could I get my toothbrush out?"

She glanced to the small leather toiletry bag at the end of the white marble counter.

"I can't sleep until I've brushed my teeth and scrubbed my face, love."

"Love," she murmured to her reflection. "He wishes."

She knew it was a common pet name used by the Brits, but the word annoyed her. There was no love between the two of them. Although she did sense a bit of twisted, lustful curiosity on both their parts.

"What are you doing in there? Maybe I shouldn't be listening...."

Clad in only a towel, Becca snatched the diamond, opened the door and slid past Dane. "Knock yourself out."

The velvet pouch lay on the bed. She grabbed it, put her stone in with the other, then stashed it in her laptop bag. Then Becca strode to the serving tray and picked over the food. Half a dry cracker with a bit of cream cheese spread stuck to the white paper liner. Almost appealing. But the half bottle of white wine did appeal. Alsace Grand Cru, 2004. Tilting it back, she drank a healthy swallow.

The bathroom door stood open, and Becca noticed for the first time that Dane had removed his shirt. Wearing just the tuxedo pants, he bent before the sink, scrubbing his hands under the faucet.

It might have been the exhaustion, it may have been the wine, but Becca wasn't about to analyze her next move.

Wine bottle in hand, she strolled into the bathroom and pushed up to sit on the double-wide, two-sinked vanity next to Dane. Her pot of Cié de Peau Beauté moisturizer sat to her right. Setting the wine down, she picked up the cream and screwed off the cap. The scent of almonds mingled with the lavender steam.

Dane rinsed his hands. "Almost finished. Though I'm thinking I should shower again. God knows what I rubbed in when you shoved me against the building. My trousers are soaked. Smells like petrol."

"No hurry." She scooped up a wodge of cream and rubbed it over her elbow. The moisturizer came with a very small spoon for doling out slowly. Becca always tossed the thing. "Do you want me to get out?"

That question sparked the most delightful look from Dane.

"Suit yourself. That stuff smells good," he said around the washcloth he scrubbed over his face. Why were men so rough with themselves? "You put that cream all over?"

"Sounds like a need-to-know question to me."

He patted his neck with the towel. "Smells expensive."

"Four hundred dollars for six ounces."

"Christ. I could make a bloody car payment with that."

"That little toy you drive cost that much? It looks like something a kid would dump out of a cereal box in the morning."

He flicked off the water and tossed the wet hand towel to the floor.

"Slob," Becca muttered.

"Snob," Dane countered. Crossing his arms, he leaned against the half wall at one end of the bathtub. Muscles in his biceps flexed sinuously with his movement. The man worked out. And Becca didn't mind staring.

Another wodge of cream. She started down her other arm. "Tell me about Dimitri."

"Love—"

"Seemed for a moment there in the club you knew he wasn't Turkish."

"Like you said, we both heard him speak."

"Yeah, but you also knew his name."

"Lipreading."

He did have a knack for keeping his story straight.

Skating her eyes over his flesh, Becca felt a flush of warmth within. The man was a surprise underneath the swank attire. Firm muscles, even the beginnings of a six-pack. He hadn't struck her as the sort who would have the discipline to work out.

"So you like it when people watch, eh?"

"I was playing a role, Agent Dane."

"A role you assumed with ease. We call people like you honey traps in the trade."

"As they say, you can lure more flies…" Torn between a ridiculous attraction and the need to remain professional, she felt the moral side of her begging to be obeyed. "Despite your digs, I am experienced in the field. You, on the other hand, were positively mortified."

"For you, love, for you."

"Give me a break. If the situation were different I think you would have liked to join in."

"No threesomes for me. Christ, the man touched my arse."

She smoothed cream across her forearm and thought for a moment. For all the mental turmoil he'd caused her today… "So what if it had been just the two of us?"

Dane's posture changed. Every part of him curved toward her. "You propositioning me?"

"Maybe."

"Better than a proper no."

Becca laughed, loving his easy surrender to her flirtation. She was a little tipsy from the few sips of Grand Cru, added to the absinthe fumes she'd inhaled from Dimitri's kiss.

"So, did you get a buzz from that hit of absinthe you took at the club? Or were you faking?"

"I'll never tell."

Ah yes, need-to-know. And what she wouldn't pay for a peek into all his secrets.

Becca closed her eyes and leaned back against the mirrored wall above the vanity.

"All right, let's see if I can ask something you will answer…. Have you ever been married?"

"Never."

"Serious girlfriends?"

"Two. One in school, the other a few years ago. Next question?"

"How old are you?"

"Thirty-two."

Six years her senior. Not an enormous age difference. He'd been around a few times, had seen the world.

"What about you?" he asked. "Dare I ask a woman her age?"

"Twenty-six. But I act older, yes?"

"But you look younger."

"One point for you on the knowing-what-to-say scale. So, why'd you transfer from Scotland Yard to MI-6?"

"I see Lester has been filling your ears." He shrugged. "The quick down-and-dirty? My father was MI-5. He was killed in the line of duty. I thought I could do more good in Six because of their further reach, you know?"

"Do you know the person who killed your father?"

"I do." He inhaled heavily and shook his head. "It's not something I feel comfortable talking about." A catch in his voice stopped him for a second. "Just know I'm not going to do anything rash. My job comes first, before all.

"Anyway, now it's my turn. How did you get into the gemology business? Shouldn't an heiress spend her days with her Manolos up in the manicurist's chair and her servants asking her which diamonds she wants to wear with her outfit?"

Becca gave a loose shrug. She was feeling the wine.

"If not the life of leisure," Dane pressed, "then I'd think you'd be playing the circuit alongside Daddy."

"I didn't feel the music as my father does. You know, in your bones, like the trance music at *verte*. I can play anything, but the emotion isn't there, and I didn't know how to make it happen."

"You're kind of weak on the whole emotion thing."

"Whatever." She slid off the vanity and grabbed the wine bottle.

"You see?"

Yes, she did see, but she wasn't about to acknowledge the truth he'd discovered. Becca could hardly waste her time caring what others thought of the choices she made in life. Perfection demanded one curb emotion. It was as simple as that.

"You know what I've figured about you?"

"Hmm?"

"You've never dated outside your social set."

"Why should I?"

"So being with me…well, it's like slumming, isn't it?"

"What makes you think I would even consider *being* with you?"

"Oh, that's harsh." He crossed his arms.

It was harsh. She knew it, and yet she didn't feel it. It was a conditioned response.

But a surprising reaction followed.

Becca leaned forward, drawing Dane to her by his shoulders, then kissed him. At first he resisted—in anger or surprise? But quickly his hands eased around her shoulders and over the plush towel to land on her bottom. Stepping closer, he insinuated himself against her body.

He kissed like a dream. Not too soft or tentative. Not demanding or trying-to-prove-himself manly. Just right. Secrets be damned, this man touched her darkest desires with ease. Whatever he needed to know about her could be had.

"This is insane," he muttered against her open mouth. "You don't want this. You're tipsy."

When he started to draw away, Becca pressed the heels of her palms to the counter behind her and leaned back.

Was he right? Did the wine make her react?

While part of her knew that must be the case, an even bigger part said, *You want this. You need this! Don't let him talk you out of it.*

He stepped backward. "I think I need a cold shower."

"You don't like kissing me?"

"Kissing you is brilliant, beyond brilliant. But that's the problem. I'm not going to take advantage of you just to get my rocks—hard as they are—off."

"I'm not drunk, Dane." She caught the towel wrapped around her as it began to part beneath her arm. The action exposed her right leg and thigh all the way up to her stomach.

"You're just trying to fulfill a need, is that right?"

"Maybe. Why are you backing away? I would have expected you to jump right in. Don't I attract you? Am I the wrong social class for you?"

"Becca." His back hit the doorjamb.

She stood up and moved closer until she was only inches from him. "You're sending me mixed signals, Dane. You know what that's called in musical terms?"

"Should I care?"

"Playing a countermelody."

"Yeah? Well, there's no one to witness this little tango. One of us could end up getting burned."

Becca tugged her towel tighter. She wanted to fling it away and stride naked across the room. Straddle Dane and have sex with him. But he'd made his opinion clear. He wasn't interested.

Grabbing the cream from the counter, she strode past him and heard him slam the bathroom door shut. Setting the pot of cream on the desk, she plunked down on her bed in a huff.

The shower started. Becca stared up at the ceiling. Stretching, she reached for the lamp and dimmed it.

Dane was right. This—whatever it was—was wrong.

But she was…well, horny, damn it. She was wet, and not because she'd just taken a shower. She ached for satisfaction.

Slipping her hand over her hip, she nudged up the towel and eased her fingers into the heat Dane had created. Closing her eyes, she exhaled. She was very efficient at getting herself off. He'd never know. The shower would disguise any whimpers that should escape.

Oh yes, no turning back now. Images of a solid, hard

man visited her thoughts. Just to imagine his ripped abs
glancing over her nipples, and that kiss…

Becca arched her back. She was close to coming. Part
of her brain protested. No, this was wrong. He was in
the next room! The other half said, *So what!*

And she released, spilling out the day's tension.
Giggles bubbled out. Anxiety swept away on waves of
satisfaction.

Breathing heavily, and sighing, Becca suddenly realized the shower had stopped.

The bathroom door was open.

Dane stood in the doorway, towel around his hips,
and his toothbrush dangling from his mouth.

Chapter 15

For a moment Becca, elbows propping her up on the bed, smiled at Dane. She was in the zone. One more giggle slipped out.

He snatched the toothbrush from his mouth. "In-sodding-credible."

His astonishment did not override her high. Allowing her head to fall back onto the pillow, she let out a satisfied sigh.

Tension: obliterated. All the day's stresses: gone.

One MI-6 agent: gobsmacked.

Still smiling, Becca sat up on the bed, ensuring her towel was pulled down to her thighs.

Dane stood in the doorway like a Ken doll waiting for direction.

"Do you always brush your teeth in the shower?"

"Woman." He strode to the alcove but stopped a good distance from the end of her bed. Spreading his arms to encompass something he couldn't wrap his mind around, he exclaimed, "You've just come gloriously, and all you can ask is where I brush my teeth?"

She shrugged. "Told you I could take care of myself."

"I guess you can." He tossed the toothbrush to the bedside table and sat at the end of the empty bed, his back to her.

And while she should be feeling embarrassed, even shameful, not an ounce of either stirred Becca's blood. She was sated. Relaxed. Ready to drift off to sleep.

Dane's shoulders glistened with water from the shower. His moist hair stood up in spikes. He swept a hand across the back of his neck, then turned to her, switching from a smile to a grimace, and then to an expression of utter confusion. He didn't know what to say!

Reaching behind her head, Becca gave a punch to the pillow and leaned back. "It's a great tension reliever."

"Oh ho? And now you expect me to sleep next to you in this little narrow bed after…that?"

Drawing up her legs, Becca slipped them under the toile de Jouy counterpane. "Yes."

"Bloody incredible!"

Dane walked around to the opposite side of his bed and tossed back the sheets with an irritated fling. He fingered the towel wrapped about his hips. Even in the dim light Becca saw something had risen to the occasion.

Admittedly, this situation was fast becoming uncomfortable. He wouldn't actually expect her to…? No. And she wasn't about to offer.

"Don't tell me you sleep in the nude?"

"Usually, yes," he said, a note of uncertainty in his voice. "I hadn't expected to be sharing the room."

Becca flicked off the table lamp. "There."

In the few moments of utter darkness that followed, she listened as Dane slid between the crisp sheets. Naked. Now it was too dark for her to get a proper glimpse of British arse. Would it be tight as his pecs? Mmm.

Stop it. Already satisfied, remember?

A streetlight beamed through the narrow crack in the draperies, slicing a line across the ends of their beds. Steam from the bathroom seeped out in lavender clouds, further coaxing Becca to sleep.

It was utterly silly that she had done such a thing. And to be caught?

She snuggled into her pillow.

She was aware that Dane didn't lay down, but instead sat up in bed. What could she say? Apologize for taking a moment for pleasure? Hardly.

"So," he began in a whisper, "do you always giggle after you come?"

"Not always." She turned toward him, and propped a hand under her head. "Sometimes I cry."

Two beats of silence, then, "That must go over well with your lovers."

"It's not like sobbing crying," she said defensively. "It's more like tears of joy silently streaming down my cheeks. You know, everything comes out all at once. It's a tremendous release."

"Sure. Release." His sigh seemed to slowly siphon off his own tension.

"You can go ahead," she offered, feeling a bit of a tease. And more powerful for it. Hell, it was the wine. She'd never been much of a drinker. Two chocolate martinis and it was time to tuck her in.

"Go ahead and do what?" The question echoed across the room.

"Take care of yourself. Jack off."

He gave a snort of laughter. "Not bloody likely."

"Shy?"

"Bloody rot. You want me to…? Not in a million—it's—a man reserves that for when a woman is not available."

"Ah. What makes you think I'm available?"

"And a bloody good-night to you, New York."

"I *am* high maintenance, remember."

"So that's what they're calling it now." Dane shuffled down into the sheets and said not another word.

Smiling to herself, Becca turned over and closed her eyes. Score one point for self-maintenance chick.

At 5:00 a.m.—less than four hours later—Becca's cell phone rang. Which meant Zeek was working late.

"We lost each other last night."

"Couldn't be helped." Becca strode across the dark room, mining for shoes. She'd been awake for about twenty minutes and had been in the process of dressing.

"I've got an identity for Pink," Zeek said with a yawn. "Katarine Veld. She's associated with the Russian Mafia, known for burglary, money laundering, black market military trades, all sorts of nefarious deeds."

"Russian Mafia, eh?" A glance determined Dane

slept still, the counterpane shoved down to reveal his bare chest slowly rising and falling. "What about the info I sent you on the Turkish prince?"

"That particular face is being a bit more elusive. I'm tracking him through all databases. What makes you think he's Turkish?"

The question of the moment.

"I don't. I think he's Russian. At least he spoke it fluently last night. He's posing as a Turkish prince, and has been photographed hobnobbing with the elite in New York. Do a search on Dimitri Boratov."

"So that's why MI-6 nudged in on this one."

"What do you mean?"

"Six has been after the Russians for a while. Last year they took out a couple of MI-5 agents, tortured and killed them."

My father was killed in the line of duty. Dane's father?

"Though, as I understand it, the MI-5 deaths weren't Mafia related."

"Hmm, so if Pink is also Russian—"

"I didn't say she *is* a Russian. Actually, Ms. Veld is Nordic, of Icelandic descent. More like a mob moll, if you ask me. She the prince's girlfriend?"

"I'm not sure. She met up with another man at the club. Lots of skull tattoos and a roving tongue. No, I wouldn't say she belongs to Dimitri exclusively. So what's the word on Lester? Did he screw me?"

"Maybe, maybe not. Agent Arlowe arrived to find him near death, a breathing tube tight about his neck."

"That's not the way those things are supposed to work."

"I know," Zeek said. "Anyway, our guess is Pink followed the stone after Scotland Yard arrested the thief that ended up committing suicide."

"Which means she had to have followed Dane and me to Paris."

"Unless she's getting cues from someone higher up. You got the stone from the auction, yes?"

"Yes, and more." Becca looked to the nightstand next to Dane's bed. She'd completely forgotten about *two* diamonds! "Pink handed the diamond over to Dimitri. And then he made the exchange with me. Of course, I didn't give him an option."

"Excellent!"

"Even more excellent? *Both* stones were in the exchange."

"No kidding."

Becca could hear the furious tapping of computer keys in the background.

"I've made a note of that."

"Zeek, what the hell is going on?"

"What do you mean, Becca?"

"I can't help but feel my objective isn't really the diamonds. The CIA isn't as keen to nab the stones as I hoped."

Zeek's sigh registered as a warning tingle at the back of Becca's neck. "All I can do is verify your suspicions by stating that indeed your objective has been altered. I've nailed the origin of the diamonds."

"I thought it was Amandus Magnusson?" Becca asked.

"Almost. He got them from his son. One Uther Magnusson, nanotechnologist and utter genius."

"I know Uther."

"Really?"

"From when we were kids. He was a little hellion who used to take piano lessons from my father. I remember him well, only because one time my father had to run an errand and he left Uther alone for an hour. The kid disassembled Father's grand piano."

"Precocious little prick, eh?"

"To put it lightly. How's he involved?"

"Not sure. But the CIA can verify someone has been snooping around his laboratory. Someone with a Russian first name."

"Interesting. So the CIA has been following him all along?"

"You were chosen simply to follow the diamonds, Becca."

Until now. So the CIA had been playing the need-to-know card as well. Bastards. The least favorite part of her job? Protocols. Becca sighed, and prompted Zeek to continue.

"We've questioned Uther's father. He said his son is away. Doesn't have a location. As well, his girlfriend has been elusive—we haven't had opportunity to question her. Uther is very secretive. But I have managed to track his credit card to a flight to Berlin a week ago, and I'm currently chasing electronic transactions. Can you guess what your new objective is?"

"Get to Uther?"

"You got it. He's the only one who can answer the big question. What is in the diamonds."

"And who is after them. Obviously, the Russians."

"Yeah, but didn't you mention Agent Dane is keen to nab the stones as well?"

"Right. I wonder what MI-6 wants with it?"

"I'll search the cyber-alleys, see what I can come up with. Just don't let the rocks out of your sight. Right now I'm being told they don't want to send in agents to get the diamonds yet. Don't bother asking why. I don't know. But keep your enemies close, if you know what I mean."

Behind her, Dane's snore rattled softly.

Becca nodded. "Thanks, Zeek. I'll keep the diamonds in hand. Tickets to Berlin, then?"

"They'll be at Will Call at de Gaulle. You depart in an hour. Oh, and Becca? After you've located Uther, you're to return to the States with him. He's ours. We'll take things from there. Talk to you soon."

He's ours.

So much in those two words. Becca hung up the phone and finished buttoning her shirt.

Did Zeek mean Uther was working for the CIA? Or did she merely imply the CIA intended to claim Uther upon his return? Return, meaning capture. A capture that might see him forever removed from his life, family and friends to do the government's bidding.

Behind her, Becca heard Dane move. From the corner of her eye she saw him sit up and wrap the sheet around his waist.

He groaned and wandered into the bathroom. The tail of the sheet got stuck in the door. Another loud groan echoed out from the bathroom. The sheet disappeared with a tug.

How was Uther involved in this goose chase of diamonds and crazy Nordic women?

Dane emerged from the bathroom. "Where are my bloody trousers?"

Becca nodded toward the floor by the bed. "They're probably dry, but they look a little crunchy to me."

"Crunchy will do. Who was that?"

"CIA. They've discovered the source of the diamonds. A nanoscientist. Seems his father might have accidentally sold the stones without realizing they may have had more than monetary value."

"Pure dead brilliant of you, New York."

He should thank her. It was more information than he was willing to share.

"I'm surprised, though." She stood and folded her laptop shut and shoved it in her Gucci bag. "I find it hard to believe the old man would sell something he knew was of value to his son. And of what value would a ten-carat stone be to a nanoscientist?"

"Besides the obvious? Millions?"

Becca shrugged. "The Magnussons are old money."

"A tax bracket you're familiar with?"

"Yes. Intimately." Becca winked as Dane smirked. "So, you see, Uther, the son, doesn't have to worry for cash."

"I imagine nanoscientists require a bit of dosh for their experiments."

"Hmm. Maybe. Still not making the connection to the Russian Mafia."

"Russian Mafia?" With the sheet wrapped about his waist in Zulu fashion, Dane inspected his wrinkled trousers, avoiding eye contact. "When did they become sussy?"

"Pink is linked to the Russian Mafia. Our man last night—"

"Your Turkish prince?"

"He was Russian. And I think you know something about him you're not telling."

"You may be wrong."

"Dane." She approached, tugging the trousers from his hand. His pecs tensed as he took a step back, like a wary dog. "What are you not telling me?"

"I never not tell anything." He frowned. Even he, apparently, had trouble deciphering that statement.

"Fine. Have it your way." She made to hand back the trousers, but something slipped from a pocket. Becca caught it. His passport. Without thinking, she splayed it open with her thumb. A small head shot photo was paper-clipped inside.

Dane snatched it from her, along with his pants. "Just a passport, love. You've seen one…"

"Right." Hiding something. Again. "Two can play at this game."

Grabbing up her laptop and surreptitiously slipping the diamond pouch into her pants pocket, she gave a parting scan to the room. "Our flight to Berlin leaves in an hour."

"Berlin—"

But she'd already walked out the door.

Chapter 16

The de Gaulle was busy even in the early morning. Their tickets picked up and tucked in Dane's pocket— he obviously wasn't about to let her hold them unless she traded for a diamond—and their flight took off in fifteen minutes. Becca kept the rocks in the velvet pouch in the pocket of her wool slacks. Not secure, but she wasn't about to risk losing her laptop bag or putting the diamonds in an airport safe. Already one exchange had gone wrong. Keeping them in hand was the only option.

She mentally crossed her fingers, hoping she could tie things up in Berlin and make it home in time for the gala. Should she not make it, Lucy had Sherri Grant, a fellow Gotham Rose club member, at the top of her list for replacement hostess. Of course, with the time change she did have more than a few hours to work with.

She sat next to Dane in the boarding lobby on one of the hard plastic chairs designed for maximum discomfort.

Along with the slacks, she'd changed to a snug red V-neck Ralph Lauren Black Label cashmere sweater Kristi had sent along. The pink silk Louboutins were a new favorite, so she wore those again.

Dane tipped up her shoe. "You've worn these once already. Won't that screw with the very fabric of the universe?"

Laughing, Becca decided it was difficult to fault a man who knew his designer shoes.

"You got the rocks?"

"Don't worry, they're in good hands."

"I'd feel a lot better if I could hang on to them."

He punched a fist into his palm, and when he did it again, Becca intercepted, catching his fist with both hands. The amount of tension she felt surprised her.

"Do I piss you off, Dane? You make it so much fun to push your buttons."

"This coming from a master button manipulator, eh, high maintenance?"

She tightened her grip on his fist. "Go ahead, take your best shot. All this pent-up anger of yours is obviously meant for me."

"You've got it all wrong, love."

"Prove it. Tell me what I need to know."

Pulling free of her grip, Dane slumped against the plastic seat. He shrugged his shoulders and considered for a moment. "We're not playing for the same team. You should know better than to ask."

"And here I'd always thought the Brits and the U.S. were partners?"

"MI-6 is international."

"Uh-huh." Man, the guy was closed tighter than a steel safe. "All right then, don't forget, I can play your game. But tell me this, is your *team* on the side of the good guys or the bad guys?"

"Good."

"Promise?"

"I can't promise anything."

There was more going on behind those sneaky blue eyes. Information about Dimitri Boratov, she guessed.

Your objective has been altered. You're to locate Uther.

So why did she feel compelled to chase after Dimitri? He was key; she sensed it.

"Work with me for just a minute, will you?" she asked. "A genius scientist imbeds code, or something, inside two ten-carat diamonds."

Dane nodded. "Sure."

"What for?" Becca wondered. "What is the significance of the diamond? Why not hide the code on a disk?"

"Disks are easily readable and stealable."

"Obviously the diamonds are, too."

"True. But not so destructible."

"Good point. Now the Russian Mafia is after the diamonds, or so we suspect. And very possibly…MI-6." She waited for Dane's reaction, but didn't get the affronted protest she'd expected.

"What about the CIA?" He tossed out the question. "Just because you're working for them doesn't mean you have a clue, New York. Are you charged to bring back evidence?"

"That's usually what one does on a case like this."

"Fair is fair then. We've both got the same goal."

"But why? I want to know what's inside, to decipher the code. Maybe some kind of military secrets?" She perked up. Her thoughts began to hum. "I was able to erase the first diamond. An erasable code…that makes some kind of sense."

"For military use? Not when the method of delivering the codes is in such a sought-after item as a diamond."

"What if the diamond was the payment? The recipient receives the information, erases it, does whatever the code requires of him, and then…sells the gem."

"It would make for easy crossing through airport security checks for a terrorist," Dane agreed, looking toward the gate they would pass through shortly. "Not with a diamond so large, but if it were smaller, and set in a ring or necklace."

"We've got to talk to Uther."

Her cell phone jingled and Becca answered.

"Rebecca?"

"Mother?" She hadn't heard from her for weeks. Last conversation they'd had, Emily had been calling from a mobile box phone in Sri Lanka, part of her crusade to help bring learning supplies to schoolchildren.

"Rebecca!" Her mother insisted on using her birth name, despite Becca's insistent claims to its stodginess. "I tried to get hold of you all day yesterday. And now you greet me like that?"

A pinch to her right arm alerted Becca. Dane unobtrusively nodded across the aisle to the bookstore thirty feet away. A man dressed in dark blue jeans and a pull-over black sweatshirt peered at them over the top of his upside-down book.

"He's been watching us," Dane said as he lifted Becca's elbow and she stood. "Follow me. Keep up your conversation."

"Rebecca?"

"I'm here, Mother. From where are you calling? Are you still in Sri Lanka?"

She hooked her arm in Dane's and they walked, as a couple, across the aisle to look over the lighted kiosk that displayed a map of the airport. From the corner of her eye she noticed the suspect tilt his head and say something. *To no one around him.* Must be wired.

She verified with eye contact that Dane had seen the same. He tugged her along. Together they walked past the man.

"I'm in Tuscany for a week, dear. Flew in last night. Your father insisted I take a mini-vacation. He's right— I needed this rest. But I can't wait to get back to work-ing with the children. They are so eager to learn!"

"You're a wonder, Mother."

"You know me, I have to keep busy."

No, she didn't really know her mother, precisely be-cause she was always so busy.

"Are you excited about the gala?" Emily never for-got a reason to get dressed up and don rivers of jewels.

"Yes, it's going to be marvelous," Becca replied. "I wish you could come."

Dane suddenly tugged her to the right, down a long

hallway that led to the restrooms. No one else was in the hall. Their mark followed at a distance.

With a nudge, Dane gestured toward the women's room.

"I think your father will be flying in for the event," Emily continued.

Becca paid partial attention to her mother, fixing the majority on the thug behind them. She stopped at the door to the women's room and blew a kiss to Dane, who stood at the men's room door. She didn't want to step inside, but their pursuer would expect it. She did so.

Becca dodged to avoid the swoop of a fist. Phone hand swinging out for counterbalance, she twisted up and intuitively delivered a right fist to her attacker's gut. A bleached blonde in a pink velour sweatsuit let out a guttural squawk. Pink.

Where had she come from?

"Rebecca?"

She kicked high and caught Pink under the jaw with the toe of her shoe. "Right here, Mother."

Pink wielded a white plastic pick. The weapon slashed over the arch of Becca's foot, leaving a gash.

"You don't sound well. You're breathing heavily. What's wrong?"

Tossing the cell phone into one of the sinks, Becca gripped Pink by the throat and delivered another punch. Pink slid to the floor, knocked out cold, blond curls bounced over her left eye.

Becca retrieved the phone. "I'm fine, Mother. You said Father was going to be in town? He hasn't called."

"His tour just ended. He's coming home to rest as

soon as things are tied up. He should be there soon, unless he takes the red-eye, then look for him Sunday morning."

"I will, Mother." She prodded Pink with the toe of her shoe. "I'll try to contact Father, see if he plans to make the gala. I've some business to take care of first."

"Is it a man?"

Becca smirked and toed the plastic pick away from Pink's leg. Zeek would need to send an agent to take care of Pink. "No, Mother, it's not a man."

She bent and patted down Pink's jogging suit, shoulder to ankle. No other weapons. Katarine Veld, eh? How did she always know where to find Becca? She hadn't been able to shake this tail since London.

A quick walk through the three stalls didn't produce a hidden purse or backpack.

"I should let you go, Mother." Becca grabbed Pink's left wrist and dragged her into the farthest stall. "Happy Valentine's Day."

"You, too, sweetie. You would tell me if it was a man, wouldn't you?"

Becca strode to the door and peeked out. Dane stood outside the men's room. He gave her a thumbs-up as she walked to him.

"Yes, Mother. But I promise, no men in my life at the moment."

Dane gave a mock pout.

"Talk to you soon." Becca clicked off.

"I'm not a man?" Dane hooked his arm in hers.

"I thought you were a big boy," Becca teased.

He nodded to a passing officer, who hastened by and into the men's room.

"That was fast."

"I called security. My people will be in touch with them as soon as possible."

"Send one to the ladies' room as well."

"Really?"

"Pink was waiting for me in some atrocious velour number."

"Well, this little adventure is getting bloody interesting."

Dane flipped open his phone, redialed security and directed them to the ladies' room.

"Our flight just issued last boarding call," Becca said. "Let's get out of here."

Sabrina Morgan poked around inside the refrigerator, looking for a snack. A few dehydrated carrots lurked at the back of the highest plastic tray. Three eggs wobbled on the second. Uther literally lived on Mountain Dew and sliced ham on rye. So unhealthy.

She'd arrived at his apartment on Madison Avenue well after midnight, wanting to surprise Uther, but he wasn't home, so she'd let herself in. She hadn't been able to reach him for days. But that wasn't strange. Twice since she'd met him, he'd left for spontaneous "breathers." She knew exactly where he was.

He'd promised to be home by morning.

They would attend the Grace Notes gala, where they planned to officially appear as a couple after their recent engagement.

Sabrina couldn't help wondering when Uther would spring the big surprise he'd been teasing her about for weeks. It had better be before the gala.

Deciding on a glass of water, she pressed a heavy tumbler against the ice-maker tab in the door of the fridge. The ice machine hummed and growled, but it didn't make the usual crushing noise.

"Did he forget to make ice again? Sometimes that man can be so absentminded. Amazing he is a genius."

She tugged open the freezer door and pulled out the huge white ice cube tub. It was full of half-moon cubes.

"Something must be jammed."

She probed the ice cubes to the base of the plastic tub, where they funneled down to the waiting glass. There was something big stuck in the shoot. She pulled it out. What a strange piece of ice.

"Yes!"

Chapter 17

Germany—Berlin

In The Know with Rubi Cho
Über-Geek in Love.
Model/actress Sabrina Morgan and scientist Uther Magnusson have embarked on a whirlwind romance, tripping the light fantastic last night at Cream. Miss Morgan wore an almost-see-through sheath designed by Vera Wang, and was not afraid to dance beneath the disco ball. Uther, puppy-eyed and stylish in Zegna, attended his lady all evening. Who says molecules and atoms have to be dull?

Uther kept the month-old clipping from Rubi Cho's New York gossip column in his front jeans pocket. He liked to find his name in the newspapers—even the gossip column. Now he gripped the clipping and squeezed until he heard the paper tear.

He'd just hung up after talking to Sabrina. He hadn't called her for days, and had been missing her. She hadn't missed him, obviously, because she'd suggested he not take an early flight home, but instead remain in Berlin for his final day.

What she had been excited about had shocked the hell out of Uther. She'd found the diamond.

And he'd thought he'd hid it in the perfect spot.

How could Sabrina have made such a way-out guess what it was for? An engagement gift? Sure, they were recently engaged, and he had planned to buy her a gift, but why did women's minds go there?

And for him to have allowed her to believe it?

He had to do something.

Sabrina had put herself in danger.

The DomAquarée Radisson was located on the River Spree, although Becca knew to pronounce it *schpray*. The German language, oft considered abrupt and rough, fascinated her. She had visited the biosphere reserve Spreewald, about fifty miles southeast of Berlin, a few years ago, and would never forget the gorgeous rain forest cut through by various streams and tributaries from the major river.

The hotel had opened in 2004. Its main attraction, the

Aquadom, coaxed visitors from far and wide. It featured a massive aquarium that ran down the center of the hotel lobby. Twenty-five-hundred tropical fish swam in one million liters of water, amazing young and old alike. Visitors could take an elevator ride right up the center. It was the German equivalent of a budget Sea World.

The cab let off Becca and Dane outside the hotel. The streets, as well as the sidewalks and rooftops, were coated with snow. Cars each wore a white toupee, and a man across the street riding a wobbly bicycle drew a wavering black line in the snow behind him.

Though it was early morning, it actually felt a little warmer here in Germany than in Paris. Becca guessed it must be in the low thirties. The air smelled clean, fresh and icy. Holding out a gloved hand, she watched as thick flakes landed on the brown leather and slowly melted into a darker stain on her palm.

Dane, stomping snow from his shoes, stepped up beside her. "You willing to expose your cover to get close to this guy?"

She'd told Dane she'd known Uther when they were younger, but they were far from friends.

"I have no intention of doing so," Becca said. "We'll have to go after Uther in a roundabout manner. I don't know if he'll remember me, but I'll play it by ear until I can be sure."

"Pretty convenient the CIA picked a freelance gemologist who just happened to know the key figure in this mission." Dane walked onward, leaving Becca startled as hell.

"What are you implying? That I was—"

"Picked as bait? Clever Americans."

"We had no idea Uther was involved. Zeek just—"

"Suit yourself," he called back, and strode inside.

Dane's ideas were farfetched. The road had led to Uther only this morning. And Zeek was telling her all she knew.

There was not time to debate Dane's theory. Becca joined him alongside one of the lighted media stations in the lobby. White epoxy flooring stretched like a calm sea. Red, blue and green lights illuminated the base of each modern white reception station, flashing in rainbows across the floor.

"We'll have to get a room," she said, forming a plan. "Just for cover. We are *so* not staying here."

"Why?" Dane asked. They both looked up at the eight-story-high column of water and fish and…terror. "Ah. Your hydrophobia thing."

A shiver crept across Becca's scalp. "It's so *much* water."

"But it's contained."

"What if the glass cracks?"

"I suspect the tank is made of high-impact plastic. Tell me, is it rational or irrational, your fear?"

"What's the difference?"

"Rational—you almost drowned as a child. Irrational—you think you will drown."

"A little of each."

"Some fear is good, you know. But just in case, you can hold my hand."

"That's nice, but—" she slipped her hand from his seeking fingers "—I'm a big girl."

* * *

After some flirtation with the male clerk at registration, Becca was able to procure a room right next to Uther Magnusson's.

"He's staying on the sixth floor," she told Dane. "Let's go up and check it out."

The elevator stopped off at the sixth floor, opening to reveal the spectacle of refracted blue light shimmering across the curved white walls that embraced the lobby. Becca strode down the hallway, with Dane in tow.

Arriving at room 612, she paused and listened. The faint buzz of a television was muffled by the door.

Stepping slowly backward to room 610, she inserted the keycard and entered, but remained by the open doorway, one eye on Uther's closed door.

Lemon scent wafted through the room. A double bed blocked a direct path to the desk neatly arranged with a small steel lamp, alarm clock and phone. Everything was done in dark woods, with white linens and padded chairs. Asian-inspired and clean.

"So what's the plan, love?" Dane smoothed his thumb over her wrist. The silver band he wore was warm, a part of his flesh. That he took such liberties touching her didn't trouble her as much. It actually eased the aching inner part of her that needed consolation. "You going to stand there all day and wait? Not very covert."

He knew her secrets.

Becca looked at Dane with new wonder. He *knew* her secrets. Every bit, about living the covert lifestyle and the life of an heiress.

"I…"

So why didn't he feel like more of a threat? Instead, he felt like a missing piece. A part that could easily fit into her life.

Right. But not both of my lives.

Because the socialite would never date out of her social set. And the spy, well, she preferred Zen sessions to commitment.

"Want to talk about it?" he asked her.

"No," she said. Instead she tapped his ring. "But tell me about this."

He shrugged. "It was my dad's. His wedding band. Mum wanted me to wear it."

"She's alive?"

"Yes, and well."

Uther's door suddenly opened and Becca shoved Dane into the room. She called as if she were leaving, "I'll take a coffee with two creams, honey."

"What?" Dane answered.

Becca stepped back into the hallway and collided with Uther, dropping her keycard. "Oh! I'm so sorry."

Uther bent to retrieve it. All arms and legs and loose-fitting khaki jeans, he looked more a pimply skateboard freak than a scientist. Three-inch-long brown hair was gelled to a scruffy yet alert bouffant at the front of his head and left to fall helter-skelter halfway back.

In his early twenties now, he'd graduated high school at twelve and from MIT summa cum laude at sixteen, Becca recalled reading.

He handed her the plastic entry card, avoiding eye contact.

Becca touched his shoulder, forcing him to look at her. "Do I know you?"

Dane opened the door and leaned against the door frame. Uther shot him a fleeting glance. He shuffled a hand up one arm and, bouncing from foot to foot, tilted his head and studied Becca. "You do look… Becca?" His sullenness abruptly faded and his mouth spread in a thin-lipped smile. "I can't believe this. Becca Whitmore, Reinhardt's daughter?" He did a quick imitation of playing the piano keys. "The twentieth century Mozart?"

"Yes! Oh, my gosh. Uther? Little, precocious Uther Magnusson, who will never be allowed back in our house after the piano incident?"

"Piano incident?" Dane repeated from the doorway.

"Oh, Uther, this is my…boyfriend, Aston. We've arrived for a weekend. Aston, this is Uther Magnusson. He once took piano lessons from my father."

Dane offered his hand, and Uther shook it magnanimously.

"And the incident?" Dane prompted.

"I took apart their grand piano," Uther said proudly. His spread-legged stance might be what held up his loose jeans, Becca mused. A bit of striped boxer shorts peeked above his waistline. "After finding the neatly arranged parts, her father chased me out of the house, a freshly penned symphony rolled into a tight weapon. I would have stayed and put it all back together."

"And I'm sure you could have," Becca said. "So Uther, funny running into you halfway across the world. Let's see, you are some kind of scientist now.…"

"Nanotechnologist with a focus on biopolymers and quantum manipulation."

"Oh, yes! Lately Rubi Cho has been reporting your and Sabrina's every move."

"When she's not reporting on you. You're always hosting a bash and raising money for—what is that charity?"

"Grace Notes."

"Right, right. I never thought the paparazzi would have an interest in me. It's all Sabrina." Uther sighed. "She's so beautiful. She's a model, you know."

"I think I read that about her. You've dated for a while?"

"Two months!"

"Ah, so it's a whirlwind romance?"

"It's true love."

"So why aren't you at her side right now? Are you here for some sort of symposium, or whatever it is you scientists do?"

"Um…" He ran the heel of his palm through his gelled hair, flattening the left side. "I come to this hotel a lot. When I…you know…need to think." Suddenly animated, he bounced on his heels. "It's my favorite place. I've got an in with the aquarium elevator operators and they let me ride it by myself."

"Oh." Becca turned to Dane to hide her wry expression from Uther. "How fun."

"Becky loves the water," Dane interjected. "She can't wait to check it out."

"Er, right. Uther, *Aston* was going to run down to the lobby to pick me up a coffee. Would you like him to get something for you?"

"Actually, I was—"

"I'd love to sit and chat for a while. Catch up on what you've been up to. Unless you're busy? Oh, I shouldn't even suggest—"

"No, I guess that'd be cool, Becca. A few minutes to talk to you. You're working as a jeweler now, I hear?"

"A gemologist. I'll take it black," she said to Dane, who, after nodding and crossing his arms tightly, made his way down the hallway. "Thanks, Aston!"

"Anything for you, Becky! Can I bring back something for you, Uther?" Dane called.

"I'm fine, thanks."

"So, why don't we step inside my room?" Becca offered.

"You two don't have any luggage?" Uther wondered as he strode inside and inspected the room.

"We're…" Oops "…waiting for it. It was misplaced at the airport. The concierge promised to taxi it right over as soon as they find it."

Uther nodded. He stood at the end of the bed, arms folded over his chest.

"So tell me about your work, Uther. I always knew you'd go into something like science. You're so smart."

"Genius. With a 168 IQ. I've been studying nanotechnology since puberty. Ah, it's kinda boring to a layman." He wasn't going to relax too easily.

Becca mock punched him in the arm. "Loosen up, buddy. You look tense. Sit down. Is anything wrong?"

He remained standing, arms seeming to tighten.

"Uther?" She moved in front of him and bowed to

look up into his brown eyes. A touch to his chin melted his rigid stance. "You're nervous."

"No. It's just you, Becca."

"*I* make you nervous?"

"Not like you think. I mean, you're pretty and all, but I do have a fiancée."

"Oh? Oh! You don't think I was—? What's wrong, Uther? Is something going on with Sabrina? I really wish you'd sit—"

"I shouldn't be here right now." He fled for the door.

"Is it something I said?"

"No, really, I just…" He scrubbed a palm over his scalp again. The gelled hair protested angrily. "I just got off the phone…"

"With Sabrina? If I'm keeping you from anything—"

"No! Well, sort of. I've got a speech to work on. I'm speaking on fluorescent nanoparticles in two weeks in Venice."

Fluorescent nanoparticles?

"Is that like nano code?" Becca said, trying to pry more info from him.

Uther paused in the open doorway to the hall, then turned to walk out onto a balcony that circled the lobby and looked over the aquarium. Shadows and light from the aquarium danced across his face. "You know about that kind of stuff?"

"It's a guess." She shrugged. "Is it like ion beam branding?"

"It can be used for that, yes, but on a whole new level. The branding is still relatively new throughout the diamond industry."

"Yes, DeBeers diamonds, basically. Not a lot of jewelers are familiar with the process. And the equipment to brand the diamonds costs close to a million dollars for initial setup."

"Wow."

"What?" she asked coyly.

"You know a lot."

Becca shrugged. That was the extent of her knowledge. "It is part of my trade to know such things."

"I suppose." He looked to the floor, his hand twisting on the balcony railing. Unsure? Wanting to spill something? Or just a quirky scientist?

"Nanotechnology is the ultimate level of finesse," he announced. "For now. The pico-nuts are starting to come out of the woodwork. Pico is a measurement even smaller than the nano."

He bit his lower lip.

"What is it, Uther?"

He lowered his voice. "I'm in trouble, Becca."

"Oh?"

"Deep shit kind of trouble."

"Maybe I can help."

"No one can help me. Especially not a gorgeous heiress on vacation with her boyfriend. I shouldn't have said anything. What an idiot!"

She didn't want to lose him now that she'd gotten him going. "Maybe talking about it will help?"

"I…" He stared at his stiff and open palm. "I don't know what to do." Fingers clenched to a fist. "I should take an early flight back to New York. But what if they follow me? I'd be leading them right to Sabrina. I don't want to endanger her. But now—she's got it, Becca. She's holding the ticking time bomb. They'll find her. They'll hurt her to get it. She needs me!"

"Who are *they*, Uther?"

He held her gaze for what seemed forever. Finally, he inhaled sharply. He loosened his fisted hand with a shake of his fingers. "We can't talk here. There's only one place we can go where I'll feel safe."

"Let's go."

Chapter 18

The elevator attendant wore a blue T-shirt with the Aquadom logo blazoned in yellow across his left pec. Uther scampered up to him and began to chat.

The Atrium bar circled the base of the round aquarium. Forming a generous C, the bar was lit from below with colored lights—pale yellow, then red, then various other hues. Visitors sitting at the bar could look up for an excellent view of the lower levels of the fish tank.

The entire structure looked as if a giant halogen lightbulb with glowing prongs had been set on end, waiting to be pushed into a socket.

"Come on," Uther said with an urgent gesture. "We've got it all to ourselves. But be quick or someone will notice."

"I don't know...." Becca uttered, because to say "It freaks the hell out of me" would have been rude. "Maybe if we just grabbed that coffee and stepped outside for a few minutes?"

"Becca, it's thirty degrees outside. Come on. The elevator ride only takes a few minutes."

A few minutes? How slow did the thing go? She could ride from the lobby to the eightieth floor in the Empire State Building in about forty-five seconds.

"Becca," Uther pleaded. "Please, I need your advice."

An opportunity that might reveal the entire plot behind the coded diamonds.

Staunching a moan, Becca reluctantly followed.

The base of the tank was suspended one story above her head. She stood below a million gallons of water. A *million.* That was more than a thousand, or even a hundred thousand.

"No." Becca stepped back.

Was she willing to compromise the entire mission because of a million gallons of water?

Is your fear rational or irrational?

Logically, she knew it was more irrational.

Did she really want to notch up a negative point in the reliability column?

This is what you do. You push out of your comfort zone and thrive for having done so. You want this. Just...take a step!

Impulsivity streaked through Becca's system. She wasn't about to turn away. It was a simple elevator ride, not a wild and crazy roller coaster adventure.

"Hold on." Becca forced her legs to move.

"There's no one else," Uther coaxed. "We'll have the elevator all to ourselves. You don't like fish?"

Just as Becca decided to turn and make a run for it, she felt Uther's fingers thread through hers. Yanked into the elevator, she spun and gripped the stainless steel handrail in the center of the circular glass bullet.

"Come on, let's go up to the second floor."

"The second floor?" Becca craned her neck. Yep, there was a spiral staircase in the middle of the elevator that led up to a second observation deck. "What the hell is this, a condo?"

Entombed within an oddly muted blue cylinder of eerie sea life, she drew two quick breaths through her nose. Yes, air, there *is* air in here…. Becca took the first of the spiraling steps.

There was no reason to be so fearful. She'd never nearly drowned, or anything remotely similar. Just a minor mishap in the hot tub one summer at the Hamptons. Her knee had gotten sucked tight to the drain at the center of the tub. The water level had covered her mouth but not her nose. Her girlfriends, after much silly panic, had had to turn off the tub to free her. Bruised and bloody, her flesh had been shaved raw.

It wasn't a good excuse. Many people had suffered real disasters in water and at sea. She just did not like water in great abundance.

Halfway up the staircase, Becca glanced to the side. Realization pulsed nervously in her gut. She was inside a huge fish tank.

Uther bent and peered down the staircase from

above. "Becca, look at that gorgeous water. God, I love this place. It makes me feel safe."

Very well. As she'd announced to Dane, she was a big girl. Gripping the handrail tightly, she reached the second floor.

Uther stood at the perimeter, his palms flattened to the clear acrylic as the elevator began to rise.

"You come here a lot, Uther?"

"Whenever I've got a difficult formula to work out, or if I've overworked and need to relax. See that fish? His name is Sunshine. He's an Oriental Sweetlips. Isn't that cool?"

Becca tilted her head and forced herself to look into the tank. She wouldn't know an Oriental Sweetlips from a trout.

"Relax, Becca, we're safe now."

"Really? You feel safe enough to talk to me?"

"Do you? I can feel your tension, Becca. Chill out. Think of it as a return to the womb." Uther stretched out his arms and then clasped them across his chest.

The womb? Not unless there had been sea creatures swimming around inside the womb with her.

Uther pressed a hand to her shoulder. She stiffened, even though it was not her wounded side. "I'm sorry. I had no idea you were so frightened. I needed a place where I could be sure no one else could hear me."

"Why do you think you're being followed?"

"I don't know."

"Tell me about it, Uther."

"She found the stone."

"What!"

"It's a flawless ten-carat, heart-shaped diamond. I hid it. Sabrina found it. And now she thinks it's some kind of wedding gift."

"Another diamond?" Becca whispered, turning her head quickly so Uther wouldn't hear.

"She's in danger, Becca. And it's entirely my fault. I've got to tell you this. I know it won't help me, but you're a woman, maybe you can think of something. There must be some way to get Sabrina to ditch the thing before it's too late."

"You want her to ditch the diamond?"

"It's a death sentence, Becca. That diamond had all my data for a project I've been working on for the government contained within it."

"You're…working for the government?"

He's one of our own.

"Since when did you start working for the government?"

"Since they gave me no option but to do so. Becca, I can't go into detail, but I've developed technology to encode diamonds with crucial field data that can be used by the military for very sensitive missions."

"Coded diamonds? Like the ion beam branding?"

"Yes, but the beauty of my coding is it can be erased, leaving no trace of evidence to fall into enemy hands."

Using nothing more than a simple UV light.

"That's unbelievable, Uther."

"Fluorescent nanoparticles, Becca. Quantum dots that can be altered with simple light beams. Highly luminescent particles embedded during the branding process. They fluoresce pink!"

She nodded, taking it all in.

"With the use of a single excitation source—an ultraviolet light—those particles can then be erased. In the field! The operative receives instructions for whatever, and then he erases the code and keeps the diamond as payment."

"Like…spy stuff?"

"Exactly!"

"Clever."

"Fucking genius is what it is." A triumphant fist punctuated that declaration.

"But aren't operatives paid a salary? A diamond, that's a big payoff."

"The mercenaries who will be using my technology don't get salaries."

"I see."

"Besides, the diamonds are just the beginning. I've plans to use cheaper, less obvious methods of transport. I've so many ideas. Well—I can't tell you. Anyone. Not even Sabrina."

"And yet you're hiding out in a hotel in Berlin and now fear for your girlfriend's life?"

"I sensed something wasn't right. People were following me. I made a break for it. I had to. But first I copied all my data. Sabrina wasn't supposed to find that diamond, Becca. It was my backup copy."

"Backup? There are…more copies?"

"Two—but both are safe. I think they're looking for anything that will lead to my research."

"Who are *they?*"

"I…can't say."

"The U.S. government?"

He scrubbed the heel of his palm over his left eye. With an exclamatory gesture, he declared, "It might be the Russians, it could be the United States government. Damn CIA agents were checking in with me once a week."

"The CIA is involved?"

"Yes. No. Oh! Maybe—but you didn't hear that from me. Hell, you don't really understand all this stuff, do you?"

With a snotty flip of her hair over her shoulder, Becca momentarily assumed socialite mode. "Of course not."

So the CIA had known all along what was contained within the diamonds?

"No, I know absolutely nothing beyond galas and fashion week." She sighed, hating that lie, and finding it strange how the lies she hated most were the ones about her real life. Had the socialite become the mask? "What do you think I can do for you, Uther?"

"Could you talk to Sabrina? Convince her to put the diamond back. Like, pretend she never found it. Say I was feeling bad, that I wanted to surprise her. That'll give me a chance to hide it again, in a better place."

"Why would Sabrina listen to me? And wouldn't she be suspicious?"

Uther pressed his forehead to the curved wall. "I am so screwed."

And so was Sabrina if Dimitri found her before Becca could send an agent to whisk her off to a safe house. A call to Zeek was in order, but not in front of Uther.

"Who are these Russians you mentioned?"

"You wouldn't understand, Becca. It's like spy stuff

and covert action going on all around me. Everyone wants the technology I've hidden on these diamonds. Fortunately, I stashed two of them safely with my—I can't tell you."

With his father.

Obviously, Uther was unaware his father had already sold them. Why had Amandus betrayed his son? As well, Uther had to be completely unaware that MaryEllen Sommerfield had been shot in the head for one of them and that the CIA, MI-6 and even the Russians were tracking the stones across Europe.

"I'm sorry to lay all this on you, Becca. You were always so nice to me. Even held the door for me when your father chased me out of the house."

"If he would have caught you he would have bent you over his knee for sure." She smiled to think of that long-ago, lighter moment.

Once again she had been called to help Uther escape. But from whom?

"I want to help, Uther." Without blowing her cover. "Why don't you go back to New York, to Sabrina, and I'll…accompany you."

"For what reason? Are you going to chase off the bad guys? Ha! Besides, Sabrina said I shouldn't rush back."

"But don't you plan to attend the gala?"

"Of course. But my flight doesn't leave until later. No sense in rescheduling. So what are you doing here?"

"End of a vacation. We're leaving today to get back in time for the event." Oops. Bad lie. Hadn't she told him they'd just arrived?

But if Uther noticed, he didn't say anything.

"I should have left as soon as I got off the phone with Sabrina." He splayed his arms out, then dropped them wearily. "We can go back down."

"Down? But aren't we at least halfway up?"

"I think so…."

The elevator had stopped moving. Neither one of them had noticed. Six stories up in the aquarium, Becca and Uther hung suspended in an eerie column of water.

Becca pressed her palms to the thick acrylic and tried to see beyond the dark waters. "What the hell?"

Chapter 19

The woman had boarded the elevator with Uther. Were they working together? Who *was* she?

He hadn't gotten intel on her yet. She'd given him a false name—Becky—at *verte*. Had played the airheaded sexpot. Why did he feel as though he'd met her somewhere *before* last night? And where was the blond man who had wanted to watch?

Dimitri searched his memory as he toyed with the small plastic injection dart hidden in the palm of his hand.

The Atrium bartender whisked an ice drink for him. Dimitri didn't like fruity drinks, but it offered him the longest period of time with the bartender's back turned.

Dimitri had been in Europe for a few days. The past month had been spent getting close to Magnusson and his kind. High society. Ha! The women nipped and tucked themselves to horrendous masks and the men paid for them to do it. Money wasn't money unless it was old. They judged you by the watch on your wrist and the shoes on your feet.

But he'd insinuated himself fairly well into the charade—as Prince Dimitri Boratav.

Is that where he'd seen the bitch? At one of the society events he'd attended, flirting profusely with the hags and smoking thousand-dollar stogies with the old chaps? Hmm…

It didn't matter who she was; she was in his way.

Time to sweep the rubble under the carpet. Katarine had proved a failure, but his other contact had recently scored. He'd tie up loose ends here in Berlin, then move on to New York.

Aiming the dart gun up and at the underside of the acrylic aquarium, he delivered a projectile that would cling and remain there. A minute amount of polymer explosives were contained within the device. Impact would activate the timer.

The bartender turned and flourished the hideous pink concoction of crushed ice. A little yellow umbrella shielded the neon-green straw.

Dimitri nodded thanks and laid a five-euro bill on the white plastic counter. Then he flicked out his mobile phone and dialed 110. No reason to endanger the entire hotel. He wasn't a monster.

Now all he need do was go fishing for a scientist.

Paper coffee cups in hand, Dane had almost made it to the elevator when red lights flashing outside the hotel caught his attention. A black van was parked out front. Two officers in black fatigues and helmets conversed vehemently.

Dane sipped at his hot cream-doused coffee. New York was busy getting the goods from Uther, so he had a little time.

Abandoning Becca's coffee on one of the white plastic reception kiosks, he walked outside to investigate. He slipped his free hand inside his jacket and produced his badge.

"Agent Aston Dane." He flashed the officers his credentials. "MI-6."

"Word travels fast, Agent Dane," one of the German officers said in pristine English.

"I am here to assist," Dane said, knowing the vague offer usually tendered information in return.

"Sergeant Kiel, BND," the officer replied. He handed a heavy black mobile phone over and made a gesture for Dane to listen.

The clunker of a communications device looked as if it had been unearthed from two decades earlier. Setting his own coffee on the hood of a parked car, Dane held the phone with both hands to his ear. He introduced himself, stating he'd just arrived on site.

"Agent Dane, there's been a bomb threat in the hotel. I am organizing a squad to go in and investigate, but we have to evacuate immediately. My guess would be the bomb has been placed somewhere near the Aquadom. There's been no valid reason given for the threat. The caller said we'd have enough time to get people out. Can you assist my men to organize an evacuation, Agent Dane?"

"I'm on it."

A sodding bomb? The assassin should be using a gun. To take out one person, not an entire building filled with innocents.

And where was Becca? Still inside, with the scientist. Bloody hell!

Why had the elevator stopped?

"Is this normal, Uther?" Becca asked.

He pressed his palms to the curved acrylic next to her and peered out. "Never happened before. Maybe there's been a power outage throughout the building."

With the gentle hum of the elevator mechanics silenced, standing inside the column eerily muted her senses. Becca let her gaze stray upward, along the acrylic ceiling of the elevator. Was there a way out of this watery hell?

Her gaze fell to eye level. A black fish with white polka dots and yellow lips hovered before her. Staring at the human fish in the tank?

Why was it all so dark? If the power for the elevator had gone out, surely she would still be able to see the hotel lights reflecting through the water. Had power gone out in the entire building, as Uther had guessed?

Getting an idea, she rushed down the curving stairs. The keypad was on the first level. The steel emergency box was locked, no key in sight, nor breakable glass. What kind of rinky-dink operation was this?

"It must be an electrical problem," she called up to Uther.

"Oh no!"

"What?"

"What if…oh hell. I can't believe this. They found me!"

They? The Russians Uther had told her about? Not a very logical deduction. If someone intended to take out Uther, why suspend him in the middle of an aquarium?

"They're going to get me," he shrieked. She heard what sounded like his forehead pounding the acrylic. "I don't want to die, Becca."

"You're not going to die, Uther."

"Like you would be any help!"

"Yeah, well…" She let it go. Better leave him to panic on his own. She needed to figure this out.

Where was Dane?

Remembering that she was not alone and abandoned with no means to save herself, Becca tugged her cell phone from her coat pocket. She didn't have Dane's number.

"Nine one one," she muttered as she started to dial.

"It's 110," Uther corrected in a wail. "In Berlin. That's the emergency number."

"Thanks." Erase 911. Dial correctly. The phone rang endlessly. Then a metallic German voice, female, but void of compassion, announced a thirty-minute hold.

Becca pressed her forehead to the cool glass and her palms to each side of her face. Now was no time for panic.

Dashing up the stairs, she scanned the ceiling again. There were many steel clasps and bolts that secured the circular panel in place. And *yes*—

Her cell phone rang. When she clicked on, Dane immediately started in.

"Becca, everything has gone pear-shaped. The hotel is being evacuated. You've got to get out now."

She peered hard through the crystalline depths of blue water and noticed that, indeed, the lobby teemed with blurry images of little, fast-moving bodies.

"Evacuated? What for?"

"There's been a bomb threat. The building must be evacuated by 0945 hours."

"Nine forty-five?" she muttered frantically.

"The bomb is timed to go off at ten o'clock. We've got about ten minutes. Wherever you are, get your pretty arse outside."

"Do we know what sort of—" she turned her back to Uther "—device?"

"Not a clue. The BND is sending in a bomb squad as we speak. But they don't have much time. Where the bloody hell are you, and is Uther with you?"

"Yes, he's with me. Dane." Becca looked to Uther, whose shaking fingers clawed at his neck. Sweat beaded his forehead.

"What? Becca, where are you?"

"We're in the aquarium elevator, Dane. It stopped when the electricity went out."

"Christ."

"Yeah, a little prayer would fit the bill right now."

Chapter 20

It was ridiculous to stand and wait for a rescue that very probably would never arrive. The bomb squad would be focused on their task. It would be risky to bring in a rescue team with less than ten minutes to detonation, but certainly it should be attempted. Becca hadn't a clue about the protocol for something like this in Germany.

"What are we going to do?" Clinging to the iron railing that wrapped the staircase, Uther pleaded with Becca. "What did your caller say?"

She patted her jacket pocket where the cell phone rested. Should she tell him they were sitting on a bomb? A lie would keep Uther calm. But he was a big boy. He deserved to know he might be dead in ten minutes.

Drawing a deep breath and exhaling in her most yogic manner, Becca worked for a gentle beginning, then announced, "That was my friend Aston. There's been a bomb threat."

The man chuffed out a breath and pushed his fingers through his hair. He pounded a fist against the transparent wall of the elevator. "No!"

Drawing in a shaky breath, Becca summoned her resolve. Reinhardt Whitmore had not raised a whiner or a complainer. He'd raised a daughter who could do anything she set her mind to. And the Gotham Roses had trained a woman who could think on her feet.

"A bomb squad has been sent in," she explained. "But we're not going to stand around waiting for rescue. We need to do something."

"Like what?" Uther shrieked. "They're going to kill me!"

"No one is going to kill you, Uther." Becca kept her tone from rising too high, and drawing a breath, she spoke calmly. "Think about it. Why would anyone who wants what you've got kill you? How would they get the information after that?"

"If I'm dead all they need to do is get the diamonds with my research in them."

"That's not going to happen," Becca said evenly. "Just stay there and…chill. I've had a look around. I can figure something out."

A silly thought entered her head. What would Batman do? He'd find a way out. And he wouldn't panic. And should Robin be at his side? Batman would surely involve him in the process.

"On second thought, if you're doing something, you won't have time to be nervous." She shrugged off her coat and let it drop. "Give me a boost, will you? I want to check the ceiling. There's got to be an escape hatch, some means to access the elevator for repairs. Whoever is after you, he's not going to win. Let's do this."

Uther bent to offer clasped hands. Becca stepped onto them and, using the curved wall for balance, was lifted to touch the ceiling. Pressing her palms and fingers along the cool acrylic surface, she found a latch. Yes! A release switch for a door opening into the elevator shaft.

"Found something. I think we can crawl out."

"To where?" Uther shrieked. "We're stuck on the…the sixth floor. We can't crawl up two stories!"

"Yes, we can," Becca stated. She leaped down from Uther's grasp and placed a hand on his shoulder. "There's an access ladder concealed by a fake coral reef that climbs the length of the elevator shaft. Primitive, but serviceable. You can do this."

"No."

"Uther!"

A morbid resolve tightened his gaping mouth. "And why can *you* do it? You're so calm. And tough. Shouldn't you be crying or wailing for Daddy?"

"Uther, please." Slapping his shoulder, she nodded confidently. "I'm used to working under pressure. You know my father—he's a stickler for perfection. Can't be seen onstage until it's all worked through, all the angles and tangents have been planned for and the sweat has been sweated. You must have an idea of what working under pressure is like."

"I do. Yeah." He swallowed. Becca could feel him relax.

"Say it," she coached. "I can do this."

He gave her a nod, a surety that indeed he would give it a go. "I can do this."

"So let's do it together." She wasn't about to mention how time was quickly dwindling. That would only make him shake all the more. "You go first."

"How will you get up?"

"You can reach back down and pull me up. Can you do that?"

He nodded and stepped onto Becca's knee, then, reluctantly, into her clasped hands. Uther managed to climb to the top of the elevator with minimal grunts.

"There is a ladder," he called down, "but it's so narrow. The steps are wide enough for—"

"One foot," Becca agreed, as she bent to shuffle through her coat for her cell phone, slipping it into the pocket in the front of her slacks. "Be careful. Take your time." But not too much time, she thought to herself. "First pull me up!"

Uther's head and arm popped back into the elevator. Becca jumped and clasped his sweaty hand—and slipped down again.

"Oh man," she muttered, then shouted up, "Wipe your hand on your pants, Uther."

"Sorry, I'm like a slimy fish. When I get nervous I sweat—"

"Just do it!" she commanded.

The hand reached down again. This time it was clammy but not as slick. Uther had a good grip, and there were muscles somewhere beneath all that saggy clothing. Becca dangled from the opening as he pulled her through.

Her cell phone rang as she crouched on top of the elevator in the eerie, watery shaft. Not separated by two layers of plastic now. Just one. And why did that frighten her more than the potential of a bomb obliterating her world?

"Go." She gestured for Uther to begin the climb, while she clicked on her phone. "What?"

"Becca," Dane said, "you should know the hotel determines it'll be another ten minutes before they can get the backup generator working, and the lift back in order."

"Not a problem. Just tell me the guests have been evacuated."

"All of them. But you—"

"Have taken matters into hand. We're climbing out of here. See you in less than ten minutes."

"Great. Er…Becca?"

She did not like the tone of his voice.

"Tell me, Dane. I don't even have ten minutes, do I?" She glanced up. Uther had reached the top of the access ladder inside the elevator shaft and was beating against the door that opened to the observation deck, and a steel catwalk that connected the aquarium to the ninth floor.

"Just hurry, love."

"More or less than five?" She had to know.

"Becca, I—"

"Dane!"

"Three. Hurry."

Uther managed to open the observation deck door and crawl onto the catwalk. He peered down at her and the ground floor below, and shouted, "I don't see a bomb squad—"

His shout was abruptly cut off. Becca searched for him through the thick layers of acrylic. Gripping the steel stairs inside the shaft, she started to climb, but stopped when she heard a voice. It wasn't Uther. It was…Russian.

"No. Way!" she muttered.

Mounting the steel rungs as quickly as she could, she still took a good thirty seconds to reach the top. She pulled herself onto the catwalk.

At the other side of the steel landing stood Dimitri, with his arm locked around Uther's neck. "Ten seconds left. You'll never make it!" He blew her a kiss, then wrestled Uther upright and started running toward the ninth-floor stairway entrance.

Dimitri had the wrong person. Becca was the one with the diamonds in her pocket.

Ten seconds?

The sudden pulse below her feet moved her to action. Clinging to the steel railing, she heard a dull thumping noise beneath her. The sharp cutting slice of cracking acrylic came next. She looked down and actually saw an ice-blue zigzagging crack race up the side of the aquarium. Fish dodged and disappeared from the perimeter of the tank.

Another pulse vibrated beneath her feet like a giant belch. Air had entered the aquarium.

Was that it? Had the bomb gone off? Had the explosives merely cracked—

"Whoa!" Vibrations shook the catwalk. Becca gripped the railing and raced toward the ninth-floor landing. The heavy vinyl-wrapped cable threaded through the posts of the railing quivered like a plucked guitar string.

A loud splintering noise behind her clued Becca that the tank had broken. Acrylic groaned as it separated in jagged panels and fell to the floor below. A huge wave of water gushed, sloshing and tearing at everything in its path.

She turned her head to see the entire side of the aquarium slide like a wall of ice severed from an iceberg. Beside her, the support cable threaded through the railing zinged through the poles, unraveling like a loose thread in a sweater. The catwalk twisted and she slid backward. Grasping the railing became slippery work as the walkway bent downward.

Despite her slick grip, she worked her way up the sloping pathway. Slapping her palm onto the carpeted floor of the ninth level, she struggled for purchase with her fingers.

She couldn't grab hold. With one hand gripping the railing, she dangled nine stories above ground. One shoe slipped from her foot and landed in the ocean below.

At least the structure of the building remained sound. So far.

Trying again, Becca managed to grip the railing post bolted onto the ninth floor. But no matter how desperately she tried, she couldn't work herself up onto the carpeted floor. Light as she was, her body weight hung heavily from her arms. Her right shoulder hurt like a mother, but even the searing pain couldn't prevent her from trying to save herself.

Not like this.

The snap of steel bit at her shoulder. The looped end of the support cable wrapped in clear vinyl swooshed through the twisted railing and landed on the floor before her. Becca grabbed for it.

With the cable still attached to the railing post, the steel catwalk frame snapped from the ninth floor. A heavy steel bolt zinged past Becca's face. The force of the detachment sent her flying backward. Her body swung out wide, like Tarzan grabbing a rubber band vine instead of a real one, and then soared back toward the interior rooms.

Clinging desperately to the looped cable, Becca braced herself for impact against the concrete wall. But instead of crashing into it, she was suddenly falling, the cable dropping her quickly.

With a snap, she stopped, dangling six stories from the lobby floor.

Becca clung to the cable with both hands. She managed to lift her legs to avoid the slice of a massive piece of acrylic that sailed past.

The steel railing groaned. And bent. Her body dropped another story or two.

Looking up, Becca saw that the catwalk railing had gotten hooked on the top of the now-exposed elevator shaft. It was still moving, the topmost end bending downward. The cable she clung to was attached to the railing. With each creak of steel Becca felt herself drop lower.

The entire structure would fall soon.

She had to risk it. If she waited for the catwalk to snap free she'd be crushed. Or sliced open by a big shard of acrylic.

Another downward plunge happened so quickly she felt her heart leap to her throat. She'd dropped another few stories. Becca swayed, feeling like a fish on a hook, about to join the hundreds of colored fish flopping about in puddles and pools on the slick white lobby floor.

Counting to three, she swung toward the far wall. The cable loosened. She descended.

And leaped.

Chapter 21

The aquarium had been torn apart. Dane struggled with the three German police officers who kept him from running into the hotel following the spectacular crash that had literally shaken the asphalt.

He'd seen Uther, helped along by an unidentified man, run to safety seconds after the explosion. Grabbing a BND agent, Dane pointed them out, and sent him to secure Uther.

Now, less than three minutes after the disaster, the hotel manager had cautioned that the entire building could come down if the explosion had threatened the integrity of the structure.

"Bugger that, she's still inside!" Dane shouted to the officers who held him back. "There's a woman inside."

"Bleiben sie hier!"

Stay here? Wrong.

"It is not safe!"

Dane continued to struggle. Much as he'd been working in opposition to Becca the past few days, there was no way he could turn and walk away from this disaster without her. New York was one hell of a tough woman. But she wasn't a superhero. He should have been at her side to protect—

Catching sight of the slender, drenched figure walking through the shattered lobby doors, Dane stopped struggling. A massive chunk of acrylic—part of the aquarium—sliced through one of the doors in her wake. She didn't blink or turn.

"Un-sodding-believable."

She'd made it. The New York dame had actually made it!

"Let me go."

Dane tore away from the officers and ran across the parking lot toward the most incredible sight he knew he would ever see.

Shivering, and soaked from head to single shoe, Becca stumbled across the parking lot, which was littered with fresh snow. Fat snowflakes fluttered from the sky. She held something in her hands, both cupped to her chest. At the sight of him, she cracked a weary smile.

"Been for a swim," she said, her words slurred.

Dane got to her as she toppled into his arms. The black-and-white fish she'd had hold of slipped free and landed on the snowy pavement. He supported her so she could stand.

"Dane?"

"You're safe, love. I can't believe it, but you made it out."

"The fish. You gotta save it. No innocents should suffer. It wasn't their fault."

"I'll get an agent on it. Right now I'm more worried about the warm-blooded creatures."

Nodding to one of the horror-stricken people loitering on the sidewalk, Dane silently ordered he tend the fish. Which, surprisingly, the man did.

"That was an awesome ride."

"I'll bet. Did I tell you already you're an incredible woman?"

"You can tell me again. Did I…" Shivering violently, Becca coiled against Dane's chest. Her lips were already beginning to blue. "Did I mention I don't like large bodies of water?"

Despite himself, Dane chuckled.

Dane had conjured a thick wool blanket from one of the ambulance techs, and somehow Becca had been given a pair of boots. They were five sizes too big for her feet, and made her feel as if she was clomping about in cement blocks, but they kept back the cold, so she wasn't complaining. But somewhere along the line she'd lost her gold choker. Which pissed her off.

Dane hadn't let her get more than a foot away from him while he tried to locate the officer he'd sent after Uther.

"You find them?" she prompted.

Dane looked around. Weary-eyed civilians milled about in scattered crowds. "I still can't place the officer

I sent after them. Sod it! I didn't even recognize Dimitri. He was in the hotel?"

"He plucked Uther off the top of the aquarium as we were making our escape."

"You still have the stones?"

"Right here." She patted her left pocket.

"Can I...hold them?"

"You never give up, do you, Dane?"

He embraced her. The warmth emanating from his body and seeping into Becca's pores felt ridiculously calming. "Relax. Go sit inside one of the ambulances before you turn into an ice-pop. You okay?"

"Perfectly fine. Just a couple more bruises to add to my collection." A monstrous sigh formed a cloud in the chilly air before her. Unable to disregard a silly worry, she muttered, "What about the fish?"

"Fish and Wildlife has been called in to salvage as many as they can." He tapped her skull. "I meant, are you okay...in here. I can see you've got bruises and scrapes, but what are you thinking? Talk to me, love."

"Stop calling me love. I'm not your love."

She stomped away, hands on her hips. The movement exposed more of her flesh to the cold air, but she couldn't even summon a shiver. A sweep of the parking lot revealed moaning and crying civilians, and a barrage of police vehicles and ambulances. As far as she knew, everyone had gotten out safely.

Had this been a result of Dimitri's attempt to take her out? Why such a drastic process when a simple bullet to her brain would have sufficed? So many could have suffered, or worse, died, had the hotel not been cleared.

And now he had Uther Magnusson.

Turning abruptly, she slammed into Dane's body. It was difficult to push away from his dreamy warmth. She wanted to hug him. To wrap her legs and arms around him and suck out all the heat. And so she did.

Snuggling into his trench coat and tucking her head against his neck, she closed her eyes and stilled her thoughts.

Dane tugged the blanket firmly about her shoulders. Then he slipped his hands up under the wool and around her back, pressing her even closer to his body heat. "Take all you want, love—sorry, Ms. Whitmore."

A tear threatened, but Becca stopped the urge. Much as she wanted to coil up and have a good old bawling session, now was not the time. Secret agents did not cry. They got the job done. No tears, no fears.

But Dane was right. A little fear never hurt.

Standing in oversize boots that wouldn't allow her to step too close without crushing his feet, she leaned into him and clung mindlessly. Ah, body heat. Delicious. "You can call me love."

"You're remarkable," he whispered in her ear. "In-sodding-credible."

"You've mentioned as much. *You're* warm."

"Much as I'd like to stand and hold you until the sun sets, I want to get you inside. I don't want you looking like old polka dots over there."

"Who?"

"The fish you walked out with. It'll be fine—don't cry. I'm here."

She released a few tears. Couldn't be helped. She'd

been dangling a good ten feet from the floor when the cable had snapped and she had jumped. She had survived the Great Water Disaster. She had…faced her fear.

"I did," she murmured. A sob segued to a choking laugh.

"Did what, love? Is that real laughter or have you gone a little loopy?"

"It's real," she assured him. "I've faced an irrational fear and come out alive."

"That you did. I'm proud of you."

And that surprising affirmation made her feel even better.

Now it was time to focus. "Do they know who planted the bomb?"

"We got an anonymous phone call, traced it to inside the hotel. BND is working to decipher it right now."

"Right. Well, I'm making a guess it was Dimitri." She pulled far enough away to look at Dane's face. The warm contact was replaced by a gush of cool air. Struggling against her body's desire to snuggle and her logical need to finish the task, she felt logic win. "Is there any way we can view the hotel's security tape?"

He nodded. "Right. Good idea."

It took a virtual act of God to finally convince the building inspector to allow one BND agent inside the hotel to acquire the security tapes from the office. Half an hour later, in the comfort of a warm van outfitted with surveillance equipment, Becca and Dane scanned through the morning's tapes.

There were no signs of anyone approaching the gigantic tank to plant or press any sort of substance against it. They scanned through the tapes of patrons sitting in the Atrium bar. Dane proposed an indirect method of delivery.

Becca repeatedly played back a few minutes of tape featuring a tall figure in a dark baseball cap. He approached the bar, sat down, spoke to the bartender. While he waited for a drink, he pointed his finger at the base of the aquarium. A quick call on his cell phone followed. When his drink arrived he paid, then left. Didn't even take a sip.

She pointed the man out to Dane.

He leaned in for a closer look. "Can you notch that one up, Hans?"

The security technician assisting them tapped his keyboard. The screen shot increased fifty percent, but it made the face blurrier.

"It's got to be Dimitri," Becca said. "He was wearing all black when he took off with Uther." She pushed back her heavy, wet hair. "Can I get a match on that time, Hans? See if it coincides with the phone call to the police warning of the bomb?"

Hans tapped on a few keys and the digital recording forwarded. "It matches."

"He's our man," Dane said.

"What time is it?" Becca asked.

"Noon," Hans replied. "There is coffee in the emergency vehicles."

"Thank you, Hans. But we'll take it to go. I suspect Uther and Dimitri are on their way to New York."

"What for?" Dane asked.

"Sabrina Morgan."

Dane shrugged.

"I'll tell you about it in the taxi." Tugging the blanket about her shoulders, Becca stepped outside onto the slushy asphalt, but gave a protesting whimper when Dane pulled the blanket completely off.

"Here." He shed the fleece-lined trencher from his shoulders and swung it about hers. "Wear this, and button it up so you don't flash anyone."

Becca flipped up the hem of her torn red blouse to survey her exposed skin. "You don't like the style?"

"Personally, I love the teasing bit of belly button. But, besides the frostbite, I think you're a more conservative dresser."

"Frostbite bad."

"Body heat good," he offered as he hugged her close. "We'll have to get you proper shoes, as well."

"Louboutins?"

"How 'bout a sexy pair of Jimmy Choos?"

Nestling her head against Dane's shoulder, Becca gave the latter some consideration. "Choo. Good."

The cab to the Brandenburg Airport blasted blessed heat into the back seat. Jimmy Choos had not been available; the closest stores offered cheaper fare. The best Dane could manage was a pair of flat white boat shoes from a tourist shop outside the hotel. But they felt like Cinderella's glass slippers when her prince put them on her feet.

Trench coat buttoned up to her neck, Becca dialed Zeek to report.

"What's going on, Becca? You don't sound right."

"Bomb. Big one. Lots of water." She sighed and shrugged a hand through her still damp and slightly crunchy hair. "I'm fine. But the target has been kidnapped."

"Uther Magnusson?"

"Currently headed toward New York, is my guess."

"Is that a good guess?"

"Yes. I need an agent put on Sabrina Morgan. She may be in danger. She also holds a third diamond with the same data coded inside the crown."

"We were not aware there was a third. Excellent work, Becca. I'll get an agent right on it, take the diamond into evidence and post operatives at JFK."

"Great, but I'm already forming a backup plan in case he slips through customs. If we can get to Sabrina first, maybe I can lure Dimitri to me."

"Don't take unnecessary risks, Becca. Just secure Uther."

"I can't do that unless I attract Dimitri. Don't worry, I have an idea."

There was a pause on Zeek's end. "You ditch MI-6 yet?"

"Haven't tried."

"Be careful."

"I always am." Becca tugged the lapels of Dane's coat to her chin. "Talk to you soon."

Too weary to even click off, Becca laid her head back against the seat. If luck held out, they might apprehend Dimitri and Uther at the airport. But in the event that scenario didn't pan out, she must figure out a plan for New York.

Dimitri had been posing as a prince?

An idea emerged. Though risky to her cover, it would lure the Russian right where she could nab him.

She scanned through her list of contacts on her cell phone and found Rubi Cho's number. It rang once, and Cho, in her usual perky voice, announced she would listen only if the caller had something juicy to say.

"Have you gone to press yet?"

"Becca Whitmore! In print, yes. But if you have a scoop, I can post something online. What is it?"

"I've got a big scoop for you."

Chapter 22

New York City

As suspected, there was no sign of Dimitri or Uther at the Brandenburg or JFK airports. Likely Dimitri used an assortment of aliases and disguises. Perhaps even had a private jet. Instead of demanding to scan the security tapes on the Berlin end, both Becca and Dane decided it was best to hop a flight to the States.

Becca used the flight to catch a few desperately needed z's. They stepped onto U.S. soil at 3:30 p.m. Gotta love flying across five time zones.

Jake, her butler-driver, was waiting at JFK International. He didn't so much as lift a brow when Dane followed Becca into the back seat of the Hummer. Instead, he handed Becca a charged cell phone battery and a laptop with Rubi Cho's column *In the Know* on the screen.

While Dane helped himself to Perrier, Becca read the column.

"All right to crack this open?" he asked her.

She peered over the top of the computer. Dane shook a small tin of beluga caviar. "That's what it's there for. Neither of us has had much to eat the past day."

"Love you, love." He dug in with gusto.

Nodding graciously, she decided the moniker didn't bother her so much anymore. If he wanted to call her love, more power to him. It was just a nickname; didn't mean anything.

Cho's column introduced a new face to the ranks of society: "Meredith and Charles Pearce have given birth to a healthy baby girl, already tricked out in Baby Gap and a diamond-trimmed rattle from Barneys."

Becca recognized the next name as a fellow agent.

"A certain Gotham Rose club member, Tatiana Guttman, was seen tripping the light fantastic with a well-known Apprentice. They looked snug on the dance floor, but do you think he'll be fired again before the week is up?"

It was the final note that caught Becca's attention.

"Watch for the debut of a rumored flawless ten-carat beauty of a diamond to appear around model Sabrina Morgan's neck. The young Nordic beauty became engaged to über-geek nanotechnologist Uther Magnusson, of the Manhattan Magnussons.

"Tune in to the Grace Notes gala at the Waldorf Astoria tonight, Valentine's Day, to see if the twosome can be captured in a sweetheart snuggle."

Nordic beauty? Why did that description of Sabrina bother Becca?

Her cell phone rang. Zeek reported that Sabrina Morgan had been secured at a safe house, as well as Amandus Magnusson.

"Did you get the diamond?"

"It's been sent to Alan Burke. He's setting it right now. Sabrina didn't want to give up that beauty." Zeek snapped her gum and made a quick apology for the noise. "I understand you'll be wearing it later this evening?"

"I don't know how else to nab Uther."

"Sabrina was directed to leave a message for Uther at her home, stating she'd meet him at the gala if she didn't hear from him sooner."

"Great. If both Dimitri and Uther suspect Sabrina will be at the gala, then it's certain they'll be there. Thanks, Zeek."

"They pulling a fake for the evening?" Dane wondered as he licked a fingertip clean of caviar.

"A fake? No time, we're using the real thing."

"Risky."

"Yes, but if Dimitri knows what he's looking for, it may be risky to use anything but."

"You're the germologist," Dane said.

Becca noticed the tin of caviar was empty. He hadn't. The stuff cost a thousand bucks a can!

She shook her head and smiled. He had.

"Where's a proper place to get a bit of shut-eye in

this town? I didn't sleep a wink on the flight—too much turbulence."

"I've a guest room. I'm sure Jake has it ready."

"Really? You inviting the arsehole into your home?"

She set the laptop on the seat between them and hooked her elbow across the back, turning to face him. "You accepting?"

"I wouldn't think to refuse."

"I should hope not. I believe you owe me some serious toadying for all that caviar you just snarfed down."

"I'm starving, love. Is there a pub we could stop by and get a sandwich before your big to-do?"

"I don't know, this is New York," she said slyly. "We're not big on restaurants here."

"Very funny."

"I've food at my apartment."

"Really? Who'd have thought, the pampered princess does her own cooking."

"I wouldn't go quite that far. Jake makes a mean Dijon chicken salad sandwich."

"Sounds minimally exciting. But I'm all for food of any kind. So what's the skinny?"

She handed him the laptop, but when he yawned and tapped the computer with the Perrier bottle, she took it back and read the column out loud.

"That your doing?" he queried.

"Yes. This means Dimitri will know exactly where to find what he's looking for."

"You honestly believe you can lure Dimitri to you with that gossip column? He won't even see it."

"I'll take my chances. If he's got Uther with him,

he'll be sure he calls every place Sabrina could possibly be. As far as Uther knows, Sabrina is meeting him at the gala."

"Sounds a long shot."

"Have you a better plan?"

Dane closed his eyes, shook his head and then punched a fist into his palm. "I should have taken Dimitri out at the club."

So he really had known then. Becca hadn't suspected anything less.

"I thought the diamonds were your objective?"

"They are, love."

"And yet taking Dimitri out appeals to you? Why didn't you have him arrested when we had a chance? You're still keeping secrets from me."

"Love—"

"Secrets about Dimitri Boratov that I should have been told from the get-go."

"Sounds like the CIA—your own people—were keeping you in the dark. Just because you've got some moves and have the secret phone number to the CIA doesn't mean you get to— I'm sorry. I don't mean to snap, but I am charged to bring back evidence, and thus far, I'm at zero and you're at three." He yawned again. "Care to share?"

"You need some sleep. We've only got a couple hours before we need to tog up again."

"You're changing the subject."

"You bet."

Dane tapped the laptop. "Those gossips columnists

must be your bane, eh? You ever get caught with your slip exposed, so to speak?"

"When David and I were engaged we made the column every time we went out. I don't understand the fascination. We're normal folk."

"Normal folk don't flash Centurion cards or carry thirty-thousand-dollar mobile phones."

Becca shrugged. "The exterior may be a little more fancy, but inside, we're all the same."

"I don't think so. How many New York heiresses spend their free time tracking criminals?"

"Maybe just the one," she said with a smile. "Or maybe just enough to keep the good ole boys on their toes."

A hand-me-down from her grandmother, the thirty-second-floor apartment on Park Avenue provided a generous twenty-five hundred square feet space and was priced at a cool twelve million.

"You can take the guest room," Becca offered Dane as they entered and she deactivated the alarm. The boat shoes made squidgy noises as she strode across the high-gloss marble floor to the kitchen. "There's an alarm clock you can set."

"Goody. Don't want to miss the big show. Is this guest room close to your bedroom?"

"Why do you ask?"

"I'm pretty tired." Dane stretched out his arm, flexing the muscles beneath the fitted sweater. "I don't want to be kept awake by your 'maintenance.'"

"Very funny, Dane."

Becca set her Gucci bag and cell phone on the rose-quartz-topped island. "Can I offer you a drink before you go to sleep?"

"I'll pass. But I wouldn't say no to one of those chicken sandwiches."

"Jake'll fix us something soon as he comes up from the garage."

"Gotta love that man Jake. Point me in the direction of the shower then, and I'll be out of your hair until munchies."

He followed her directions. Becca slid onto a bar stool, watching as he padded off toward the bedrooms.

First thing on her list: check in with Lucy. Becca felt a twinge of guilt for being away so close to the gala. Certainly if she had been in town, she and Lucy would have gotten together to go over details.

Now she was back and stepping into the shoes of a socialite. *Can you walk in them? Do you want to?* Or did she crave the feel of dangerous spike heels and secrets?

If things went the way she expected, she might have to wear both sets of shoes tonight. The very reason she had been selected as an agent was because of her real life. But lately, balancing the two roles was becoming more of a challenge.

Chapter 23

At 5:00 p.m.—an hour before the gala began—Becca passed through the elegant wrought-iron doors of the brownstone on 68th Street that served as the Gotham Roses' home.

Italian marble stretched across the lobby. A doorman prompted her for her coat, which she kept; the Berlin chill remained with her. The faux mink-trimmed wool duster was more fashionable than warm. It was the gloves and a smart hat that kept her from the cold.

Renee's secretary, Olivia Hayworth, spied her on the video console and immediately buzzed her in. Becca had little time, and should go directly to Alan for briefing for the evening, but not until she saw Renee. Asked her the burning question.

Had she been bait?

Passing by Olivia's desk, Becca nodded to the freckle-faced beauty, who usually wore her hair in a loose, blowsy bun that emphasized her elegant bone structure and drew attention to her exquisite blue eyes.

Tugging off her gloves, she walked on past the main floor tearoom, which was right off of Renee's office.

The two hundred members of the Gotham Roses would never guess covert activities took place literally beneath their feet in the basement.

And should they ever wonder? Well, no explanation so decadent as a secret agency would occur to the socialites.

Renee's office was a generous-size room with seventeenth century French furnishings mixed exquisitely with modern touches like a cappuccino machine and a huge plasma screen, the latter of which functioned as a monitor, a surveillance screen and a television.

Not taking the time to do more than shower and change clothes since her arrival, Becca wore moisturizer and some clear lip gloss, and had pulled her hair back into a messy ponytail. She was still in agent mode.

Pausing before knocking on the door, she tugged down the simple violet cashmere sweater she'd slipped on over the clingy wool slacks. Dane hadn't seen her sensible Prada boots because she'd left him asleep with a note to meet her at the gala.

Part of her wanted to nab Dimitri on her own. Part of her thought partnering with Dane wasn't so dreadful. An even bigger part of her screamed for her to pull herself together—she was made to go it alone.

"Come in," a calm female voice called through the door.

Fresh white tea roses scented the room with a hint of spice.

"It's good to see you, Becca. How was Europe?"

"A whirlwind. Not so cold as New York."

"We're having a bit of a snap." Renee gestured for Becca to take the chair across from her desk.

Becca crossed her arms and paced to the wall opposite the desk, where the plasma screen hung. Her back to Renee, she centered her brewing emotions. Anger. Curiosity. Even doubt.

"You've obtained the diamonds?"

"Both of them." Becca turned and, arms swinging, strode to the center of the room. "They're at my apartment in a safe. Will they be claimed by CIA or the Gotham Roses?"

"That's need to know. I'll send someone to retrieve them."

Need to know. Not what she needed to hear right now.

"Of course. Jake will accommodate whomever you send."

Renee dismissed the absence of evidence easily. She was all-business. But for the struggles she had faced with her husband's incarceration, she literally glowed. "I have information on Agent Dane that will interest you."

"You have information on everyone, Renee," Becca replied. "Not interested."

Renee gave her a long hard look. That had been a very curt reply. But no one told Becca with whom, or when, to have a liaison.

"Very well." The older woman crossed her legs, gathering her composure. "Have you been briefed for tonight?"

"I'm meeting with Alan as soon as I leave you." Allowing the anger to simmer up, Becca pressed her fists to the edge of the ornate desk and spoke as calmly as her agitated nerves would allow. "Please tell me the CIA had no idea they were after Uther and his technology from the get-go."

"You're speculating, Becca."

"Speculating!"

Renee sat back in her chair and gazed at Becca. The woman was impeccable in style, manner and determination. Normally she could quiet Becca's ire with just a look.

But not this time.

Standing and shaking out her arms, like a boxer working off tension, Becca asked, "Who wants Uther? The CIA? FBI? Some black-ops arm even you don't know about?"

"I can't say."

But she did know.

"The Governess?"

"I can tell you we have Uther Magnusson's best interests in mind. If he should fall into the wrong hands—"

"Damn it, Renee, I was chosen because Uther knew me. Is that right? No one cares about Dimitri. He's just a mule carrying the cache to the States. The cache is Uther Magnusson. A prize that might be won only by sacrificing an innocent, Sabrina Morgan."

The two woman locked gazes until Becca finally blew out a breath and offered a brisk apology. She ran her hand over her hair and tapped her booted foot.

"Why does this particular case bother you so much,

Becca? Yes, we are aware you know Uther, but you two are not close."

"No, we're not."

"Then what is it? You've done this before. You've been trained. You are required only to know what you need to know, and to look beyond personal connections, yet if need be, to use those connections."

"I know." Need to know. Right. She'd been too hard on Dane for something that was just part of his job.

Renee tilted her head and leveled a hard gaze at her. Becca was fully aware of all the woman and her family had suffered at the hands of the good old boys. Everything was personal to her. And how she held herself together in the face of opposition was to be admired.

Pursing her lips, Renee sighed and splayed a hand in surrender. "The CIA was worried Uther would fall into the hands of the Russians or, even worse, although we hope unlikely, the Duke. Uther Magnusson is an asset we can't afford to give up."

The Duke. Another moniker for a face Becca didn't know, but had only heard about. The Governess's nemesis. The man authorities believed was rich, powerful and behind some of the worst crimes imaginable. But his wealth and status had managed to protect him, conceal him and make him untouchable. Rumor was that the Governess believed the Gotham Roses might be the key to rooting him out. Some Roses were rumored to be dedicated solely to that purpose. Certainly it was possible the Duke would be looking to get his hands on Uther, whose technology could make him millions in the black market. But all signs pointed to the Russians.

"There might be a mole," Renee admitted, almost reluctantly. "We believe someone may be tipping off the Russians as to Magnusson's research. They're poised to nab the scientist as soon as he goes public. That's all I can tell you."

"A mole." Events from the past few days passed through Becca's thoughts. "Zeek?"

"She's being watched. I don't believe so, but she won't be in on the operation this evening."

"Agent Arlowe?"

"She's been assigned in Croatia. Again, unlikely."

"The Russian Mafia's reach is far and sticky. It could be anyone."

"Mafia— Becca, are you aware Nazarova is SVR?"

She lifted a brow. "Nazarova?"

Renee tapped out a few keys on the flat screen embedded in the desk before her, and the picture of Dimitri appeared, along with his stats in green text. "He's been in New York for the past month, posing as one Dimitri Boratav—"

"Yes, yes, as a Turkish prince. Nazarova, eh?"

Russian intelligence? She and Dane had only speculated. Or had she speculated when Dane had known all along?

"Zeek implied Dimitri was Mafia. When did that information come in?"

"A few hours ago. Until then we'd thought him Mafia, as well. We've been keeping an eye on him but hadn't been able to blow his cover until now. Thanks partly to Katarine Veld's arrest."

"What does the SVR want with Uther?" Stupid question. Same thing the CIA wanted him for. And MI-6. Nano-coding to be used by their country's military.

"So I'm trying to lure in a Russian agent? Why? He's already got what he wants—Uther."

"I suspect Dimitri would like the diamonds, as well. A backup, in case Uther won't be cooperative."

Renee spoke of Uther as if he were some kind of…equipment.

"We'll do everything we can to protect Miss Morgan and him. Everything in *my* power."

"I understand."

"You did lead Nazarova to Uther."

"I didn't lead—" But she had. Dimitri had to have followed her and Dane to Berlin, to the very hotel where Uther had been hiding out. "No. The mole. It was someone else."

Renee pondered the idea. "Possibly. Can I trust you'll be on top of your game tonight?"

"I always am."

"You'll be wearing two hats."

"Yes, that of socialite Becca Whitmore and that of spy. Tell me this—is my objective merely Uther Magnusson, or does nabbing Dimitri somehow figure into the game?"

"We are not interested in Nazarova. But you will be competing against MI-6 tonight. What's your relationship with Agent Dane?"

"Partners."

Renee's condescending stare bored right through Becca's exterior armor and into her heart. She saw things even Becca couldn't yet recognize. "Fraternizing with foreign agents, even if they are allies, is a no-no, Becca."

"I'll put it on my list."

Not an answer Renee appreciated. Tough. There were too many hands in the cookie jar. Becca didn't have time to fight for anything but the biggest piece.

"I know you don't want to hear it," Renee began slowly, "but I must inform you—Dane's father was MI-5."

"He told me that."

"Did he also tell you it was Nazarova who tortured and then killed him for refusing to expose MI-5 secrets?"

Becca had stored the few facts about Dane's father for further thought. She hadn't had opportunity to think about them, but now it was as if she had known all along. Dane and the SVR…there was a connection she was missing. She needed to shake through the past few days and focus.

"Thank you, Renee." Inhaling a calming breath, she held it in. "I should be going. Alan is waiting."

"You can use my entrance," Renee offered. She pressed a button on the desktop console and the sliding door to her powder room opened. The cooling system hushed out a stream of chilled air.

"Becca, you're one of my best agents. On occasion I've turned my attention to your private pursuits. But I trust you'll do what is best for the agency, and not yourself."

"I will." She sighed and turned in the doorway, leaning against the partition. "You know…" Dare she bring this up? She had always been able to talk to Renee; the woman would understand. "It's different with a fellow agent."

The softer side of Renee emerged with a gentle smile. "It is. You think your secrets are safe. And yet…the secrets are actually doubled, Becca."

She thought about that. She and Dane knew each other's cover. Bonus points for that. But could they ever know whom their ultimate alliances were to? Not unless he confessed his secrets. How many more did Dane still keep? Subtract multiple points for needing to know.

"Thanks, Renee."

Becca walked into the closet stocked with every designer label of the season. Turning to the wall of shoes, she pressed a keypad to reveal the glass elevator tube that would shuttle her down to the underground operations. Leaning forward to the biometric panel, she waited for iris recognition to verify.

Dane's father had been tortured and murdered by Dimitri?

I was lipreading.

Oh, Dane. What the hell was he up to?

A moment after Becca had left the office, Renee's phone rang. It was the Governess. She rarely called, and when she did, her voice was altered with a digital scrambler. Keeping her identity a secret was of utmost importance, even from Renee, although Renee had her beliefs about who her mystery boss might be.

"Everything prepared for the snatch this evening?"

"I've got one of my best agents on it."

"Yes, Becca Whitmore. The woman who allowed MI-6 to accompany her to New York?"

"He's within jurisdiction."

"You protect your girls foolishly, Renee. I trust no one. Not even MI-6. The Brit could be on the Duke's payroll. Uther Magnusson is key. The CIA can't afford to lose him. Put an extra agent on Whitmore. I don't trust her, either."

Renee leaned back and tapped her desk with a French-manicured fingernail. "I trust her."

"You're not calling the shots tonight. If you can't handle the situation—"

"I'll see to the arrangements," Renee broke in. "Have a pleasant evening."

"I'm going to need more eyes tonight," Becca explained as she sorted through the various gadgets on the black steel countertop in Alan's shop. "The Waldorf ballroom is huge. The expected attendance is pushing one thousand. This sort of scenario is filled with distractions. We need to pinpoint our suspect before he sees me. He's ID'd me in the Aquadom elevator. I can't wear a disguise because I'm expected to host this evening. My two worlds are converging head-on."

"Usual operational procedure," Alan noted.

"Yes, but for some reason, tonight I expect one hell of a nasty collision."

"No problem." He beamed. The young man's stylish, midnight-blue Paul Smith suit accented his lean frame and straight shoulders. He must have plans to trip the light fantastic later. "I've got everything covered. Kristi's got a fab gown. I think red for tonight?"

"Red's good. So long as it's not too tight. I want ease of motion to move about."

"And leg room for running."

"And good sturdy shoes."

"Sounds utilitarian," Alan said with a pout.

"Well, certainly I wouldn't frown at a pair of Marc Jacobs."

"Good girl! So here's the plan." Alan opened up a black jeweler's case to reveal a pair of chandelier earrings upon a bed of black velvet. Much more delicate than the Paris ones. "We'll have a Rose agent, Sherri Grant, posted at the entrance to take pictures of every person who crosses the threshold. You know Sherri, yes? She's the cute one with the dimples and red hair. Love those catty green eyes of hers! Anyway, photos will arrive here—and with Zeek—and the faces will be matched in our database."

"I know Dimitri. I can ID him, no problem."

"Yes, but will you be all places at once?"

No, she'd be dancing a delicate line between socialite and secret agent.

"If he doesn't have an invite he won't enter through the front door. The CIA will have operatives posted throughout, posing as waiters and staff."

"He'll come through the front door," Becca said, a startling fact dawning like a lightning bolt to the brain, "because he has an invitation."

Chapter 24

Alan gaped. "What?"

"I invited the Turkish prince, Dimitri Boratav, aka Dimitri Nazarova. The prince was top of my list when the invites went out three weeks ago. I didn't think anything of it, only that he was on the A list. I always invite A-listers."

"Of course. And we can hope he still thinks he's got cover as the prince."

"He doesn't know me, and may believe I was with the French police in Paris. Unless the SVR has traced me."

"A trace will only tell them about the heiress." Alan brushed his fingers through the dark brown hair coiffed in a side part over his forehead. "Don't worry about it. This might make things a little easier. So, Sabrina is secure, and Uther—"

"The Nordic beauty," Becca said absently, then, more focused, asked, "Alan, do you have a file on Sabrina Morgan?"

"I'm sure I do."

"Bring it up, will you?"

"All right." He spun about and tapped on the computer keys. A file of names scrolled before him, while Becca continued her thoughts.

"So, just wait-staff undercover tonight?"

"About half a dozen," he said over his shoulder

"We'll need more."

"What about that Brit I hear you toted back to New York?" Kristi arrived to display a delicious couture gown with a thick froth of brilliant red fox fur edging the collar. "So you've already picked a dance partner for the evening?"

"It's his case, too," Becca said. "But don't expect us to be pulling any Fred and Ginger moves."

"Uh-huh." Kristi smirked and exchanged a look with her brother.

"What about you?" Becca petted the fox fur. "You going to be twirling on the dance floor?"

Kristi sighed. "Not tonight."

"Trying to convince her to give Internet dating a go," Alan whispered conspiratorially behind his hand. At Kristi's scathing look, he spoke up, "As for myself, I've a sweetie waiting to meet me later and we'll trip across the ballroom. It *is* Valentine's Day."

"I had forgotten," Becca said as she pushed her fingers deep into the fur. No romance or roses for her tonight. "You find anything yet, Alan?"

"Strangely, no. There are five Sabrina Morgans in the city, but none match with the one we've got sitting in a safe house. This is most curious."

"Keep looking. I'm going to change."

"Hurry back," Alan called. "You do want to see the pièce de résistance!"

The dressing room behind Kristi's office was ultra-modern and scented with vanilla oil. Two walls were lined with gowns, shoes and accessories such as purses, scarves and hats. Behind gossamer white drapes was a well-lit dressing room.

Becca slipped in and quickly stripped and pulled up the red gown. Stepping out to stand before a three-way floor-length mirror, she studied her image. Funny how a well-fit designer dress made one's confidence level soar.

The froth of luscious fur nestled against her neck and veed down to her décolletage, where it caught up the slinky red silk sheath. The fur was actually detachable. One simply had to decide how much cleavage one wanted to reveal. Not too much, to begin with. This was a charity function.

Smirking at her silliness, Becca sat on a sleek white leather chaise to slip on her shoes—sexy red numbers with straps and sparkles. There were little crystals sewn along the strap that crossed over her toes. Dane would appreciate them.

Dane. Becca would miss the man of many talents, in-cluding his remarkable ability to recognize designer footwear.

Too bad he played for the wrong team. Or did he even

play for a team? And now to know Dimitri was really SVR, as Dane had suggested early on…

Kristi entered the dressing room, toting her makeup case with two hands. She set it up on the vanity next to a shampoo sink with a *thunk*.

"You're going to need some makeup to cover those bruises. Yikes, Becca, what have you been up to?"

Becca twisted toward the mirror to check the bruise on her elbow Kristi was looking at.

"Dodging flying cars. Fleeing drunk Russians. Swinging from an nine-story cable over a giant fishbowl."

"Oh. Well then. To be expected."

Laughter felt so right, and the two of them shared a couple bursts.

After a session of makeup, not too midnight-sultry, but understated glamour, Alan invited them back out to his workshop. He fastened the chandelier earrings to Becca's ears and explained how they worked. They were similar to the pair she'd worn in Paris, but without a camera.

"Let me guess," Becca said, "the earrings have microphones in them?"

"Actually, these nifty pretties are your audio output, through which you'll hear me. The Waldorf ballroom is a WiFi hot spot. We just checked it out before you arrived. You can't go anywhere without standing in a hot zone. We'll pick up your transmissions wherever you go. Even the ladies' room."

"Comforting. I think. So where's the microphone?"

Alan ran the back of his hand over the fur at her collar and waggled his eyebrows flirtatiously. "Microfilaments embedded within the fur. It's a stunning achievement, if I don't say so myself."

"Took him days," Kristi said over his shoulder. "And despite the fact that I'm against fur, I had to do the happy dance with him when it was complete."

"The tiny filaments within the fur are so thin you won't be able to detect them. Each contains a nanosize microtransmitter at the tip," Alan continued enthusiastically. "Kind of like those prelit Christmas trees, but without the gaudy flashing colors."

"Cool." Becca ran her palms over the fur. "Will it crackle with interference if I do this?"

"Shouldn't, but don't get nervous and start rubbing," Alan cautioned. "It's got a close range, less than a foot, so only your voice will be transmitted. Unless someone whispers in your ear or invades your personal space."

"Hmm," Kristi purred, "like a certain blond Brit?"

Becca rolled her eyes. "So what's the MO on Sabrina Morgan?"

"Zilch."

"What? Don't you find that strange?"

"Very strange. I've contacted Zeek who's cross-checking her database. I'm sure it's a glitch, but I will leave no stone unturned."

"Speaking of stones… Where's the star of the show?"

Alan clapped his hands together and rubbed them gleefully. "It's a beauty!"

After a search of the Park Avenue apartment, Dane came up with nothing beyond that the woman liked her silky La Perla underwear and fruity smelling creams.

But he didn't believe she would tote the diamonds around the city with her. One option was turning them in to evidence; an agent could yet be on the way to retrieve them. The other…

He pushed open the pocket doors to her bedroom closet and kicked aside a scattering of shoes that would likely pay his rent for an entire year.

"But pretty," he muttered as he eyed them. "On her gams, nothing but the best."

The smile that creased his face caught him so off guard, Dane knelt there for a moment just taking it all in. He pressed a palm over his heart. The woman had imprinted herself onto his psyche. And erasing her wasn't an option.

But he wasn't about to let a sexy laugh and killer gams throw him off his game.

As suspected, behind the shoes stood a small black trauma safe, utilized for storing jewels and documents by the wealthy set.

With a crack of his fingers and a loosening shake of his hand, Dane set to work.

"You said you had the diamond."

"It was…misplaced. I will get it back."

"Veld!"

"Dimitri, do not raise your voice to me. I've been playing nice with the CIA the past eighteen hours. I had no choice but to let it go. Did you get the scientist?"

"*Da,* but he is useless without the information on the diamond. Claims it would take months to recreate the formula without his notes."

"We will have the diamond before tonight is over. You stay hidden until I bring it to you. Did you go on-line and read the New York gossip columns? They are going to attempt to draw you out by using the diamond as bait. Foolish Americans."

"Bring it to me, then I shall reward you."

Chapter 25

Red and white and silver and black. Everywhere. And what didn't sparkle flowed or flickered or smelled of roses and chocolate. The Waldorf's balcony boxes were draped with swags of fully opened thick red roses with heads larger than a man's fist. Silver confetti glittered on the red carpets and traveling minstrels dressed in red-and-white harlequin costumes serenaded the attendees.

The table settings were extravagant mixes of roses, red candles and luscious sweeps of white chiffon, all grouped about white-and-silver carousel horses. It had been Lucy's idea to do a Carousel of Love theme. Everything sparkled as if a fairy had swooped in and dropped the motherlode.

Indulging in a chocolate-covered cherry so sweet and juicy it was the perfect kind of sin, Becca turned, licking her fingers, to see Lucy approaching.

Spills of glossy garnet curls flowed to Lucy's elbows and slithered across her deep violet gown. A heart-shaped neckline accentuated her buxom figure. Her signature white lily was tucked above her right ear. She absolutely beamed. "It's perfect, isn't it, Becca?"

"Flawless," she agreed with a sardonic smirk. Flawless as a ten-carat diamond? Or flawless as an MI-6 agent's lies?

And who was she to throw stones?

Becca wrapped the long silver cord of her satin purse about two fingers. "When do the children perform?"

"Early. Seven-thirty is what I've planned. They'll promenade through the ballroom, instruments in hand, wearing perfect little black-and-white suits with red cummerbunds. They are so cute!"

"What are they playing?"

"The *Midsummer Serenade*."

Becca's jaw dropped, but she could not form words. The purse cord drew tight about her fingers. "My father's piece?"

"The one he composed for you." Lucy gave a sheepish grin, then paused. "Don't be angry, Becca, it's such a beautiful piece."

"I'm not angry. Not at all. It's a very difficult piece. What about the cadenza in the third movement?"

"Well…"

Oh no. She couldn't possibly expect…?

Lucy had a way of saying things without uttering a word. Such hope and expectation glittered in her deep green eyes.

"There's an extra violin in the office. Please, Becca?"

Becca raised an arm to touch a suddenly aching temple. Not good. Not this evening. Not…children.

"Too much danger," she whispered, turning away from Lucy.

"Oh, Becca, it would mean so much to everyone."

Becca put up her palm. Drawing in long breaths, she altered her focus. She was trained to anticipate the unexpected. Protecting children from a maniac SVR agent? Hell.

"It's still an hour and a half until showtime," Lucy chirped. "Think about it. I'll touch base with you in a bit. Oh, baby." She gripped Becca's wrist. "Did I ever mention how much I appreciate the Italian designers?"

At Lucy's appreciative growl, Becca turned to discover what had piqued her assistant's base instincts.

A vision of chalk-striped Zegna approached, striding across the black-and-white-checked ballroom floor. Perfect Italian tailoring, from the fitted sleeves, to the short jacket, to the slender trousers. A micro-dotted red tie shimmered beneath a swanky grin.

"Who is that?" Lucy playfully nudged Becca in the side, but Becca ignored her. "Is he yours? Where did you get him?"

"Mine? Er, Agen—Aston—er, London. Just a… friend from London."

"Nice."

"I'll talk to you later, Lucy. I'd better go say hi."

"Say hi from me, too. Ask if he's got a brother!"

Dane stood, one hand cocked at his hip. The tailored shirt knew how to work the ripped pecs. A heart-shaped wreath of bloodred roses on the wall behind him framed him like some kind of treat waiting for a taste. And he simply stood there, waiting for her to come to him.

Cheeky swank.

But she had no difficulty crossing the room.

Becca found herself turning into Dane's proffered embrace. She spun, and he caressed her from behind as if in a Fred and Ginger dance move.

He leaned in and whispered, "That is a posh frock, love. I adore fur. It's soft and touchable. Just like you. But where's the rock? Are you hiding it in the depths of your soft, buxom—"

"Agent Dane," she warned.

"Back to formalities, I see. Very well, then. Ms. *Whitmore*."

"So you like the dress?" She smoothed a hand over the fur, hoping to cause interference on Alan's end.

"That's what I said. But I like you better. Bruises and all."

"Can you see the bruises? I thought I'd gotten them all covered."

"You did. You're a bit uptight tonight, love."

"I am surveilling."

"I know, but there's a dozen CIA agents wandering the room, doing the same thing. Some acting none too subtle. See Slim over there?"

Becca spied the tall, lanky waiter decked out in tails and white gloves. He pressed a finger to his ear and spoke. With no one in the immediate vicinity.

"Don't you Americans train your spies better?"

"He could be one of the wait-staff. They all wear headphones to communicate with the kitchen."

"Oh?"

"Yes. But shouldn't you have known that? Haven't you cased the place? And now that I think of it, how are *you* here? Did you present an invitation?"

Oh, cold one.

"As much as you wish to keep me from the party, I persevere."

Dane swept her into a waltz pose, one arm stretched out, her hand firmly held in his, then pulled her against his solid, muscular body. "You know I don't follow the rules."

"Oh, I know. I've also figured out you've been after Dimitri from the get-go."

Dane's breath brushed across her cheek. He hadn't an answer for that one.

"Sergei the Dog," she said. "An SVR snitch. He's why you jumped on the case. I would have figured it out a lot sooner, but you were perfectly fine with letting me believe Dimitri could be Russian Mafia."

"As I explained, MI-5 was out of its jurisdiction, love—"

"That doesn't explain either suicide. If the men feared the Mafia's retaliation, sure, but if they knew they were working for the SVR?"

"You don't know the SVR well, do you, love?"

"The driver?"

"As far as MI-6 can determine, there was a mistake. The suicide driver was connected to Katarine Veld. He had either intended to scare you or drive the car just far enough into the shop to grab the diamond from you, then leave. Poor bloke misjudged braking distance, is my guess."

"Is that the truth? Because if not, I don't even want to listen."

"Ah, I think I begin to understand. Have you had a direct order from up high? Superiors admonish you to keep your distance from the foreign agent?"

They'd yet to make any sort of dance move. Becca felt conspicuous standing there, ready to dance but not doing so.

"Nothing's changed," she answered. "We've always been working against one another."

"Good on you, New York, you've finally accepted that fact. Another fact—MI-6 has been monitoring Dimitri's activities. Oh, you left the pretty stones in your apartment, by the by."

If he had— "So my guess is you stole some diamonds this evening?"

"Only took what had been mine in the first place."

"Did you get that, Alan?"

"Ah, so *Alan* is listening in. Hello, Alan. MI-6, here."

"Cad," echoed in Becca's left ear. He had that one right.

"Come, come."

Becca shuffled reluctantly behind Dane as he led her to the dance floor. Brushed by silks and taffetas, she smiled at people she recognized. The air smelled of chocolate and roses, and had a gaiety that worked against her ultrasensitive nerves.

Stopping in the center of the dance floor, where they were surrounded by dozens of couples swooping by, Dane drew Becca to him and skimmed his thumb along her cheek to her lips, the silver band glinting beneath the crystal chandeliers.

"Shall we dance?"

An irresistible offer. One that should conjure an easy answer—no. But to refuse after he had dragged her out here would surely draw more curious stares than she wanted.

"I haven't yet made the rounds," she hedged.

Her next inhalation drew in his Burberry cologne. Never before had she smelled such an enticing man. And while he rubbed the secret agent the wrong way, the woman inside wanted to eat him up, to drown in his taste and in the rough texture of his being.

"Don't worry," he said soothingly. "The CIA is in full force. Your crew is listening in on every word we mutter. And I've met your Sherri Grant at the door. Gorgeous young thing. She the photographer?"

Blinking to dispel the intoxication she felt, Becca nodded. "Actually, she's a magazine fashion editor. Just here on business."

"Right. All on the up and up. Nothing covert there. I like your ladies' cover. New York heiresses taking down the bad boys."

"He knows?" Alan hissed in her ear.

"Dane."

"Ah yes, all a bit of hearsay, innit?" He leaned in and spoke next to her ear, and his every word sent a visceral thrill across Becca's shoulders and scalp. For some reason, him knowing made her feel free. "Don't worry, Alan, just a guess."

A brush of his breath across her neck seeped into her bare flesh with an erotic shimmy. "Now, I know you've got to make the rounds, introduce yourself, make nice, talk up the big donations, but I think this dress calls—no, it absolutely screams—for an entrance, and I won't take a sodding no for an answer."

Before she could protest, Becca once more stood aligned with Dane's fine physique, palm to palm, ready to dance. She looked to the side, avoiding aquamarine passion and intensity as if her very life depended on going to hell.

To their right a couple spun close and the man dipped his partner. The beat suddenly changed and the lights dimmed.

"A slow dance," Dane murmured in the devil's tempting tease. "What a lovely start to what may prove a harrowing evening. Loosen up, love. Where's the sexy secret agent I know and love? The woman who thrives on danger?"

Christ, he was laying it on thick.

"Relax, Becca," Alan said in her ear. "We don't have any information yet. Your Brit is right. Act natural."

She struggled to keep a balance between agent and socialite, while a disembodied voice in her ear was giving her dating advice.

To hell with discipline. Time to dance.

"Let's do it."

And for the next two minutes nothing in the world existed except their embrace and the intoxicating gaze of a most frustrating man.

He knows your secrets.

The secrets double….

Had she for one moment considered Dane a romantic prospect? A safe choice she needn't fear would flee at her secrets?

Silly girl.

And yet…

"Laugh for me," Dane suddenly said, middance.

"What?"

His cheek nuzzling against hers sent a shiver of possessiveness directly to her heart.

"I adore your laughter. It makes everything right."

"Oh?" She looked at him askance, deciding her next move. "Do you want plain laughter or…a giggle?"

He purred. "I'll take the laughter now and save that giggle for later, love."

As they moved slowly about the dance floor she was aware of all the curious stares taking in her and her handsome partner. Whispers fluttered from ear to mouth to ear. Who is that? We've never seen him before. He's holding her so close.

"Who's that?" Dane wondered.

Becca spied Rubi Cho, her trademark purple rhinestone cat glasses glinting with her movements. The slender Asian gossip columnist wore pink floral Betsy Johnson fringed in red roses just above the knee. She winked at Becca, and then snapped a photo as Dane nuzzled her ear.

"Gossip columnist," Becca moaned. "I'm sure we'll be reading about our engagement by tomorrow morning."

"Sounds promising."

"You willing to cross the ocean and start a new life?"

"You making an offer?"

Becca couldn't help a smile. "Never."

"Then we've nothing to worry about it. Prepare for the big finale."

Dane's hand slid down her back and Becca felt him move in. His leg hugged her thigh. He was going to dip her. She reacted in kind, falling into the move. And there, beneath a massive crystal chandelier, she looked up into Dane's eyes and fell—

"Becca, there's a glitch."

"What?"

Alan breathed in her ear. "Sabrina Morgan just walked through the door."

Chapter 26

"I thought—isn't she at the safe house?"

"She was. Damn." Alan never swore.

"Do not tell me the CIA has pulled her out to use as bait." Renee had promised they would keep Sabrina safe.

"No. I've got Zeek on the other line. They are as surprised as we are."

"I thought Zeek was off the mission?"

"Oh yeah? I didn't get that memo," Alan replied stonily, which implied that he had, but he didn't care. Zeek had been working the mission all along, her input was invaluable to them.

"Sherri reports she looks calm but is holding herself stiffly. She's alone. Dimitri has not been sighted. I think you should go say hello, quickly."

"I'm on it." Becca relayed her plan to Dane. "Cover me?"

"You asking me? I thought we walked parallel paths."

"Fine—"

"Love." He squeezed her hand. They still stood in a dancer's embrace, every inch of her molded against him. But the tense moment wouldn't allow her to enjoy it. "No matter what happens," he said, "I got your back."

"Really?"

He nodded.

He wanted to send her off with a kiss, but at the key moment Becca turned her cheek to receive the morsel. "Sorry," she whispered. "Everyone's watching." And she headed toward the foyer.

Dodging a gesticulating arm attached to a Fifth Avenue mogul, Becca skipped around the dance floor, nodding graciously at each "hi" or wink and wave.

She spied Sabrina immediately. Dressed in white chiffon, she wore no jewelry. Her blond hair was done up in a simple chignon similar to Becca's own style, and her wide green eyes took in the room. She looked…familiar. But of course, Becca had seen her featured in the *New York Social Diary* online.

"Becca," someone exclaimed from behind her. "That scoop you called me with?" Rubi Cho's voice dropped an octave. "She's alone."

Shit. The whole world was watching. Literally.

"Uther must be checking their coats," Becca said, then quickly dodged between two waiters and continued toward the ballroom entrance.

How had Sabrina gotten out of the safe house? There should have been a guard inside as well as two outside.

Did she expect to find Uther at the gala? Why would she risk it? Certainly the CIA had given her some clue that something very dangerous would be going down tonight.

"Sabrina!" Becca moved in to buss her cheeks. Her flesh was hot, and salty with nervous perspiration. Becca succeeded in walking her back a few steps to the wall beneath a froth of red roses. "I'm Becca Whitmore, gala chair. What are you doing here?"

"What do you mean, Miss Whitmore?"

How to do this without blowing her cover? If it wasn't already blown. Had Uther mentioned their near-death adventure to— Well, no, he couldn't have.

"Oh, well, I thought you and Uther would be together. Is he in the coat room? I haven't seen him for ages. I'd love to say hello."

"Actually, we've a room. He's coming down…later."

"You're not looking for him?"

They had a room? Something was up. Sabrina and Uther were…together?

Sabrina narrowed her green eyes on Becca. "Why would I be looking for my fiancé, Miss Whitmore? Do I know you?"

"No." But something about Sabrina felt so familiar. Her pale blond hair, that determined jut to her fine jaw… "I read Rubi Cho's online column this morning," Becca stated.

What was it about Sabrina that fired all the warning flares in her gut? Had Uther gotten away from Dimitri?

"Really? Were Uther and I mentioned?"

"Yes, and it was hinted you were going to be wearing a huge diamond."

Sabrina's jaw tightened. Malevolence flashed in her eyes. Yet, despite her stiffness, she remained gorgeous, a classic Nordic beauty. Just like…Pink.

"What do you know about the diamond?" Sabrina insisted in a low voice.

"Tell me where Uther is, and I'll tell you all I know about the ten-carat heart-shaped stone."

Sabrina gaped.

Alan said, "You're pushing it, Becca. What are you up to? Find out how she got out of the safe house."

Very well. The direct approach was always the best. Checking their periphery, Becca assured herself that no one was close enough to hear.

"You should be in a safe house right now."

A blond brow arched defiantly, but Sabrina kept her calm. "I walked out."

"You walked past three guards?"

"The guards were sleeping." Nibbling the edge of her lower lip, the woman scanned the room beyond Becca's head. Searching for a way out? But what had she to run from? Her tone changing to a warble, she suddenly gripped Becca's wrist and pulled her toward the ballroom doors. "I just couldn't stay there," she whispered. "I got a call from Uther."

"You did? When? How? I thought you said you two had a room?"

"About an hour ago he called me on my cell phone. He's here in one of the rooms."

Becca slid an arm around Sabrina's waist but the woman planted her silver heels firmly. "Tell me which one."

"Something's not right," Alan said. "Why would Uther call her? How could he?"

Becca was one step ahead of Alan. From the corner of her eye she spied Dane. He was chatting with a guest, but kept one eye on her. *I got your back.* He was out of the communications loop, but for some reason she felt more reassured by his presence than a whole force of armed agents.

"Which room?" she repeated.

Sabrina seemed to shake off a nervous jitter. "Will you take me with you?"

And walk right into a trap? 'Cause that's what it felt like. Intuition screamed for Becca to pay attention, and she did.

"Sabrina—"

"Bring her," Alan said. "You'll have backup. Just be careful."

Becca turned and hooked an arm in Sabrina's. "Sure. Then will you show me the diamond?"

"I don't—" Sabrina huffed out an irritated sound. "If you know I was in a safe house, then you know I don't have it. So where is it?"

And Becca knew she had the enemy in hand.

"Close," she admitted. She nodded toward the ballroom exit.

The elevator bays were out through the foyer. Becca smiled at Sherri Grant, who snapped a photo as they passed.

* * *

Zeek switched to Alan's channel and said hastily, "Stop, Becca."

"Why?"

"I've ID'd Sabrina Morgan. She's Louise Veld, Katarine Veld's sister."

"You mean she's—"

"Another of Dimitri's molls. They've been in place for months. Louise is after the diamond—"

"And Becca's wearing it," Alan finished. "Double damn."

They entered the elevator and the doors closed with a *ting*. Immediately, Sabrina pounced, thrusting Becca back against the metal doors and sending a shock up her spine. Raising her arms in defense, Becca reacted to the assault. An assault she had expected.

Lifting her leg high, she pinned Sabrina against the opposite wall, her knee gouging deep into her gut.

"You've got to be Pink's sister," she said.

Sabrina kicked high. Silver heels flashed. "Who's Pink?"

Catching Sabrina's ankle with one hand, Becca shoved hard. The woman flew against the elevator wall with a grunt.

"Katarine Veld. Sound familiar?" Eyeing her fallen purse, Becca knew she had to get to it before Sabrina did. Inside was a small .45 pistol.

Sabrina kicked aside the purse and slashed out a deadly, sharp-nailed claw. Becca dodged and returned with a punch to her shoulder. She spun, planning to deliver a forceful leg across Sabrina's back, but the woman gripped her ankle and twisted.

Slammed against the steel wall, Becca momentarily saw black, then twinkling lights.

Sabrina began to grope up her body. "Wire?" A knee to the back of her legs bent Becca over. Excruciating pain radiated up through her limbs.

"You are wearing a wire!" Sabrina ran her hands up Becca's sides as she slid up to stand. "Your earrings."

Gripping the clip-ons, Sabrina flicked them from Becca's ears and dropped them on the elevator floor. She stomped on them.

Having now lost the ability to hear Alan, and still not feeling firm on her feet, Becca slowly raised her hands in compliance. "Who are you?"

"None of your concern," she said, though her American accent had slipped. "My sister could not do the job right, so now I will finish it."

As Becca had guessed—Pink's sister.

The door opened on the ambassador suite level.

"Move," Sabrina directed. *"Byistro."*

Now that was Russian.

Thinking to whisper her position to Alan, Becca decided to play along for now and hope some of the other agents were on her tail. Gripped roughly by the shoulder, she followed Sabrina's directions to the left. If Uther was here, she would find him.

"Where are we going? To see Dimitri?"

"You will see soon enough."

Stopping at a door, Sabrina slid a keycard through the

lock and shoved Becca inside one of the Waldorf's large celebrity suites.

Stumbling to a stop inside the foyer, Becca scanned the room. She noted two doors. One to the right was closed. She guessed it was the bedroom. The one immediately before her stood open.

A low melody played from somewhere inside the main room. Mozart. *Eine Kleine Nachtmusik?* Seemed inappropriate for the mood, but then again…

Surveying every corner, she checked for people. Thugs. Guns. Objects of menace. A large vase of white lilies sat on the table before an oval mirror. That could knock a person out, if need be. Her purse still lay on the elevator floor, with her gun inside.

"Go!"

She assumed Sabrina wanted her to keep walking, so she entered the parlor, a large room that offered a splendid view of Saint Bartholomew's Church. A dim fake fire burned in the hearth to the left. The massive blocks of furniture made initial recognition difficult, but as her eyes adjusted to the light, and a small lamp was flicked on, Becca spied Uther.

Sitting on the floor by the fireplace, the lanky scientist was gagged and bound at his wrists and ankles. Pie-eyed, he mumbled something at the sight of her. And the woman he had thought was his fiancée.

"Becca? She's not responding to me," Alan muttered urgently. "It seems she lost the audio receivers after she entered the elevator. Where is the retrieval team? And what about MI-6?"

"He's off the grid," Zeek said. "Screw MI-6. We've got our own people to worry about."

"Exactly." Alan flipped to all-frequency. "Let's move, people, we've got an agent compromised!"

"Hand it over," Dimitri demanded. He'd appeared from out of the shadows and slipped a gun from his pocket, a slim silver number. How had he got it past security?

Dim lamplight shone over the red scratch marring Dimitri's forehead. Score one point for makeshift weapon girl.

"So, you planted Sabrina from the start?" Becca said. Even if she couldn't hear Alan, she knew he could still hear her.

Dimitri grinned. "She's good, no?"

Across the room Uther struggled.

"Sneakier than Pink, I must admit."

"Pink?"

"Katarine."

"My sister is idiot." Sabrina Whoever-She-Was joined Dimitri and snuggled the length of her silk-clad body against his. Catty green eyes slashed invisible claws across Becca's face. "She failed when she sent the car through the repair shop. Dimitri should not have allowed her to attempt the Paris nab."

"The diamond!" Dimitri ordered.

"All right, no need to get snippy." The weight of the diamond sat heavily upon Becca's breasts. Taking a deep breath, she reviewed her options. Which were minimal. But her objective remained clear. "Release Uther and the diamond is yours."

"That was not the deal. The scientist is mine."

He'd made a deal? With whom? The CIA mole? The Duke? The Russian government? But now she knew the CIA had not been compromised, because Sabrina was the mole. Having infiltrated Uther's life, only Sabrina could have known to send Dimitri to Berlin to kidnap him.

"Why do you need the diamond?" Becca asked. Stalling. The cavalry should arrive anytime now. "You've got all the information you need in Uther's head."

"Worth a million, yes?" Dimitri waved the gun frantically. "You don't think I'd walk away from so much money?"

Why had the mere monetary value never struck her as motive? He wasn't stupid. SVR wanted Uther; Dimitri planned to get paid well for the task.

"You don't know how to play the game, Mr. Nazarova. When one wants something, one bargains for it with another item. I've got the technology you want. You've got the scientist I want. You see the ease there?"

"He's mine."

"He is of no use to you. Whatever you think you can get from his mind—tortured as it will have to be—it'll never be as clear and concise as what is contained within the diamond."

"Which I have yet to see." Dimitri waved the pistol in the air. "All these questions! You don't have it on you, do you?"

Becca slowly raised her hands as he pointed the gun straight at her. After splaying and wiggling her fingers, she smoothed them over the fur, well aware she was creating havoc on Alan's end—then parted the red fox to reveal the prize. A ten-carat, heart-shaped diamond nestled in her cleavage.

Chapter 27

The slam of a door alerted all three of them. Dimitri, ears pricked and gun still pointed at Becca, nudged Sabrina. "Go check it out."

As soon as Sabrina had left the room Becca risked it all.

Bending and lunging forward, she landed on the overstuffed red couch near where Dimitri stood, and clasped his legs. He toppled. She tumbled with him to the floor. A thick sheepskin throw that had been draped over the back of the couch flopped across her face.

Momentarily blinded, she took a punch to the gut that cut off her air. Bile eddied in her throat.

Feeling his arm hook about her neck, she knew the other hand still held a gun. Moving instinctively, she dodged a slap from the weapon and kicked out, hitting what felt like a knee with her spike heel.

Dimitri was large and definitely stronger than her. One bicep could crush her windpipe. The only way of winning this struggle would be to make like a snake and wiggle away, not give him anything to grasp on to.

The silk dress did make it difficult for him to keep a sure hold. Gripped from behind by the shoulder, Becca bent forward and swung her leg back. She hooked Dimitri near the hip with a heel. Kidney shot. He went down.

The gun clattered across the tile floor.

A shot sounded, muted by a silencer. Both she and Dimitri paused in their struggle.

"Break it up, blokes."

Dane.

Tugging the sheepskin from her neck and pushing away from Dimitri, Becca scrambled across the floor to the easy chair.

Dane trained his gun on Dimitri, following the man as he rose and brushed fingers through his oily hair.

"Got everything under control, love?"

"Working on it," Becca said as she stood.

"Sabrina's taking a nap," Dane mentioned with a wink.

A glance to Uther found him struggling against his wrist ties. Becca gave a thankful nod to Dane. "Good to see you."

"You'll be changing your mind, right…about…now."

With that strange comment, Dane swung his gun toward Becca. The look in his aquamarines wasn't even close to teasing or romantic.

"What the hell?"

"Sorry, love. I've my own objectives. We never did promise each other anything, right?"

I got your back. Bastard.

"Right. No promises."

Hooking her hands at her hips, Becca looked from Dane's serious face to Dimitri's smug grin.

"You tricking him, too?" she asked, with a nod toward the Russian.

"Need to know, love."

"Fuck that. Who the hell are you, Dane? Are you really with MI-6?"

"One year, two months and seven long days. But I'm not here for a chat. We've done that."

A chill moved over Becca's scalp. Had he been playing her all along?

"The diamond, if you please." He held out a hand.

The fox fur shimmied under Becca's reluctant touch. Alan was getting every word of this. So where was the cavalry?

Eyeing her objective, Becca nodded. She was here for one thing. As for the diamond, let the chips fall where they may. "Let Uther go, and you can have the rock."

"You've got a gun pointing at you. I'm afraid you're not calling the shots. Ho!" Dane swung his aim back toward Dimitri.

The Russian raised his hands in the air in compliance.

Dane redirected his aim to Becca. "I have to take a look at the diamond first, to verify you've not erased it."

He was one step ahead of her.

"Fine." She moved her hands along the fur.

"Slowly," Dane directed.

"She could have a weapon," Dimitri snapped.

"She's clean. I frisked her earlier."

When they were dancing. And for that one moment, against all better judgment, Becca had surrendered to the mood and had fallen for Aston Dane.

A sickening rise of bile pierced her throat. *Don't fraternize with foreign agents.*

Sometimes she let her twisted fetish for the role get in the way. She felt such power when she was undercover.

Will you let it be your downfall?

No. She had an objective. The agent would fulfill it.

Yanking the diamond from its setting in the fur liner, Becca held it in front of her. Lamplight flashed in the facets of the heavy gem. Brilliant blocks of color danced across the shadowed walls. Flawless.

The complete opposite to her life.

Behind her Uther mumbled loudly, another recipient of lies—the heartbreaking, romantic, you've-been-had kind of lies that Becca could relate to in ways she knew painfully well.

A toss, and the diamond landed in Dane's free hand. He held it up, his weapon temporarily directed toward the ceiling. "Brilliant."

The secrets double....

Becca said, "You need an electron microscope—"

"Got one." Dane pulled out a penlight—the one Becca had used in Paris. When had he nabbed that? He was so far ahead in this game.

"I will pay you for it," Dimitri offered.

"Really?" After a quick inspection, Dane pocketed the rock. "How much?"

The Russian shrugged. "Half a million."

"Sounds good, bloke. But first, some info."

"Whatever you want. We will work together, yes?"

"Not so fast, Nazarova. Here's the skinny. Last January two MI-5 agents were held by the SVR, tortured and murdered. You wouldn't happen to know who was responsible?"

Dimitri grinned. "That's not worth half a million."

"You're right. Two lives are worth a helluva lot more. Priceless, actually."

"So, no deal?"

"You've got it." Dane pulled the trigger.

Dimitri's body took a bullet in the heart. Shoulders forced back at impact, his head snapping forward, he went down, landing at Becca's feet.

Eating back the scream that felt heavy and solid on her tongue, Becca carefully spread her hands at her hips, trying to project compliance. And feeling utter shock. She flicked her gaze to Uther; she felt as panicked as he looked.

Everything had gone pear-shaped.

Dane's tight jaw pulsed twice as he drew his focus up to Becca. "Claim your prize and leave, love."

For a moment she stupidly stood there, defying the man with nothing more than a narrowed gaze and two fists. Facing down a gun and a twisted set of morals.

Had this cross-country goose chase been an elaborate ruse for revenge? Whose side was Dane on?

"I don't know who you are," she managed to say. "Why not have him arrested?"

"Nazarova was a dangerous, sick man. MI-5 wanted

him dead on sight. He knew too much about the agency. I'm just doing my job."

"But what about at *verte*?"

"Don't think about it too much, New York. Just take this chance before I change my mind."

"A chance? For what?"

Dane gestured to Uther with his gun.

There was still opportunity to save the innocents.

Crossing the room, Becca helped Uther to stand. A tug to the square knot at his ankle released the tie easily. She'd worry about his hands later. "Are you okay?" She pulled down his gag.

"Becca?" His voice warbled. "What are you doing here?"

"No time. He's going to let us walk out of here. Are you strong enough?"

"Yes, I— Sabrina!"

"Let's go. I'll explain later."

Dane's weapon followed them as they crossed the room. The sensation of a gun targeting her made the hairs on her arms prickle.

"You won't get far," she said, hoping to appeal to any thread of morality Dane might possess. "There are agents combing the building."

"I'm within my jurisdiction."

And then she did look. Into Dane's blue eyes, focused solely on her. Telling lies with a Cheshire cat smile. He'd duped her. And she had let it happen.

"Bye-bye, New York," he muttered, and cocked the trigger.

Becca could take a hint; she shoved Uther toward the

foyer. He let out a shriek when he saw Sabrina's body lying facedown in the bathroom, and Becca told him, "She's fine," as she pushed him out the door.

Literally pulling him down the hallway, Becca caught the elevator still at their floor. As the doors closed behind them, she went immediately to work on the slippery white rope about Uther's wrists.

"Alan, if you can hear me, I'm safe, and so is Uther. We'll be in the lobby soon. Dane's in an ambassador suite on the thirty-second floor. Dimitri is down and whoever the hell Sabrina Morgan is is down as well."

"What about Sabrina?" Uther shrieked. "We can't leave her behind."

Becca bent to retrieve her purse. The gun was still inside. Her earrings were a total loss, crushed upon the carpeted floor. "She's a spy, Uther."

"A spy? Why are you— What is going on?"

She placed her hands on Uther's shoulders and looked him over. Might have had a bloody nose, judging from the crusted red on his chin. He smelled salty and warm, like fear.

"We haven't got time for a huge explanation. Think about it. How do you think Dimitri found you in Berlin?"

"I don't know. I told you I thought the Russians were following me!"

"Sabrina told him."

"No!"

"I'm sorry, Uther. I know you think you loved her."

"I do love her, Becca. A spy? But— Are you sure? I can't believe…" His lips curved in a smile, but the poor man couldn't muster a laugh. "They've got the diamonds. The Russians!"

He lunged for the emergency glass beside the elevator keypad.

Becca stopped him with a kick to his reaching fingers. The rhinestones on her red silk shoes glinted. "You're safe, Uther. Trust me."

"I don't trust anyone!" Gulping a huge breath, he demanded, "What will happen to Sabrina? Dimitri, he maybe forced her."

"I can't help her, Uther."

A *ting* announced their arrival at the lobby. The elevator doors slid open.

A CIA agent dressed as a waiter stood right outside. Standing next to him, Sherri Grant nodded to Becca, then spoke into her headset. "I've got them, Alan. Becca is safe."

The male agent slid a hand inside his white linen suit jacket, subtly revealing the gun strapped at his side. "I'll take Mr. Magnusson in hand."

"You'll be safe," Becca said as she escorted Uther from the elevator. Obviously in shock, the man nodded and allowed the agent to hook an arm in his.

Becca strode across the marble-floored lobby. She wouldn't look back. The man was freaked as hell. His entire world had fallen out from beneath him.

But she'd had a job to do.

"Mission completed, Alan," she said. "The target is ours. Alert the Governess her man is in hand. The mole is Sabrina Morgan."

Lucy found Becca in the lobby ten minutes later and

reminded her it was half an hour until the performance. Pleading a need for a few minutes of fresh air, Becca watched as Lucy skipped back to the gala.

The lobby was relatively quiet, save for a few lingering couples. And one set of late arrivals.

Alan crossed the lobby, with a handsome man in a white suit on his left arm. He bussed both of Becca's cheeks and introduced her to Kyle, a sun-browned model for Versace who was in town for the weekend, then asked his date to get him a drink.

"I just talked to you," Becca said, after Kyle had walked away. "I thought."

"Zeek's been monitoring you since communications were compromised and we figured out Sabrina was the mole. I couldn't sit back without coming to make sure you were safe. The CIA has taken Dimitri and Louise in hand."

"Louise?" Becca asked.

"Pink's sister."

"I guessed that."

"We just made the connection when you got in the elevator."

"I had my suspicions a little earlier. What about Dane? Any word from him?"

"He hasn't reported to MI-6. He remains off the grid. But we've got Uther, so…"

So who cared about a rogue MI-6 agent, was the unspoken end to that sentence.

Still, Becca wasn't satisfied.

"I can't believe he would leave the country without reporting to MI-6, and ultimately, the CIA."

Common sense said, *Let it go.* He hadn't shown her his objective; she hadn't shown him hers.

But intuition, and a spark of unavoidable curiosity, said, *Don't let it rest. You must have answers. You do need to know.*

A double-crossing foreign agent would want to vacate the building immediately. Which should put him…

Becca spied the blond head ducking into a cab outside the Waldorf doors at the Park Avenue entrance. "I'll be right back, Alan."

She dashed outside into the bitter cold, loosening the buttons that attached the fur to the silk as she did so.

The door to the yellow cab closed. She reached the vehicle and beat her fists on the window. The door opened.

As the cab began to pull away, Becca flung her purse inside and managed to slide into the back seat. She wasn't scared of him now that Uther was safe. "Headed to JFK?"

Dane turned on the seat and stretched an arm across the back. He didn't wink at her.

"Talk to me, Dane." Reaching behind her neck, she unclasped the fur collar. A toss delivered it outside, onto the slushy sidewalk. "I'm not wired. No one is listening."

He huffed out a breath that misted in the chilly vehicle. No response.

Becca waited. It was up to him to offer the first excuse. And that was all he would offer, she guessed. An excuse.

"What do you want me to say? You once said it yourself—it's called playing a countermelody. It's the game we play, innit, love? Spies dancing about one another, engaging in delicate subterfuge. We do what we have to. We love who we must—"

"I never loved you, Dane."

"Yeah?" He kept his eyes straight ahead; his sharp-jawed profile belonged in a Times Square sign advertising Burberry Brit cologne. The muscle in his jaw pulsed with tension. "S'all right. It didn't have to be mutual."

"Mutual? You've known me for what? Forty-eight hours?"

"About that. It already hurts."

"Don't bullshit me now. It's over. You got what you wanted by using me to get to the source. You needed Dimitri dead, didn't you?"

"MI-6 has been after Nazarova since the murders last year. That may have been reason for my seeking a transfer out of Scotland Yard."

"He killed your father?"

"I'm not saying anything that can be used against me."

Fair enough. She would never say she understood his rage. He had every right. And if a government agency wanted a man down, it could be done. No questions asked.

Dane reached into his suit pocket and drew out his passport. He pulled something from inside and handed it to her. "Here."

Accepting the small photograph, Becca leaned toward the window. The streetlights shined across a black-and-white photo of a distinguished male face with a slightly crooked smile.

"My father," Dane whispered.

Becca turned the photo over. On the reverse was another picture—of Dimitri Nazarova. She handed the photos back to Dane. There was nothing she could say.

He had gotten his revenge. But he didn't seem happy.

"It's too bad Sabrina Morgan was a plant," he said softly. "Uther is a good man. He didn't need that heartbreak."

"What do you care?"

"Despite your scathing judgment, I am not heartless. I am a warm-blooded, feeling man, Becca. A man who does what he must to keep his head above it all."

Becca turned to stare out the window. The glass was blurred with flashing red taillights and the glare of head-lights from behind.

How did a woman say goodbye to a man who had used her? And yet why did she want to pull him close and hold him? Wrap him like a frayed blanket about her needy soul?

"Are you really with MI-6?"

"Love." He turned to face her. The Cheshire cat had abandoned the cocky veneer for a softer expression. He stroked her cheek. "Your superiors have already checked me out, I'm sure."

"Is that a yes or a no?"

"I am. Still am. Will be for however long I'm able. Which is a hell of a lot more truth than you ever gave to me."

"I can't—"

He pressed a finger to her lips. "I know. You ladies keep your cover. I don't even want to understand."

The vehicle stopped. The cabbie called back, "Traf-fic jam. Settle in, folks."

They were not far from the Waldorf, a little over ten blocks. Dane still had a long ride to the airport. Yes, he didn't belong here. New York was her turf.

"So that's it." She sighed. "Mission complete. All sides satisfied, I presume? Our guys got Uther, you got the diamond with the code?"

"I'm detecting a lack of satisfaction on your part, love."

"I don't require satisfaction. I just like to know I'm doing the job—"

"Perfectly?"

"I'm going to leave," she said. "I…"

Words suddenly felt less than appropriate. And what more could she say, anyway?

Becca leaned over and kissed Dane. He was warm and open and pulled her to him. They both needed this closure. A touch, a taste, a bit of the other that would cling until a shower washed away all but the memory. She thought to straddle him, but resisted.

Don't make it more difficult. Just take one little piece.

"I'm not going to forget this," Dane murmured. The slide of his silver ring tickled her cheek. "The feel of your body, love. Or the taste of your kiss. You're the best thing I got out of this bloody mission."

"Don't kid yourself, you got several million dollars' worth of diamonds out of it."

"Nice bit of dosh, innit? Not mine, though. It'll all go to, well…"

"I know. Need to know." Becca slid from his strong arms and grabbed the door handle.

Yes, she had to do this. Walk away.

"If I ever see you again, Dane, I'll kick your arse."

"I wouldn't expect anything less."

Turning to hide her smile, Becca held back a good-bye—too final—and stepped out onto the street. Cold slush seeped under the arch of her foot. It would be a long walk in heels to her apartment, but the Waldorf was still in sight…

Her purse dangled on the end of Dane's finger. She snatched it. She'd flag down a cab, but she wasn't about to until Dane's cab was out of sight.

Fat, heavy flakes began to shake down from the sky. The night suddenly became a wonderland of reflected streetlights upon glittering new snow. Valentine's Day. How ironic. Her heart felt as if it was breaking in half, and she hadn't even been aware of sharing it.

Chapter 28

Becca returned to the gala, met by Lucy's expectant smile. After playing the *Midsummer Serenade* with the children, she then danced through the night in the arms of various handsome bachelors and grinning old coots, until 2:00 a.m., and then lingered in the background, watching couples leave the ballroom arm in arm and, finally, the cleaning crew sweep up the mess.

Jake arrived at 5:00 a.m. to bring her home, but instead, she asked him to drive her to Central Park, where he found a parking place near the Wollman Rink.

One skater occupied the rink so early in the morning. Must have snuck in, because it didn't open to the public for hours yet. Becca snuggled on a bench, wrapping around her shoulders a blanket Jake pulled from the trunk. Good ole Jake; he had everything. She might have dozed in the fresh morning air about ten minutes, but mostly, she pondered the past few days.

She had lost something on this mission. The last bit of innocence. Her love for fear. And her desire for illicit liaisons. Did she crave a Zen session? Not really. There was only one person she really wanted, secrets and all. But they were not meant for each other.

An hour later, she sat across the table from Renee Dalton-Sinclair and Alan Burke. Sherri Grant sat at the end, her face scrubbed of makeup and her red hair pulled back into a perky ponytail.

Having come straight from the skating rink, Becca didn't care if she looked like a survivor of yesterday's Saks clearance sale and a herd of credit-card-wielding women. She wanted to get this debriefing over with.

There wasn't much to say. She'd turn in her report detailing her expenses in Europe and her contact with Dimitri, Katarine and Louise.

Dimitri Nazarova was found in one of the ambassador suites, a bullet in his heart. No one stated who had killed him. Accusations against MI-6 could have far-reaching consequences. Dimitri's dealings with the black market had led to many murders, including two British MI-5 agents. No one would miss him.

"Lester Price is clean," Renee stated. "Katarine Veld nearly killed him to get the diamond. As for Louise Veld—good call, Becca. She's being debriefed as we speak. MaryEllen Sommerfield is off the critical list and is expected to fully recover."

MI-6's involvement in the operation was left entirely unmentioned. Agent Dane's name was not even muttered.

Becca fingered the pink silk purse, which sat in her lap. The fine texture reminded of her other life, the easy veneer of a socialite. So distant now. And yes, she did crave that side of her, for it provided, ultimately, an escape back to her mask.

She wanted to press her forehead to the table and close her eyes. Jake waited outside in the Hummer. A full eight hours of sleep was just steps away.

"Of course, we will keep our eyes and ears open for the sale of three flawless ten-carat diamonds," Renee stated. "They may show up on the black market. What do you think, Becca?"

For some reason it didn't feel right to condemn Dane. She knew him. He'd hand them in to evidence.

"I'm sure they'll be filtered through the British treasury." Yawning, then sighing, she nodded at Renee. "I thought we had what we needed? Uther Magnusson."

"Yes. The Governess is pleased. But it has been determined that Uther destroyed all his computer files. The only files remaining are on the diamonds."

"He can recreate the formula?"

"Of course, but it will take some time."

In other words, we didn't ask you to bring back the diamonds—but you should have, fool.

Renee held her gaze for a few moments before dismissing everyone and standing. Alan and Sherri filed out, Alan patting Becca's shoulder as he passed her.

Becca remained in her chair.

"He reported to MI-6 this morning," Renee said. She stood at the door, fanning the stack of FYI documents near her thigh. Becca didn't look up. "That's about as far as I want to take it. I'm not concerned over what Six wants or does with the diamonds, unless it involves me directly. If the Governess and the CIA want the data, they'll have to contact Six directly."

"Of course."

"Take a few days off, Becca. Have Jake pamper you. Check in with me next week, okay?"

Becca nodded, and then found the words: "Thank you, Renee."

The door closed and Becca laid her forehead on the table with a long sigh.

Adjusting her purse on her lap, she thought it felt a bit heavier than usual. The gun was lightweight titanium. She pulled open the zipper. What spilled out was not just a gun and a tube of Nina Ricci lipstick. The *click, click, click* on the table made her smile.

"In-sodding-credible," she muttered.

All three of them. Ten carats each. Flawless. Two containing Uther's code.

No matter what happens, I got your back.

Surrendering to giggles, Becca stood and shook her head. "Double-crossing arsehole."

Though it was midmorning by the time Becca returned to her apartment, the rooms were dark, for the day was cold and a storm had touched down with heavy fat flakes.

Dropping her purse and coat in the kitchen, she didn't bother to turn on the lights as she made her way back to the bathroom. She carried her gun; she'd clean it after a shower, and put it in the safe.

Unclasping the back of her dress, she pulled down the red silk to her breasts. Kicking off her high heels, she then padded into the bathroom.

The walls were tiled in small squares of recycled blue glass. The floor was highly polished, vanilla-colored epoxy resin. Citrus scented the air.

And then she noticed the shower was on.

Reacting instinctively, she crouched and thrust out her arms, gun aimed at the shower.

"In-sodding-credible," a male voice said.

Dane? Of all the nerve!

Scampering over to the glass shower wall, Becca poked the gun inside and connected with flesh. "If you think you can sneak back into my life—naked…!"

Yes, completely naked, and not at all concealed by the clear glass that surrounded the huge unit. The door to the shower was open, and water splashed on the floor.

"Take it easy, love." Dane raised his hands to his shoulders. The gun poked him hard in the temple.

"How did you get in?"

"Jake."

"What?"

"He's a cheeky fellow. I like him. Stand off, will you?"

Becca drew back the gun. Not about to back down herself, however, she remained at the shower door. Water sprinkled her front. "Why'd you give back the diamonds?"

"Because they were yours, love. You did all the work."

"I thought MI-6 wanted the information?"

"And they have it. I had a chance to have the information copied from the brilliant stone before the ball. Now you and the CIA get the gems. A mutual agreement between the agencies. I suggested it would enhance goodwill relations."

"You didn't."

"I did."

Bloody— Cocky— Brit.

Jake had let him in? Why that—

"Care to join me?"

Becca crossed her arms and slowly dragged her eyes from his water-slicked pecs, over ripped abs and lower to a very nice—

Wet fingers reached out from the shower and gestured greedily. "Can you forgive me?"

"I'm not sure." She shimmied and the dress fell to the floor. As naked as he, she still kept her distance. "You could have told me about the copy, and that you had no intention of leaving."

"I didn't know what my intentions were until you left me high and dry in the cab, love. I couldn't fathom leaving the country. I had to figure a way to see you again. My God, woman, you are bloody—wow."

Becca stepped into the shower. Catching the water from the stacked bronze jets that lined the wall every two feet, she tilted back her head and wet her hair. Hot water pulsed against her pores.

Slicking back her tresses and sliding her hands over the hardened tips of her breasts, she eyed her hungry Brit. Water splattered their bodies from all sides. It was as if they were standing in an open forest beneath a summer rain shower, except the water was warm and they'd lost their clothes.

She kissed Dane's open mouth—a slippery connection. Just as their connection had been these past few days.

But he broke the kiss and groped for her trigger hand. "Could we do this without the weapon?" He claimed her gun and set it high on a shelf outside the glass walls.

Their bodies fit together. Hard and slick, with every muscle tensing as he moved, Dane pressed her against the tiled, blue-glass wall of the shower. Frenzied kisses seared her neck and shoulders, then her breasts.

"I couldn't leave the country without one of those giggles," he murmured. "If I may?"

Becca snaked her fingers through his wet hair and steadied herself by gripping a bronze bar to her right as he went onto his knees before her.

The man was good. He knew his way around a woman. No complaints; in fact, she'd call for an encore.

Score one point for high-maintenance chick getting together with the swanky Brit.

Giggles spilled over Becca's lips as Dane stood to fit inside her.

"Amazing," he said, with a nip to her ear as they moved in unison. "You're in-sodding-credible, New York."

She hugged him to her as hard as she could. "Not so bad yourself, swank."

* * * * *

Lethally Blonde

by

Nancy Bartholomew

"Jeremy Reins, the actor, says someone's trying to kill him," Renee says after I've taken a seat in her salon. "But the evidence indicates it's just another one of his publicity stunts."

She tells me right after I've come in from a grueling sparring match with her self-defense expert, Jimmy "The Heartbreaker" Valentine. I've broken four nails, had half my extensions pulled out, and have the beginning of a nasty bruise forming under my right eye. And here is the head of the Gotham Roses spy organization, telling me she doesn't think it's even a true assignment?

"So, why not blow the idiot off?" I ask. "It's not like he's really *anybody*. Besides, he's been getting himself into a lot of trouble lately. The talk is that he has an at-

traction for kinky sex with very young men." I shrug.
"He's just an actor."

"Just an actor?" she says raising that eyebrow of
hers. "Porsche Rothschild, you know that's not true."

"Okay, okay, so he's golden at the box office, but who
cares? I mean, if he's faking it, why not just let him hire
extra bodyguards?"

Renee shrugs. "The Governess feels he's a national
treasure and Jeremy's agent, Mark Lowenstein, is married to a woman who has done us many favors in the past.
Andrea Lowenstein is saying she feels a stalker or even
a terrorist could be behind these attacks. Apparently,
Reins has done several commando, patriotic, action-ad-
venture films in the past and could be the object of a terrorist vendetta. The Governess feels Andrea Lowenstein's
concern is credible. Anyway, it's just not good to ignore
such a visible and beloved member of the public. If something really did happen, it would make the rest of the
country uneasy. We don't need to take that chance."

She smiles at me, like I'm already onboard, and says,
"We have you. With your training in clinical psychology, you'll be perfectly capable of discerning the threat
level and letting us know if we need to send a team of
more seasoned agents out to eliminate the issue."

Seasoned agents! I'm sure the entire thing with Jeremy is just a publicity stunt. But I have to admit the idea
is somewhat enticing, especially with the rumors I've
heard on the circuit about him. I like knowing the real
scoop and this will certainly be the way to find out.
Renee doesn't wait for me to accept. She assumes I will
do her bidding and continues talking.

"You'll be Jeremy's date for the Oscars and he'll be yours for CeCe Goldberg's post-Oscar charity party. That's your cover, a budding romance and your charity work," she says. "All the Roses have special charities they support. Yours will be the Miller Children's Home. CeCe Goldberg, as I'm sure you know, is not only a world-renowned investigative reporter, she is also director Spiro Goldberg's wife and quite active with children's charities. Jeremy will be only too happy to have you as his guest because he doesn't want the rumors about his sexuality spreading and destroying his box office appeal. You have both the name and the, er, reputation to dispel any and all doubts the public may have. I'm sure he'll be only too happy to stick to you like glue and show you all around the Paradise Ranch as well as the rest of L.A."

I ignore the comment about my reputation and instead roll my eyes at the mention of Jeremy's estate—the Paradise Ranch. How *nouveau riche*.

"You know," she says, "with your almost photographic memory and your graduate level course work in clinical psychology—and your family name, of course—you could be most useful to the Gotham Roses, should things go well with this assignment."

Good old Renee, dangling that golden carrot in front of me. I can only become a permanent fixture in her elite undercover organization if I prove to be successful in my mission in Los Angeles. If I wind up blowing it, I'll be useless to the Roses. Of course, I am not about to blow it. Sneaking around spying into the secret lives of my fellow rich and famous comrades sure beats attend-

ing the endless party circuit and listening to dull stories
told by dull people. I'll actually have a life—even if I
can't tell anyone about it!

❤ SILHOUETTE®
Sensation™

RIDER ON FIRE by Sharon Sala

With a hitman hot on her trail, undercover DEA agent Sonora Jordan decided to lie low—until ex US Army Ranger and local medicine man Adam Two Eagles convinced her to find the father she had never known and the love she had never wanted.

TO LOVE, HONOUR AND DEFEND
by Beth Cornelison

Someone was after attorney Libby Hopkins and she needed extra protection. So when Cal Walters proposed a marriage of convenience to help him win custody of his daughter, she agreed. Close quarters caused old feelings to resurface, but Libby had always put her career first. Could Cal show Libby how to honour, defend *and* love?

HER LAST DEFENCE by Vicki Taylor

Doctor Macy Attois and Texas Ranger Clint Hayes were racing to track down a diseased monkey—before it fell into the wrong hands. As time ran out, the intensity rose...and so did the heat. Clint had always kept his emotions hidden, but he faced a stark choice—walk away or give in to the passion he and Macy had found.

On sale from 15th September 2006

Available at WHSmith, Tesco, ASDA, Borders, Eason,
Sainsbury's and most bookshops

www.silhouette.co.uk

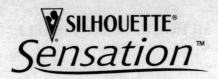

0906/18b

FLASHBACK by Justine Davis

Bombshell: Athena Force

New information about the murder of the Athena Academy founder had FBI scientist Alexandra Forsythe jumping to investigate the decade-old case. With the help of special agent Justin Cohen, Alex discovers the trail leads straight to Washington's corridors of power—and that those she loves are in danger from the ruthless killer...

DEADLY REUNION by Lauren Nichols

Ike Walker was determined to prove to his ex-wife Lindsay Hollis that he wasn't responsible for the death of her brother —and that she would help him to do so. Bringing the killer to justice stirred memories, and passions, which Lindsay would rather forget. But as they closed in on the killer, was there a second chance for the love they thought was dead?

LETHALLY BLONDE by Nancy Bartholomew

Bombshell: The IT Girls

Porsche Rothschild's life had always lacked focus. But when the Gotham Rose spy ring tapped her to be undercover bodyguard to a Hollywood bad boy, the spoiled socialite suddenly had a purpose. With the actor facing death threats, Porsche rallied his entourage, and his handsome manager, to the cause of keeping the cool in Hollywood!

On sale from 15th September 2006

SILHOUETTE BOMBSHELL

Presents

RICH, FABULOUS...AND
DANGEROUSLY UNDERESTIMATED.

They're heiresses with connections, glamorous girls with the
inside track. And they're going undercover to fight
high-society crime in high style.

August 2006
THE GOLDEN GIRL *by Erica Orloff*

September 2006
FLAWLESS *by Michele Hauf*

October 2006
LETHALLY BLONDE *by Nancy Bartholomew*

November 2006
MS LONGSHOT *by Sylvie Kurtz*

December 2006
A MODEL SPY *by Nathalie Dunbar*

January 2007
BULLETPROOF PRINCESS *by Vicki Hinze*

0906/46

SILHOUETTE®
INTRIGUE™

DESERT SONS by Rebecca York, Ann Voss Peterson, Patricia Rosemoor

Don't miss this thrilling collection brought to you by three of Intrigue's favourite authors. Journey into Southwest America to meet a trio of Native American heroes and the courageous women who help them to face a most unusual enemy—a murderous Pueblo with black magic on his side!

THE SHEIKH'S SAFETY by Dana Marton

Neither Dara Alexander nor Sheikh Saeed was happy when the hard-as-nails secret agent was assigned to be the sheikh's bodyguard. Once Dara rescued Saeed from a corrupt king's prison, sparks flew. Could mutual passion be enough to hold this mismatched couple together?

BODYGUARD RESCUE by Donna Young

Someone wanted nuclear physicist Kate MacAlister's secret formula badly enough to kill for it. Now the only way to keep one step ahead of her enemies was to join forces with the seductive bodyguard Roman D'Amato. But could she trust her life to the man who had broken her heart all those years ago?

URBAN SENSATION by Debra Webb
Eclipse

As a homicide detective, there wasn't much Rowen O'Connor hadn't seen. But her newest case was testing even her iron will. Then former FBI agent Evan Bunter reappeared in her life and things got out of control. Could they solve this case with their lives—and hearts—intact?

On sale from 15th September 2006

Available at WHSmith, Tesco, ASDA, Borders, Eason,
Sainsbury's and most bookshops
www.silhouette.co.uk

'It's scary just how good Tess Gerritsen is.'
—Harlan Coben

Twenty years after her father's plane crashed in the jungles of Southeast Asia, Willy Jane Maitland was finally tracking his last moves. She recognised the dangers, but her search for the truth about that fateful flight was the only thing that mattered.

Closing in on the events of that night, Willy realises that she is investigating secrets that people would kill to protect. And without knowing who to trust, the truth can be far from clear cut...

19th May 2006

MIRA

4 Books
and a surprise gift!

We would like to take this opportunity to thank you for reading this Silhouette® book by offering you the chance to take FOUR more specially selected titles from the Sensation™ series absolutely FREE! We're also making this offer to introduce you to the benefits of the Mills & Boon® Reader Service™—

★ **FREE home delivery**
★ **FREE gifts and competitions**
★ **FREE monthly Newsletter**
★ **Exclusive Reader Service offers**
★ **Books available before they're in the shops**

Accepting these FREE books and gift places you under no obligation to buy, you may cancel at any time, even after receiving your free shipment. Simply complete your details below and return the entire page to the address below. You don't even need a stamp!

YES! Please send me 4 free Sensation books and a surprise gift. I understand that unless you hear from me, I will receive 6 superb new titles every month for just £3.10 each, postage and packing free. I am under no obligation to purchase any books and may cancel my subscription at any time. The free books and gift will be mine to keep in any case.

S6ZEF

Ms/Mrs/Miss/Mr ....Initials ....
BLOCK CAPITALS PLEASE

Surname ....

Address...

....

....Postcode ....

Send this whole page to:
UK: FREEPOST CN81, Croydon, CR9 3WZ